ENDORSEMENTS

For those who love art, history, and solving mysteries, this novel takes you on a true art detective voyage, blurring the line between truth and fiction. Historically accurate, the reader can enjoy "meeting" Rembrandt, trusting the author. Sensitive and captivating—a great homage to the Master.

— ZHENYA GERSHMAN, ART HISTORIAN AND REMBRANDT SCHOLAR,
CO-FOUNDER & PRESIDENT OF PROJECT AWE,
FORMER PROJECT SPECIALIST AT THE J. PAUL GETTY MUSEUM

This riveting story of the captivating Yusupov Rembrandts carries the reader through tumultuous events from 1660 Amsterdam, to France, Russia, and England, to 1942 Washington. The Lady evokes the enigmatic attraction of Rembrandt, and the values, both reverential and material, that have accrued to the artist.

— AMY GOLAHNY, LOGAN RICHMOND PROFESSOR OF ART HISTORY,
LYCOMING COLLEGE, WILLIAMSPORT, PENNSYLVANIA;
PRESIDENT, HISTORIANS OF NETHERLANDISH ART;
AUTHOR, *REMBRANDT'S READING*

Frederick Andresen's novel, The Lady with an Ostrich Feather Fan, is a revelation about how intricately historic events, human lives, and pure chance are intertwined in time and connected through art. A fascinating story of the thorny journey of two Rembrandt's paintings and their owners through almost three centuries of European and Russian history, and the feat of salvation of this priceless art from the turmoil of the Russian revolution by the ingenious Prince Felix Yusupov. We admire Rembrandt for the elevating magic of his creations, and thank the author for the ennobling experience of reading this book.

— TATIANA SOLOBAEVA, SECRETARY OF THE BALTIC SEA REGION
UNIVERSITY NETWORK; INTERNATIONAL RELATIONS,
ST. PETERSBURG STATE UNIVERSITY OF ECONOMICS, RUSSIA

Andresen has painted a full and fascinating picture of Rembrandt, 17th C Amsterdam; 18th C Russian and European history, all the way to 1942 America. His depictions of Prince Yusupov and the Rembrandt paintings, of Petersburg and Moscow and Paris, of Napoleon and Rasputin and the Russian Revolution overflow with rich sensory and historical detail. This beautiful tale is difficult to put down as we follow the paintings on their dangerous journey over almost three centuries, through a war-troubled world, to a place they can call home.
— JERI CHASE FERRIS, AWARD-WINNING AUTHOR OF TWELVE BIOGRAPHIES AND HISTORICAL FICTION, THE 2013 SCHULZ LITERARY AWARD AND A GOLD MEDAL FOR "BEST NONFICTION BOOK OF 2013"

For 282 years, two paintings, the products of Rembrandt's creative transformation, lived more exciting lives than many of us will know. This is the riveting tale of the Yusupov Rembrandts challenging journey from 17th century Holland, through the wars and revolutions of Europe and Russia, to a final home in America and the fame they so richly deserve.
— FRANZ MCLAREN, AUTHOR OF THE *CLARION OF DESTINY* SERIES

"Andresen's book covers a dazzling sweep of history that jumps centuries, countries and conflicts, and serves to remind us that every work of art that survives the test of time has its own unique story."
— SARA JOYCE ROBINSON, PROFESSOR IN WRITING, NATIONAL UNIVERSITY

THE LADY
WITH AN
OSTRICH-FEATHER FAN

**The Story
of the
Yusupov
Rembrandts**

**A HISTORICAL
NOVEL**

Fred Andresen

FREDERICK R. ANDRESEN

Published by Aviara Press
Contact: info@aviarapress.com

Library of Congress Control Number: 2015909890

ISBN: 978-0-9965020-0-9 (paperback)
ISBN: 978-0-9965020-1-9 (ebook)

Printed in the United States of America

Dedication

*This work is dedicated
to those special men and women
who devote their time, energy, and life
to the preservation, conservation,
and appreciation of fine art.*

"...artists do not live so their lives might
be art, but so that their art might live."

TABLE OF CONTENTS

PREFACE

AUTHOR'S NOTES

Where does it begin?

WHERE AND HOW DOES A STORY START? Stories are always there, but they have to be discovered. They have to be revealed.

One afternoon I was in the National Gallery of Art in Washington, DC and I happened to call a friend who asked if I knew of the Yusupov Rembrandts. I said, "No," and then I went to see these famous portraits. In an hour or so, I had the start of a story. Why? It was the eyes—the eyes of the lady in *Portrait of a Lady with an Ostrich-Feather Fan* and her partner in *Portrait of a Gentleman with Tall Hat and Gloves*. They set me wondering about the message in the eyes of those mysterious characters, especially the woman's eyes—Rembrandt's woman.

The portraits, for almost half of their 282-year journey, were the pride of the largest art collection in Russia, that of the famed Yusupov family, the richest family in eighteenth and nineteenth-century czarist Russia.

The story is about the power of love wielded by a courageous line of women, descendants of the woman in the portrait. It was their destiny to protect these famous Rembrandts from the threats of European revolutions, destructive invasions, obsessive men, and American law, until the paintings finally found security in a principal American museum. It is a quest through the ages for identity and fulfillment—the eternal search for home.

I present the story as *historical fiction*. What does that mean? My approach is to clearly know what is *known;* and to clearly know what is *not known,* then to work the known into an illuminating drama. It is somewhat mystical when I find how the exciting drama seeps out from between the colorful, historical facts. A frequent result of carefully examining history is the discovery of unintended consequences of well-planned events. Often these unexpected happenings are life changing, and sometimes even humorous.

I have spent years researching what is recorded and known about these paintings and their exciting journey through history, from their birth in seventeenth-century Holland until they found their current home in the National Gallery of Art in Washington, DC. There, today, the world can stand in front of many of Rembrandt's masterpieces and dream up their own story.

Part of my research took me to Amsterdam where I enjoyed an invaluable visit with Ernst van de Wetering, the leading authority on Rembrandt and head of The Rembrandt Research Project. I asked him a question, "What did Rembrandt think–about life, women, government, church, his work, himself, etc.?" Van de Wetering said, "We don't know what he thought; only what he represented, and that is for you and me to decide. And we may disagree." However, we do know what could have impacted Rembrandt's thinking—death all around (the plague), the restrictive Calvinist church, the recent break from the Catholic Bourbons, his chronic financial irresponsibility, the women in his life, his son's devoted life, and untimely death.

Rembrandt wrote nothing. He expressed himself with his brush. Amy Golahny says it well in her book, *Rembrandt's Reading,* "Rembrandt's greatness lies in his mastery of illusion in the service of narrative...." He conveyed "subtleties of expression, a style that dazzled the beholder with technical skill and conveyed psychological complexities." Hence the eyes of *The Lady...*, which captivated me and started the discovery of the story.

It has been a special and fulfilling experience to bring this tale all together. I am pleased to share it with you.

ACKNOWLEDGEMENTS

GRATITUDE GOES WELL BEYOND words to so many who have graciously helped me over the fifteen-plus years that this historical novel has been under research, development, writing, and publication.

First, I must thank the person who started it all. When I was visiting the National Gallery of Art, in Washington, DC, I called Priscilla Roosevelt, author of *Life on the Russian Country Estate*, to say hello. She asked, "Do you know the Yusupov Rembrandts?" My answer to her was negative. I then visited the portraits, and in an hour and a half I had the start for this story.

From the beginning, staff members at the National Gallery of Art, in Washington, DC were greatly supportive, in particular Arthur K. Wheelock Jr., Curator of Northern Baroque Paintings, and Anne Halpern, in the Department of Curatorial Records.

Also in Washington, DC, I had the critical assistance of Ronald Moe, of the Library of Congress, author of *Prelude to the Revolution: The Murder of Rasputin*.

In Amsterdam, I had the gracious help of Ernst van de Wetering, head of the Rembrandt Research Project, and Jaap van der Veen, Curator of Historical Research & Head of the Rembrandt Information Centre.

Elsewhere, others have been generous with their time and assistance: Amy Golahny, Professor of Art History, Art Department, Lycoming College, Williamsport, Pennsylvania; President, Historians of Netherlandish Art, and author of *Rembrandt's Reading*. Also, Idris Rhea Traylor Jr., historian and administrator at Texas Tech University.

Supporting and editing the Russian chapters were Evgeny Maksakov, Steve Shelokhonov, and Tatiana Solobaeva, all from St. Petersburg.

In addition to all the varied professional and literary support that has been so valuable, the focused development that a written work must have is a very good and experienced editor. I am so grateful for Loretta Hudson's professional expertise and commitment.

And then there were my friends and relations, well-read and well-traveled, and interested in the artistic subject of this book. A major help in her reading and productive criticism was Cali McClure of Laguna Hills, California. Another, and with most critical assistance before the work actually saw the light, was the professional proofreading and final editing of Fred and Jane Andresen, my son and daughter-in-law. Such educated and experienced sharp pencils were so crucial to the final form.

HOLLAND

1660–1760

CHAPTER ONE

THE HOPE

Amsterdam
Wednesday,
December 12, 1660

ANNEKE OUDERGAARD, her baby on her hip, pushed out the shutters and looked down the three stories to the Westerstraat where she saw Captain Henryk van Hoeten put a coin in the outstretched palm of a street boy and point him to the two shiny black horses harnessed to his coach by the snow-filled gutter. The boy ran to hold the impatient team that was snorting and shaking.

"Look at him, Mauriana. Isn't he magnificent?" Anneke put her hand over her mouth, holding back the rest of the thoughts she usually recites when talking about the father of her child. She was proud of Henryk, who had first gone to sea at fourteen. Now, with his own ships leading the lucrative Russian fur trade, she felt sure this man was ready to build his family and fortune, as a proper Dutchman should. Anneke loved him dearly. Still, she worried that Henryk's proposal had been the result of obligation.

While she looked down at her future husband, he glanced up at the window where she stood. The corners of his mouth curled upward in a broad smile when he saw her.

"He does love me," Anneke said.

Mauriana took the sleeping baby, blond little Saskia, from Anneke's arms. "Never doubt that, dearest. Now you must hurry."

Anneke laughed. Her burdening sense of guilt would soon be lifted. Her beloved daughter, born out of wedlock, had no father in the eyes of the Church and was, therefore, forbidden to be baptized as a Christian. Her marriage to Henryk in three days would change that.

"I am hurrying, Mauriana," said Anneke. "I'm almost ready. Sea captains will wait on the wind, but not on a woman." Anneke raised her arms in praise. "It's like coming to the end of a dark and sleepless night," she sang. Standing in the morning light, Anneke's voice dropped to a whisper, her hands coming to her lips as in prayer. "I know that whatever may lie ahead, with the comfort and strength of my love beside me," she looked toward the window and smiled, "nothing can harm us."

"You are poetic, madame." Mauriana smiled. "Now the dress." She gathered up the heavy black wool. "He'll wait on you, my dear, as he does the wind."

"I hope so." Anneke shrugged. She sat at her dressing table. "But, today is equally important." Looking into her mirror, fluffing her golden curls, she added, "I don't want to look like some country farm maid for The Master."

With a pad of felt she wiped a bit of rouge from a small porcelain dish and touched it to each cheek. "Ah, too much," she said, quickly rubbing some off, and then spreading the rest out with her finger, giving herself just a hint of pink.

Mauriana slipped the dress over Anneke's head, and attached the wide lace-trimmed cuffs. Over her shoulders she wrapped the lace collar, fastening it in front, and said, "Maybe Master Rembrandt will finally finish your portrait today?"

"But, first!" Anneke's mind was elsewhere. She pointed her finger in the air and slipped to the small writing desk in the corner. She took a quill and wrote quickly on the open vellum pages of a leather bound journal, remembering, as she passed her fingers over the vellum, her sea-captain father who had given her this diary as he left years before, on his last journey to the Dutch East Indies—a trip from which he never returned.

"Really, madame, you must hurry," Mauriana insisted.

Anneke replaced the quill after writing only six sentences. She blotted the ink, and closed the journal. "Yes," she whispered, "Home, we know, is not a place; it is where we belong to each other. And our answer will come—soon."

Straightening, she said, "Ah, Rembrandt. He is months overdue, so unpredictable. How he depends on the light. 'We wait on the sun,' he says. 'It doesn't wait on us.'"

Anneke lifted her chin as Mauriana centered the linen bow of five gathered ribbons onto the collar of her dress, fixing it with a little gold pin shaped like a flower.

"Henryk is a generous man," said Anneke. "Without all this, I would be in the poorhouse and little Saskia in the orphan home."

"But, you're free now," said Mauriana. "No longer your mother to care for. You're in the prime of life—so don't ruin it by being late."

Anneke slipped the gold bracelets onto her wrists, the matching ring onto her finger, and the gold necklace around her neck. "I'll be back early to finish the wedding dress," she said.

"We'll both be waiting for you."

Blond little Saskia, in her white cotton gown and lace cap, was fast asleep in the corner crib.

"You're like a mother to me, Mauriana." Anneke gave the nurse a kiss on the cheek. Grabbing her long coat and fur hat, she flew out the door and hurried down the narrow stairs, struggling to keep from tripping, holding onto the railing with one hand, and with the other, lifting her dress as it ballooned over five petticoats. After four steps she stopped, turned, and said, "Mauriana, three days. Our home. We will be together—in our home."

CHAPTER TWO

EXPECTATION

Amsterdam, 1660
Same day

"AMSTERDAM," ANNEKE SAID as if talking to herself, "hides its obsession with money behind a curtain of stiff white collars and clean front stoops." She turned to her betrothed to make her point as they rattled down the cobblestone Breestraat, a street wider than most in this city of canals, and narrow, gabled houses, and shuttered windows. From under his tall hat, Henryk's dark eyes admired his wife-to-be. She returned his smile, then turned to the window, watching the passing houses.

"Don't be ungrateful, my dear," he said, looking at her out the top of his eyes. "It is a city that has brought me a comfortable bit of wealth and security, which we will share, don't forget."

"Yes," she placed her hand on his and turned to the window again, "but it is hard to be happy under the judgmental eyes of those Calvinist predicants. They frown on the least hint of happiness."

"Not for long," he said squeezing her hand.

She knew that beyond those coveted doors, Dutch pride was displayed on white plaster walls in portraits of rich merchants with satisfied expressions. Soon there would be two more, painted by The Master himself.

Crossing the bridge over Sint Anthonies Sluys, the carriage clattered to a stop across the street from a row of those substantial homes. The driver jumped down and twisted open the latch of the coach door. Henryk stepped out and with one hand holding his hat against a sudden gust, offered the other to Anneke as her shining black boots touched the wet pavement stones.

"Being with you is my life," she said. With a finger she brushed aside a dark curl, kissing him on the cheek.

She looked up at the red brick house at Number 4, The Breestraat, four stories tall and one story wide, the house of Rembrandt Harmenszoon van Rijn.

She knew the house well, especially the artist's second-floor studio with its cracked, yellowing walls. Faded rectangles remained like ghosts where the works of Titian, Brueghel, van Leyden, and even Rubens once hung. The studio, Anneke remembered, was always too cold or too warm.

CHAPTER THREE

THE PAINTING

Amsterdam, 1660
Same day

FROM THE CORNER OF HIS second-floor window, Rembrandt looked down on the pair. He watched Henryk speak to the driver, then turn and take Anneke in his arms so their lips brushed. Rembrandt smiled, remembering how his wife Saskia and he had done the same. The sting of Saskia's death still lingered in his heart, although she had now lain for eighteen years under the cold floor of the Oude Kerk. Death from the painful plague was almost expected—at any age, at any time. How was it that he had survived? Still, his heart warmed in gratitude for Hendrickje Stoffels, who had filled his life after Saskia with love, care, and good cooking.

The artist closed his eyes, inhaling the scent of the linseed and walnut oil, the smoldering peat in the fireplaces—the smell of his studio, his home. His subjects were late, but he understood, knowing they had other things on their minds. No matter, he thought. Henryk's portrait was finished and Anneke's almost so. They were not the ordinary Dutch merchant couple with money—Henryk and Anneke. Their obvious love for each other persuaded him to paint their portraits. It was their eyes—the story was always in the eyes. Rembrandt wiped his brushes with a clean rag, stroking them as if they were pets.

He watched the woman on the street below, the sun brightening her golden locks. She took the man's arm as they strode toward the granite steps of his home, skipping around the children with their rolling hoops and barking dogs.

The cobblestones glistened with the melted wetness from the morning dusting of snow. The warm rays from the lowering sun flashed like tiny diamonds in the puddles. The ice had melted along the edges of Sint Anthonies Sluys. You can never count on December, he thought. It snows, freezing for days, and then the sun comes out, warming everything. The skating is ruined and the children are unhappy.

He heard Titus open the front door below, it making a cracking sound as it always did in the winter damp. Rembrandt was proud of Titus, his only son, a young man of almost twenty. He heard Titus greeting the couple with polite words. Rembrandt remained at the window, absorbing the winter scene; the zigzag rooftops of Amsterdam, gray smoke twisting from the blackened chimney pots, puffy clouds drifting east, unveiling a clear blue sky. He wondered why, during all those years on the Breestraat, he had resisted painting that sight. If only he could take that view with him now.

He heard Titus ushering the visitors onto the steep, winding staircase, telling them to grasp the thick rope railing.

"Good afternoon, Meester," Henryk called with a smile.

"It is a beautiful afternoon," followed Anneke.

Rembrandt continued to gaze out the window, stroking his brushes, ignoring their greetings. With inquiring eyes under bushy eyebrows, he turned to them, measuring their expressions, watching for hints of what lived behind the surface of those favored faces.

"We hope you are well, Meester," Henryk said, focusing on the artist. Rembrandt replied simply with his eyes. Henryk then glanced about the room, noticing its emptiness, except for the easels and a few chairs, and then turning to the warmth of the fireplace.

Rembrandt knew the whole gossiping town was aware these were the last days for him and his family in his comfortable home on the Breestraat. He resented the murmurings as unkind and unfair. His belongings long before auctioned to reduce his debts, he was now moving out of the house that he and his wife Saskia had bought twenty-one years before and loved so much. The city's Insolvency Office had announced that the new buyers had paid in full and could now take possession of the property. However, the pressures of penury vanished when he took a brush in his hand.

"Where will you go now?" Henryk asked.

Rembrandt grumbled an answer. "On the Rozengracht. A small place without much space to work. There are no roses—only in the name."

"It's a pity," Henryk said. "You have such success."

"Success, ha! What is success? A soldier has his victories. The merchant, his profit. My world is a dark swirling haze, without substance."

"Meester, you totally misjudge yourself. You are the most successful man in Holland, as God measures success."

"But God won't pay my debt," said Rembrandt. "The house sold for less than I paid for it." He paused and lowered his eyes. "But, let's get on with the thing at hand, yes?"

Sorting brushes, he laid some aside and picked up others. "No child this time?" Rembrandt asked.

"She's home with the nurse," said Anneke.

"Very considerate, dear Anneke." Rembrandt twisted the hairs of a brush. "Very considerate to name her after my Saskia."

"It's a musical name. Your wife was a lovely lady. She gave me an apple when I was small—a kindness a child never forgets."

Henryk spoke up, nodding toward the covered easels holding the couple's portraits, "When, Meester, are we going to see what's under those covers?"

Rembrandt hooked his thumbs into his waist sash. "Henryk, and Mrs. Van Hoeten to be," he said, tipping his head and inspecting Anneke's hair. "So we will finish today, yes?" He smiled now. "You look surprised at that prediction, my friends. I work too slowly, they say." He raised both hands and shrugged, then picked up his palette. "Time means nothing in art. If you get the moment right, it will last forever." He inspected Anneke from his easel. "And that takes time," he added. He reached forward, straightening the cap on the back of her head and smoothing her tawny locks over her shoulder. "Ha, you are the image of a proper Dutch woman, and," he nodded toward Henryk, "in the style befitting the wife of a successful Dutchman."

Rembrandt glanced toward Henryk, who was settling into a wooden chair by the fireplace. He felt a personal sense of gratitude for this opportunity to paint a successful businessman of the most powerful city in Europe. In his own small way, he felt a part of that power. If he couldn't sail the world, he could at least immortalize those who did. He was pleased to paint Henryk and his wife, hoping it would help turn around his lagging business and burdensome debt.

"Now hold the feather as before," said Rembrandt. Anneke moistened her lips with the tip of her tongue. Rembrandt stepped to the north-facing window to angle the shutters in order to throw the soft shadows just right. Then he adjusted the overhead curtain that served as a reflector. Humming a tune now, his arms folded in satisfaction, he paused before her, then reached forward and moved her hands up a few centimeters, lifting his eyes and smiling. "As always," he said, "just forget I am here. Be yourself."

The artist nodded his approval as he set the pose. She followed him with her eyes.

He picked up the palette in his left hand, dipping the brush into the thinned brown ocher. Wiping the excess on a rag, he sat and, steadying his hand on the mahlstick, trailed the brush like a feather over the canvas on the image of her right cheek and rubbed the paint with his finger. Then, he stroked her left cuff with a heavier touch, wiping it with his thumb.

"Stop smiling, Anneke," Rembrandt said. "It changes the whole image."

Rembrandt knew why it was hard for Anneke to keep her mouth composed that day. But, it didn't matter. Those eyes, those liquid brown eyes, held secrets and a quick wit. He opened the image of her mouth a bit with a fine brush of black between the lips to give a hint of expectancy for that sharp comment, or grain of wisdom, that wanted to come out. She had a pretty mouth, full and sensuous.

"How can you tell me to cease smiling, Meester?" she said when he paused. "You know what is happening in three days!" Her head remained still, but her eyes flashed.

"If you want this for your wedding, you must hold still," he said as he shot a glance toward Henryk, seeking support, knowing Anneke Oudergaard was an outspoken woman.

"Finished today, Rembrandt? Really?" Henryk inquired from his seat by the fire.

"Well, if not today," added Rembrandt, "enough to send you on your way, for a work is not finished until the artist has achieved his intention in it. Maybe a few touches here and there yet." He turned the ostrich feather a bit for the shadows to give more depth. "The feather," Rembrandt pointed with his brush, "it is like the fragility of a woman's love—so soft and dear, yet so easily lost." He rose from his chair and stood back, folding his arms. "Art, like life," he said, "needs distance. My work is not to be examined with a magnifying glass, like a student studies a bug."

He looked around, impatient, then grabbed a sable-hair brush so fine it contained only ten hairs. He spread a dab of yellow ocher onto the pallet and applied it to give more shine to the bracelets. Then flipping the brush around, he used the sharp wooden end to carve shadows into the gold, as though it was clay. With a short circular motion he formed a flower of gold in the center of the bow at her neck.

"The light is fading," Rembrandt said, taking Anneke's shoulders, turning her bit by bit. It was all about light and shadow. He sought what was within. To find the expression of character he focused the light on the face and hands. He left the rest to the mystery of dark browns and grays.

The voice in Rembrandt's head spoke to him all the time, telling him how to bring the subject's soul to life on his canvas.

"Are you hiding something?" he asked. "Your eyes, Anneke. They tell me that. What is your secret?"

Henryk looked up from his papers.

"You can't be too happy and be Dutch," the artist said. "I know the problem. Calvinist judgment!" Always there is the burden of a verdict against something beautiful that is nobody's business but his own. He thought of Hendrickje's auburn hair falling delicately between his fingers. Her green eyes as deep as the North Sea. For six years after Saskia's death he looked and waited for eyes like Hendrickje's. "If you are too happy," he said, "those jealous old men will think you are hiding something. A smile is suspicious. Let them guess, yes?"

"I must finish my wedding dress tonight," Anneke said.

Titus entered to stoke the fires and light two tallow candles on a side table for Henryk. He placed a saucer of oil on a table for his father. Rembrandt loved the smell of burning candles, the oil mingling with the aroma of the paint. He loved to see Titus, his student for two years now, stand back, silently watching him. There was learning in that watching.

Rembrandt compared Anneke's face to the image on the canvas, sensing an uncertainty, a concern in her eyes. He asked a question long on his mind. "Anneke," he paused, "what is it you want?"

Henryk looked up again, lifting his eyebrows, perhaps wanting to know the same thing.

"What is it you want more than anything?" Rembrandt asked as he dabbed a little more umber on the image of her hand, rubbing it with his thumb. "There's a yearning in your eyes."

"A yearning? Yes," she quickly answered, "for a safe home and a happy family," she paused, "and to be heard—and understood." She stopped, as if measuring her words, "Most important, what any woman wants—to be loved by the man she loves." Anneke smiled and tilted her head as if to say, "That's it."

"Ah, the same with art," said Rembrandt, "That is all a piece of art wants—to have a home, to be safe, to be admired, to be loved, to be understood."

Rembrandt kept stroking the wet paint. "But, you are not just any woman, Anneke Oudergaard. Not like other Dutch wives with their knitting in their laps."

She smiled and nodded her head.

"And what about playing that harpsichord we hear about?" he asked. "We'll listen when you return from Italy, yes?"

"Oh yes," she said, "I would play for the whole town if I could. My heart sings when I play. After mama died, Henryk sought to lift my spirits by buying me an exquisite, double-manual harpsichord from the Flemish master J. Ruckers. It has a beautiful scene of birds and flowers with a Latin proverb painted under the lid. *Music is the company of joy and the medicine of sorrow.*"

There they were, only steps away from her betrothed, discussing the depths of her heart. That is what happened to some when he painted them. He loved to expose their souls in unexpected ways with his brush.

"I am an impatient woman." She twisted the feather. "But, I have waited for Henryk and that has made all the difference." She gave Henryk a glance. "I no longer care," she said, "if I offend the unsmiling clergy. They stare at my gold jewelry as if it were stolen. It will be Saint Nicolas' Day soon, and I shall again dance in the street with the children."

Henryk smiled as he listened to her confessions. Rembrandt heard the same words while continuing to touch the image of the fan, but may have received a different message.

"Can you believe this?" she continued. "When I showed up at the Zuiderkerk to baptize the baby, they refused until I would name the father." She looked toward Rembrandt. "When I would not do that, they mocked me, asking if I thought I was the Virgin Mary, and banned me from communion."

"After that," said Rembrandt, without taking his eyes from the canvas, "I imagine playing the harpsichord in public will not be the worst affront to God, no?"

The minutes then silently passed as he continued to work on the woman's image with his broad and fine brushes, occasionally using his fingertip or fingernail.

"Now, I have a surprise for you," Rembrandt said, placing his brush in a tall, stained cup. "Come here, both of you." He moved the easel with Henryk's portrait to the left of hers and uncovered it. He lit another oil wick, moving both lights to illuminate the portraits. "Are you afraid to see what old Rembrandt has done?" He moved a bench in front of the paintings. Henryk and Anneke sat on the bench without a word, she twisting the ostrich feather in her hand.

Anneke shook her head in delight. "The dimple! You painted the dimple in his chin." She tilted her head, smiling in admiration.

Henryk pulled in his chin, puffing out his chest. "And, my dear, what about my aristocratic mustache?" He twisted it with his fingers, affecting a haughty pose. "And my noble nose?" The smile lines deepened at the corners of his eyes and he raised his eyebrows.

She reached up, kissing the tip of his nose, then tickling it with the feather. "It *is* a noble nose," she said with an adoring smile. "A very Dutch nose."

Henryk turned to the artist, "The shadow across my eyes, Rembrandt, what do you make of that?"

"I make it a big hat, Meneer. That is what it's for," the artist said. "The shadow lends mystery. Are you hiding something, too, Henryk?"

"Only," he answered in almost a whisper, "that one of my ships is long overdue from Arkhangelsk. I fear for the captain and crew." He straightened his jacket and looked toward the window. "I'm not like Bickers with his fleet of merchantmen. I have only three ships, but enough to support a warehouse on the White Sea of Russia with good Russian partners. It is not a business for the faint of heart, Rembrandt. And, Ruts," Henryk continued, "he was a handsome and clever merchant. Your portrait of him, wrapped in his sables, did not guarantee his success."

Rembrandt knew that Henryk strove hard to prevent Nicolaes Ruts's misfortune from becoming his own. That's why Henryk's portrait showed his authority and success—a Dutch merchant in black cloak with white collar and cuffs, a thin mustache, a cleft chin. There were the long curls under the usual tall black hat and in his left hand, a pair of brown leather gloves.

"It's perfect," Anneke said. "You are indeed a master." Only then did she turn to inspect her own likeness. She posed, gesturing with her hands and the feather, as if the portrait was a mirror and the image could reflect her movements. She held the feather to her mouth saying, "I'm afraid you were right. My happiness does not show."

"Maybe," Rembrandt offered. "Maybe it reflects some of my own worries at this time."

"I shouldn't be sad, though," Anneke said. "Maybe I'm afraid. I can't explain. I think maybe you have captured my inner being."

She shivered as a chill crept through the room. The peat fires had died to a bed of dull embers. The lantern cast a glow on all their faces, but threw long shadows across the floor and up the walls.

"There will never be a perfect work of art," Rembrandt told them. "There is only what the artist represents, and that is one thing to one person, and another to the next." He spread his hands before the paintings, "Now you are like poems that are seen, but not heard. What the viewer feels will be truth to him, but only him. It is no longer up to me or to you."

"Indeed, Meneer Rembrandt," Anneke said, "it is then a master painter's poetry."

"You belong together," the artist remarked, bending over and reaching between them, pointing to the portraits. "Anneke, you gesture toward Henryk with your feather, yes? And Henryk, with your gloves toward this beautiful woman? It is a symbolic union."

Putting away his brushes, Rembrandt said, "I will sign the paintings after the wedding when the paint has dried—ready for your home."

Titus called from below, "Father, supper is ready." The smell of boiled fish drifted up from the kitchen below.

Rembrandt led the couple down the narrow stairs to the *voorhuis*, the entry hall where their footsteps echoed off the empty walls. The painter lifted Anneke's coat off the wall hook and gave it to Henryk. He glanced at the floor, designed in the common black and white checkerboard pattern, but scratched and scarred from the nails of the movers' boots. He knew he would never see it repaired and painted again, since he had to vacate his home and studio by year's end.

"Henryk," Rembrandt said, "the marriage won't satisfy all their questions." He laughed, shaking his head, "Oh! Those stiff-necked preachers!" he said. "What do they know of a woman's love and the man's pain in its absence? Had the Spaniards won the war, we would be Catholic, enjoying life more, I think. With the priests you can always confess and get on with living. Hell is somewhere in the future, not every day. But, God is here for us. That's what we have to hold to."

"The ceremony is set for eleven," Henryk said. "Pastor de Groot will conduct it. I paid him double. He is a Remonstrant and more tolerant in this case. Will you be there?"

"I will," said Rembrandt.

She held out the feather. "May I take this with me?"

Rembrandt nodded. "In remembrance for your patience. Yes."

Henryk held Anneke's black sable-lined coat. She slipped into one sleeve, then the other, then buttoned the front. He handed her the black Russian *shapka* of arctic sea otter, and kissed her cheek.

"Here is for your masterful work, Rembrandt," said Henryk, handing him an envelope with the agreed one hundred guilders for the portraits. The artist laid it on the bench for Titus to count later.

Henryk pulled on his own coat, closed the double row of buttons down the front, and gathered his valise.

Rembrandt pulled open the door to a blast of cold. Henryk and Anneke stepped out onto the stone steps, their breath clouding in the cold December night. "Careful of the rime ice, my friends," Rembrandt called. "It forms even on a clear night."

Henryk steadied himself on the iron railing with one hand and with the other gripped Anneke's arm.

"Saturday," Rembrandt called, watching them descend the five steps. He closed the door, slid the lock in place, and turned and descended the narrow stairs to the kitchen below, to sit down to Hendrickje's table of creamed cabbage and peppered boiled fish.

The cold air stung Anneke's cheeks as she thought of the artist's tired face as the door closed on Number 4, the Breestraat. She absorbed the vision of the man as if she were the artist—an old man with a bush of gray hair, a scrubby beard, heavy lids hanging over tired eyes, and an upturned potato nose, wrinkled and veined. She knew he had a caustic attitude that annoyed many, yet he had a persistent, spiritual ethic that shined through. She marveled at the magic that he produced with paint and canvas. That was, she decided, what made one man's work cherished forever and another's forgotten.

Sparkles of frost hung like jewels in the yellow light of the street lamps. A large, silver halo circled the moon. The coach stood waiting for them, the horses' breath curling in the moonlight, their hooves scraping on the glistening cobblestones as if agitated by something they saw.

Portrait of a Gentleman with a Tall Hat and Gloves
Rembrandt van Rijn 1660
The National Gallery of Art, Washington, DC

Portrait of a Lady with an Ostrich-Feather Fan
Rembrandt van Rijn 1660
The National Gallery of Art, Washington, DC

CHAPTER FOUR

THE PROMISE

Amsterdam
Night
December 12, 1660

ANNEKE GASPED WHEN SHE saw the man walking toward them with long legs and short steps, reminding her of a scarecrow draped in a black sack. His hands were locked behind him.

"Good evening, Predicant Basilius," Henryk offered.

He was without hat or gloves, but then Predicants of the Dutch Reformed Church were known to tempt the devil himself, and an icy night was nothing to hide from. This familiar sight was like a walking shadow of waiting condemnation.

Basilius slowed, took three steps, then stopped, his black eyes fixed on Anneke. He did not answer Henryk.

Anneke shivered. "Good evening, Predicant Basilius," she said.

Basilius held Anneke in his accusing gaze and did not respond. Rotating on his heels as if animated by strings, he faced Henryk, eyebrows arching in judgment, saying, "Good evening, Meneer van Hoeten." His mouth twitched, and pulled up into a smirk, but only on the left side of his face, as his right side was frozen with a scar that pulled his eye askew and from there, continued to the bottom of his chin. Without a further word, he pivoted on his heels in the original direction of his walk, disappearing into shadow.

Anneke shivered again. "Discourteous man! Those cold eyes always condemning. He never even spoke to me!"

"Don't let it concern you, my dear," said Henryk. "After Saturday, you will have a husband, our daughter will have a name, and Predicant Basilius will direct his stare at someone else."

"I feel haunted," she said, "as if he has put a curse on me."

Henryk put his hand on the coach door.

"Wait." She held Henryk's face in her hands, looking deep into his eyes. "My love for you, Henryk, is forever." Her eyes demanded a response.

He pulled her closer and whispered, "I will never leave you. You will have a home, my dear. You will never be in debt again. You will be heard." His hands slipped under her collar and cupped her face in the winter moonlight. He kissed her eyes, her mouth. "I will always be by your side, my love."

His warmth comforted her, but the cold censure of the Church still chilled her very marrow. Again she shivered as if shaking off a bad dream.

Henryk opened the coach door, holding Anneke's hand as she lifted her skirts and coat and stepped into the cab.

"You are not coming with me?" Anneke asked.

"Faithful Schuyler will take you home. I must check again for news of my ship. I've been away most of the day."

She turned, leaning out for one last tender kiss, smiled, and tickled his nose with the feather.

"Tomorrow," he said. He latched the door and slapped the side of the coach. "Take her home, Schuyler. Take care of her. She is my jewel."

"Ah, yes, Meneer," the driver took the whip in his hands. "I am careful with jewels. She is safe with me."

The click of the departing hooves on the icy pavement echoed against the walls of the narrow streets. Henryk sighed and with satisfaction. "Saturday!" He glanced at the moon with its mysterious ring, and watched until the coach rounded the houses on the canal. He turned to wend his way toward the port on the slick cobblestones of Sint Anthoniesbreestraat.

The noise hit him like the shock of cannon fire. Down the icy corridors of dark houses rolled the shrill cries of frightened horses, a crash, the scraping of wood and steel, the confused shouts of men, a pause, then a crack, a splash. He feared to guess what, or who, it might be.

Henryk turned and raced toward the sound. He tripped and slid as he turned the corner, grabbing a lamppost to steady himself. He saw a carriage, its horses rearing, whinnying, and uncontrolled. The driver jumped down and ran toward the canal. A fat man in a heavy coat squeezed out the carriage door.

"What...?" cried Henryk.

He heard the driver cry, "In the water! Help!"

In the canal, on its side in a jagged hole in the thin ice, Henryk saw Anneke's coach. The horses, their eyes wide with fear, thrashed to keep their heads above the water.

"My foot!" he heard Schuyler shout. "It's caught in the reins! I can't reach the door." The canal surface was a churning maelstrom of broken ice and belching bubbles. Henryk saw no sign of Anneke.

Henryk ran to the low, stone wall near the edge of the street, tearing off his coat, ripping open the double line of buttons, and jumped into the freezing water. Taking a deep breath, he went under to open the carriage door, but couldn't budge it. He braced his feet against the carriage and twisted the handle. It broke off in his hands. He kicked in the window and taking another breath, reached in past the jagged glass, opening it from the inside. Grabbing the lapels of Anneke's coat, he struggled to drag her, soaked and unconscious, to the wall of the canal.

"Help me!" Henryk called. The driver and the fat man from the other coach were already there to pull her up. She was not breathing. Henryk bent her over the stone wall and pounded her back. Water poured from her mouth, but her breath did not return.

Henryk, shaking and heedless of his bleeding hand, took Anneke in his arms. His mouth opened, but no words came out. He stared at her lifeless body—wet hair draped across her staring eyes, and still clutched in her hand, sodden and limp, the ostrich feather.

CHAPTER FIVE

THE VISIT

A country house near Amsterdam
Evening,
May, 1698

"HERE THEY COME!" shouted Anneke. "Russians are so exciting. Princes and soldiers!" Now almost nineteen, she bounced on her toes, stretching her lean body out the open top half of the heavy wooden door of the van Hoeten home, a low Dutch country house with thick walls, small windows and a heavy thatched roof.

Squinting into the slanting gold rays of the fading sun, she called, "I see them all, Mama." She turned to confirm her mother was coming.

She watched the carriages rumble into closer view, the village dogs barking at the wheels. "There are six, no *seven* of them," she repeated with the excitement of a child on St. Nicholas' day.

Anneke's mother called from the kitchen. "*Seven?* No one told me *seven.*" Saskia Voss, tall and blond like her daughter, hurried to the half-open door, placed her hand on Anneke's shoulder, and peered around her daughter's golden locks. "You are right," her mother confirmed, "Seven! More places at the table!"

The carriages rattled along a rutted road between the floral fields of blue, yellow, and red leading up to the village with its old bent trees and crooked dirt streets. The black coaches were identical except for the third one—it was larger. The gold trim about its doors and windows flashed in the evening rays filtering through the greening linden trees that lined the road.

Watching the Russians approach, both Saskia and Anneke were excited. "But as usual they are late," Saskia said. "We met the Russians before—Henryk's visiting merchants in better times. They were always late." Holland now was abuzz with the rumors of the visiting Russians' gallantry, their generosity, and, at other times, their insatiable thirst and surprisingly bad manners.

"Mother," teen-aged Anneke shook with excitement, "Kings are not really late. It is their privilege to arrive when they please. Common folk just wait." Especially for this occasion Anneke had made a new dress of fine cotton in folds of hyacinth blue that touched the top of her high-buttoned shoes. The white lace collar framed her dimpled face and brown eyes. Centered on her collar was a family heirloom, a bent bow of faded pink linen.

"There is no king coming," Saskia said. "Remember what we were told. Also, remember…" and the mother shook her finger at her daughter, "…we are not common folk. The Dutch bow to no king." Anneke rolled her eyes, again peering down the road.

"Father," Saskia called up the stairs, "there are seven carriages. How do we feed them all?" Into her daughter's ear, Saskia whispered, "This is costing your grandfather." She held a rag to her cheek for privacy. "He's withdrawn over three hundred guilders from the bank to afford the food and these special cooks from Amsterdam. Of course he refuses to borrow against the Rembrandts."

Anneke turned and watched her mother retreat to the kitchen, first stopping under the Rembrandts, each a bit above eye level on the fireplace wall, and speaking softly to them as she often did. "How I wish you could be here with our family, today," Saskia said. "Even after all our loss, the Czar of Russia is coming to our home. Perhaps, Mother, you *are* here."

Then Henryk, her grandfather, blinking under bushy gray eyebrows, steadied himself on both railings as he descended the narrow staircase from the upper floor. Trials had creased his face and bent his body, but his trousers and jacket were pressed and spotless, as was expected from a sea captain. "We hear," Henryk said, hobbling into the kitchen, "the Czar often insists his servants dine with him."

Although it all happened before she was born, she remembered her mother telling her of her grandfather's love and support in spite of his loss of three ships—one in the Arctic ice, and another, loaded with sable and otter skins, to French pirates, and a third which he had to sell to pay his debts. She was very aware of Holland's fading fortunes forcing his retreat to the spare economy of the countryside where they now lived. All he had left of value were his precious Rembrandts.

Even young Anneke knew the Dutch Golden Age was over. Holland had fought another war with England, and their foothold in the New World had slipped. New Amsterdam was now called New York. She was anxious to meet the Russians.

The carriages clattered to a stop before the van Hoeten home. Anneke's attention was diverted by the sight of old Schuyler, a bent man in black, limping from the barn behind the house. He dragged his lame leg, which had been twisted beyond repair under the sunken carriage of her grandmother, forty years before. Although Henryk absolved him of any blame, a crippling guilt still possessed the man. That two carriages crashed on the dark streets of an empty Amsterdam just after the painting was finished and the wedding planned had always been a cruel mystery to the whole family.

"You are late," Schuyler scolded the arriving coachmen. But the Russians paid no attention to the old man speaking in Dutch.

Young Anneke focused on the gold-trimmed third carriage out of which she expected to emerge an emperor with a golden crown and ermine-trimmed purple robes. Disembarking first from the other coaches were an assortment of men, including soldiers in rich green uniforms with shining black boots and belts, hanging sabers, and gleaming brass buckles.

Anneke's mouth dropped open at the sight of these handsome men with their long sideburns, curling mustaches, and plumed hats. She watched them brushing out the wrinkles in their heavy cloaks, and lining up, five on each side on the short path that led from the gold-trimmed third coach to the door of the van Hoeten home.

One of them, Anneke guessed a servant by his simple shirt and sash, placed a small red carpet at the door of the third coach. The carriage door opened and two black boots stepped firmly onto the red square.

Anneke judged the emerging man was in his mid-twenties. He straightened, but did not stand like a soldier. Over his gray silk tunic draped a silver robe with golden rope closures. His hair was dark, hanging in curls upon his collar. He had a narrow mustache that extended just beyond the corners of his mouth. Anneke stood in the doorway with Henryk. She felt the young Russian's eyes snap onto her like a magnet. From within the coach a tap on the man's shoulder reminded him that others were ready to alight.

Next out was a gray-haired man in a royal blue cloak with golden eagle clasps at his neck. Gold chains hung from his boots. He stepped down and stood beside the door for the last man, who bent to clear the carriage roof. Like lightning, ten sabers flashed out of their scabbards and were held in a vertical salute, all precisely in line, the back edge of the blades touching each soldier's nose.

The tall man wore no rich, gold-trimmed costume, only a shining buckle on the same fitted, green uniform that the guards wore, and no insignia of rank or plumed hat. He brushed himself off and looked about, squinting at the faces peering from the cottage windows and doors. When he straightened he stood more than a head taller than the others.

Henryk, his arms around Saskia and Anneke, whispered, "That's him, Peter, Czar of Russia." The czar had a thin mustache, a high forehead, thick eyebrows, and curls reaching his shoulders. From the buzzing house staff Anneke knew they were prepared and excited that the czar was there to have dinner with her grandfather Henryk, the old fur trader, and his family.

With her hands on her hips, Saskia turned to survey the room, tight for twenty persons at dinner. A kitchen helper ran in with more chairs borrowed from neighbors. Four tables of varying heights were rearranged to make one long table. Bouquets of red tulips were centered on tablecloths of the best Dutch linen. More settings were squeezed onto the tables.

Anneke helped a servant push the family's heirloom cherry-wood harpsichord into the corner. She positioned it so that its ornately painted flowers of entwined red and gold were still clearly visible to those entering the room.

Saskia whipped off her apron. She wondered what the Russians thought as they entered the room, removing their hats as they passed through the old door frame, their boots dragging dirt onto the freshly scrubbed floor. She smiled to see them raise their heads, inhale the rich aroma of spices and food, and make agreeable-sounding comments she could not understand.

Saskia moved beside Henryk as he greeted, in his halting Russian, Czar Peter, and the other two from the czar's carriage, the older one introduced as Franz Yakovlevich Lefort, and the younger one as Aleksandr Danilovich Menshikov, who managed a glance toward Anneke, standing beside her mother. The others introduced themselves with great formality as they entered, but no one understood their names or impressive titles. Everyone seemed to be a general, or an admiral, or both. They smiled and bowed with their left hands behind their backs and their right hands over their hearts.

"Look at them, Mother." Anneke's eyes measured each of the Russians. "These are real men! They are not like the Dutch boys with their dirty hands and country manners."

Saskia gave her daughter a sideways glance, knowing Anneke yearned for the excitement of Amsterdam, or better still, the imagined thrills of Paris or London. She sighed, knowing that all the young Anneke really knew was the solitude of a Dutch village. Everything else was a fairy tale. She whispered to Anneke, "Be careful tonight, my dear. Our family has had enough surprises."

CHAPTER SIX

THE FEAST

The country house near Amsterdam
Evening,
May, 1698

A NNEKE RETREATED TO STAND behind the harpsichord where she could watch the Russians crowding into her home. It was a sight she had never imagined. First were the two men from the gilded carriage, then Czar Peter himself, bending to clear the doorframe. Then they kept coming, rifles, boots, dust, and all.

The soldiers quieted when Peter stood in the center of the crowded room. He turned, intensely examining his hosts' surroundings. Anneke's mother had told her to expect this because it was a long and first sojourn of a Russian czar into Europe. She was amazed at his attention to the paintings of landscapes, and family scenes. His inspection stopped as the two portraits on the fireplace wall seemed to catch and hold his attention. He moved on without asking questions, but twice he returned to *The Gentleman with Tall Hat and Gloves* and *The Lady with an Ostrich-Feather Fan*.

The czar's companion introduced himself to Henryk: Prince Aleksandr Danilovich Menshikov. Henryk asked, "I hear he wants to be called by a special name?"

"Peter Mikhailovich," Menshikov whispered into Henryk's ear. "His name is just Peter Mikhailovich while he is in your country. That is what he wants," Menshikov explained.

He went on to explain that the Grand Embassy was a caravan holding three ambassadors, each with scores of servants, soldiers and attendants, of which Czar Peter pretended to be one. He went on to list the many others, including four dwarfs, a monkey, and the czar's drummer—two hundred fifty people in all, plus the monkey. Anneke listened, but also noted Menshikov's glances in her direction, which she met with a smile.

Henryk gestured toward the head seat, "Please, Peter Mikhailovich, the seat of honor." To Peter's left sat Lefort, and on his right Menshikov took a seat and then motioned to Anneke, who was still behind the harpsichord. She quickly joined him. With the added set-ups the diners were crowded. Anneke and Menshikov sat with hips and shoulders touching.

Anneke smiled and out of the corner of her eye examined the handsome Russian. She was pleased to see Henryk and Saskia sitting at the other end of the table where they could keep an eye on the kitchen—but not on her.

The table was covered with delights rare in the van Hoeten household. There were silver-beaded salvers of stuffed goose in a wild cherry sauce, two braised pigs rubbed with rosemary, coriander and pepper, and platters of fish and vegetables. Wine spiced with cinnamon, nutmeg, and cloves filled large pewter decanters.

Henryk raised his cup. "We are honored," he said, "to have the Ambassadors of the Czar of Russia in our humble home." He went on to mention trust, friendship, and the things on which good and lasting business is based anywhere, but particularly in Russia.

Anneke was impressed by her grandfather's words. She smiled at Menshikov to register that. She was proud of her family's hosting of the Russian Czar.

The toasts continued in between the forks of pork and goose. With each toast they drank the full cup, and by the time the czar made his speech, some men were mumbling and slouching in their chairs, or had to be silenced to hear the czar's words.

Czar Peter stood, lifted his cup, leaned forward and said, "My friends," as he looked on the faces of his hosts, "in the approaching new century Russia's place in Europe will be a bridge between the West and East."

He paused until everyone quieted and looked in his direction. "The Czar of Russia," he said, "through his Ambassadors assembled here," looking into Henryk's eyes, "pays tribute to Henryk van Hoeten and his family, who have helped tie the bonds of understanding between Russia and The Netherlands." Anneke occasionally felt an elbow or a nudge of Menshikov's leg, along with a smile.

The Czar held his cup high. The Russians scraped back their chairs and stood, lifting their cups. Downing his wine in one gulp, the Czar continued, "We have a small gift as a remembrance of this evening."

He clapped his hands and a servant entered with a box, his arms straining to embrace it. He placed it before Henryk, after the plates and dinnerware were pushed aside. The box was wrapped in ordinary, oiled, brown paper and tied with twine as though it might contain dried fish.

Anneke stretched in her seat to see what it was.

"Open it!" Peter gestured with both hands.

Anneke watched Henryk cut the twine with a table knife and lay the paper aside. He pulled open the box flaps and his face froze in disbelief. The servant lifted out a gleaming bouquet of roses, the stems and leaves of silver, the flower petals an intricate swirl of pink gold. Saskia took a deep breath. Anneke's eyes widened in amazement.

Anneke said into Menshikov's ear, "Your czar is very generous."

"Russia is a rich country," Menshikov whispered, "It is the workmanship of Russian craftsmen. It is nothing compared to what we enjoy in Russia: magnificent palaces, golden carriages, glorious balls." He sipped his wine, shook his curls, and leaned closer, saying, "You would shine like a jewel there."

She thrilled to the warmth of their bodies touching in the chairs. She searched into his dark eyes, imagining the wonder of the world of princes and palaces beyond the boredom of a Dutch village, even beyond a rich and growing city like Amsterdam, which knew only the usual merchants, craftsmen, and artists.

With his knife, Peter struck his chalice again saying, "Henryk, please, your country..." he waved his hand in the air, "...it is so small, yet so powerful. You have no large army. You have but sailors, businessmen," and he turned to address the Rembrandts, "and artists. A civilized land, this western world. All this order and industry—he shook his head. Please tell us what we can learn from this."

Henryk cleared his throat and sipped his wine, as if searching for words. "Our strength," he said, "is in what we *do*, not what we have. There is some advantage, Peter Mikhailovich, in being small." He took another sip from his cup. "The small have no choice but to make and keep friends. We raise artists and craftsmen, and hire our soldiers when needed. It is better that way."

"Someday," Peter said, his eyes still on the portraits, "Russia will have both power and artists. It is my dream." Peter then leaned over and whispered a few words in Menshikov's ear.

Menshikov leaned closer to Anneke. "Tell me, Anneke," he said, "those portraits," motioning toward the Rembrandts with his head, "who are they?"

"They are our family," she said. "The paintings survived our move from the city. We hid them from the creditors. They are by Rembrandt, our most famous artist." She lowered her voice, "We all know the man with the gloves is grandfather Henryk in his prime. The woman...?" She shrugged. "He doesn't speak of her, but we all know it is my grandmother. There was a horrible accident before their wedding."

"Of course," Menshikov said, looking from the portrait to Anneke. "The resemblance!"

She lowered her eyes. "I am named for her."

"Ah. How nice. The bow at her neck," he added as he focused on the faded lace bow fixed under Anneke's chin.

"The woman's portrait," Anneke said, "is known as 'Portrait of a Lady with an Ostrich-Feather Fan.'"

"Your mother?" and he glanced toward Saskia at the end of the table.

"Yes," she nodded.

"And your father?" he asked.

"An officer with the Dutch East India Company. I hardly remember him," she said. "Disappeared into the jungles of Java we were told. I was only two."

"Anneke," the Russian quietly asked, "would you think Henryk would be willing to part with those paintings? For a good sum in gold, of course?"

Anneke straightened and pulled back, her hand to her mouth. The suggestion frightened her. "They are family, sir." Regaining her composure she continued, "Your request is a compliment, but he would part with them no more than he would part with my mother or me."

Menshikov nodded, sat back, turned, and with his eyes reported to the czar, who received the refusal with an understanding nod.

Then Anneke slid back her chair, folded her napkin and stood, facing the czar. "I have something for you, sir. I hope you will accept it as a gift."

"Oh? I am honored," Czar Peter said, raising his eyebrows.

She moved to the harpsichord in the corner. Lifting the top, she secured the supporting brace, displaying its underside with its painted scene of birds and flowers and, in silver and gold script, the words *MUSICA LAETITAE COMES MEDICINA DOLORUM.*

Striking his empty chalice, Peter, watching her, said, "Quiet now! We have music. *Quiet!*"

She played Couperin's romantic *Elegy,* thinking passionately about Aleksandr Menshikov, whose descriptions of Russian aristocratic life had immediately captured her young heart and carried her away as in a fairy tale.

After the last notes and the applause, she returned to the table where Menshikov took Anneke's hand and kissed it. "I am astounded," he said still holding her hand. "I have never heard a lady play a musical instrument before, not a noble lady like you—only gypsies and peasants in my country, and never a harpsichord." He held her chair and they sat. "We have no music schools as you do. The Russian Church forbids anything but the human voice." He moved closer and whispered, "It was to me the music of an angel."

She humbly lowered her head and moistened her smiling lips.

He nodded toward the harpsichord. "What does the Latin on your instrument say?"

Looking up and without taking her eyes off of his, she said, "It means *music is the company of joy and the medicine of sorrow.*" Anneke clasped her hands. "But, if a lady cannot play for others in Russia, what is she to do? A woman must be heard." She leaned forward and lowered her voice. "That is what I did for you. I sent you a message from my heart. Did you feel that?"

"I did," Menshikov said, "I want to feel it more, perhaps next time in a Russian palace." He waved the air with his hand. "There will be a new city. Peter is planning it on the Baltic. A city of palaces, the finest in all Europe." He took her hands. "I want to hear you play in my Russian palace."

The meal over, some left the table, moving out through the front door to smoke their meerschaum pipes filled with tobacco from the English colony of Virginia. But, Menshikov took Anneke by the hand and moved through the kitchen out the rear of the house. They were alone—except for one.

From the stables, old Schuyler watched the two as they slipped behind the barn. It was dark. At first Schuyler, cupping his ear, heard only mumblings. The sliver of moon offered little light, but he discerned the dark forms of Anneke and the Russian melt into one undulating body against the wall, swallowed by the shadows of the barn. Schuyler recognized the ruffling of fabric. He heard

Menshikov in low tones. Anneke was giggling with the high voice of excitement, followed by long, passionate sighs.

Schuyler leaned forward, but the sounds became masked by the merriment drifting through the open windows and doors of the house. A soldier plinked on the harpsichord. The cooks and helpers came out the back door, dumping garbage in an iron-bound wooden swill bucket on the step, throwing their dirty rags on the old planked table to be washed later, and laughing as well as complaining. An aproned cook leaned out the door, shielded her eyes, peered into the dark, shook a rag, and returned to the kitchen.

Inside the van Hoeten home the focus was intense. It pleased Henryk to be included. Around a cleared table, Czar Peter and Lefort stood with Henryk and several others hovering over a map of the lands and swamps of the Russian River Neva emptying into the Gulf of Finland. Peter, with flying hands, dramatized his plans. "There are good reasons for this city," he said including Henryk as a compatriot. "It will both protect us from Europe's greed and open our doors to its knowledge."

Henryk glanced at the clock, seeing it was almost midnight. The hint of a cool evening breeze carried the smell of burnt tobacco, brandy, wine, and the sweat of men. Some were sitting around tables with bowls of fruit. One, dead asleep with his head on the table, was poked awake by a countryman.

Heads turned as the sounds of a messenger on horseback hauled to a clamorous stop outside the open front door. The rider, drenched in perspiration, jumped down, and raced inside where he handed an envelope to the czar. Peter tore open the seal, took one look, and raised his finger to the Captain who called out the door, "In the house at once!"

Lefort and two others, who had introduced themselves earlier as Golovin and Voznitzin, both as generals and admirals, were by his side. Henryk moved behind the Russians, but absorbed the excitement. "Where is Menshikov?" Peter asked. The other men smiled and flashed their eyes toward the kitchen door.

With the opened envelope in one hand and the dispatch in the other, Peter read the message again, showing no emotion. Menshikov came through the kitchen door with Anneke, who was straightening her dress and smoothing her hair.

Peter, giving Menshikov an insulting glance, stood and turned to Henryk. With his hand on his heart, the czar addressed the whole crowd. "Henryk, Saskia, Anneke, and the whole van Hoeten household." He included the kitchen help in his gaze. They nodded in return. "We thank you all again for this wonderful evening." Peter shook the urgent message in the air. "But, we now must leave. A snake has reared its treacherous head in Russia. It must be sliced into pieces," he said. "We leave at once for Moscow." The ambassadors, the soldiers, and the servants all exchanged looks of concern.

Anneke and Menshikov shared disappointment of the night's romance cut short. Menshikov whispered in Anneke's ear, "It's what we all feared. The *streltsy*, discontented soldiers, are again revolting with the encouragement of the czar's half-sister Sophia, who wants the throne. He must strike down this revolt."

"It is a three week trip to Russia," Menshikov whispered. "All the rest of our train in Amsterdam will have to catch up."

Menshikov pulled Anneke back out the kitchen door and they stood in the hazy shaft of light from inside. She felt the firmness of his grip on her arm.

"What does this mean, Aleksandr?" Anneke asked, feeling her eyes moistening.

"It means what Peter said. We leave now." His voice was urgent and his smile short.

"But, you will return?"

He took her by both arms looking into her eyes. "Of course, my dear Anneke. How could I not return to such a beautiful and talented woman as you? You will play your music for me and all my friends in the palace I will build on the sea."

Anneke wiped her eyes. Aleksandr Menshikov gathered his robe around him and said to her, "Wait here, and don't move." He raced around the house to the carriages and returned, his arms around a heavy parcel almost too bulky to manage. It was wrapped in oiled paper and tied with the same heavy twine as was the box holding the golden bouquet.

Behind the house, in the light from the open kitchen door, he laid the parcel on the planked table covered with blood and feathers from the night's dinner preparations. Beside their feet, the swill bucket overflowed with the pungent remnants of the evening's glut. Menshikov pulled a knife from his pocket and cut the heavy twine, peeling back the paper. In the dark he took Anneke's hand and placed it on the contents.

Anneke jerked back. "What is it?"

"It is yours."

"Is it," she paused, "fur?"

"Sable. There are sixty pelts in this bundle, enough for a cloak for a princess."

She ran her hand over the fur. "It's like silk." She held one pelt up to her cheek; then with both hands, she looped it over Menshikov's head and pulled him to her and kissed him.

"The carriages are waiting." Menshikov pulled the soft fur from his neck and draped it around hers. He held her close. They kissed again. "Until I return, princess." He turned and with long strides disappeared around the end of the house.

Anneke did not sleep that night.

CHAPTER SEVEN

THE COMMITMENT

The country home near Amsterdam
Morning,
May, 1698

IN THE SUBSIDING DARK, Young Anneke stood on the spot where the gold-trimmed carriage had carried away the man she dared to hope, for a few moments at least, would open up a new world for her. At the carriage window she had seen Aleksandr's face only for a precious moment before the drivers snapped their whips and the horses strained, pulling the carriage away and up to speed.

That was five long hours earlier. The czar's silver and gold flower bouquet presented to her grandfather was delicate and rich. But, everything else about the Russians, she reflected, was heavy and big; from their cloaks which were too voluminous for a spring evening to the amount of food they had consumed, and the drink they had poured down their throats. The bundle of exquisite sable pelts, also, was heavy and large, but she smiled for that. She wondered if all Russia was like these men—heavy, solid, strong, and unpredictable.

It was a dream from which she refused to awake. She remembered his warmth as they sat at the table, the press of his body against hers, the thrill of his warmness inside her in the dark behind the barn. After the ominous message, she would always remember that shadowy image as he fled, his coat flying like wings as he hastened to keep the Czar of Russia from waiting. These were her secrets. Thinking of them made her shiver. She remembered his smell, strong and difficult to define, but after goose and pig for dinner she guessed the men all smelled the same.

Aleksandr was clever with talk, and fast with his eyes as well as his hands, but he was gentle, not like the local boys—always in a hurry.

She began a walk in the early Dutch dawn, down the avenue of Linden trees, as if she were following the Russian caravan whose dust had settled hours before. The very tracks in the dirt seemed personal to her. They were tracks with a direction. They were going away.

Framed between the tall sentinels that lined the road, planted ten meters apart by the village burghers decades before, were displayed the brilliant flower fields. The early rays of a rising sun reached like golden fingers across the flat land to brighten the floral reds and golds and blues. To the south were plots of blue hyacinths matching the color of Anneke's wrinkled dress, the floral carpet reaching to the next tree-lined road leading to its own thatch-roofed village.

A sweet aroma filled the damp breeze and Anneke pulled it into her lungs, waking her from her dream. She cherished the perfume of the fields and the moist Dutch earth. There was something secure and reliable about it. At this moment she preferred it to the smell of men with their meat, brandy, and tobacco breath spitting out promises.

Yet, inside, she twisted with indecision, between the security of where she was and the adventure of where she dreamed to be. Where she wanted to be was a fuzzy thought to her, but in the end, she knew it would not be in a common Dutch village.

Returning to the house, where she was sure everyone was sleeping, she saw a movement in Henryk's shed. It was the open-sided shed where Henryk and old Schuyler experimented with new hybrids of tulips and hyacinths, a less dangerous life than the Russian fur trade and pirates. It was old Schuyler she saw, sitting on a small stool with his face at the level of the flowers. He was scrutinizing them with the intensity of a jeweler to a diamond.

"Good morning, Schuyler," Anneke whispered as to not startle him. The man was in his seventies, but all his faculties worked well, everything but his lame left leg that stretched out straight across a padded stool.

"You are up early, young Anneke," Schuyler said without looking up.

"I am *still* up—haven't gone to bed yet."

"Ja, I know. Different kind of men, those Russians, eh?"

She smiled.

Schuyler continued to caress the leaves. He was wiping a fluid on them with a small rag. With a different liquid he wiped the petals that were a yellowish cream color with dark purple streaks reaching upward like flames.

"These bi-colored tulips," he said, "are called 'Rembrandts' young Anneke. Can you imagine why?"

"Because they look like they were painted with the Master's brush," she said. She squatted, spreading her skirt around her feet. "Why do you always call me 'young Anneke,' Schuyler?"

He turned to her and, squinting into the rising sun, focused on her for a long moment. Shaking his head, he said, "Not anymore."

Schuyler struggled to his feet, steadying himself on the thick wooden side of the flowerbed, and offered his hand to help her up. He had to look up to her as she stood a hand's width taller than he.

"We are indeed blessed, Anneke. Even as our Prince William sits on the throne in England, it is these fields and these flowers that bless the Dutch. They never fail to bring happiness. It is great to be Dutch." Taking scissors from his apron, he clipped the stem of the "Rembrandt," closing Anneke's hands around it. "Kingdoms and royal palaces are unimportant, my dear. Their gold tarnishes and their glitter fades."

Anneke looked down the road again. "Do you think they will ever come back?"

"The Russians or Heer Menshikov?"

"Prince Menshikov." She saw doubt in Schuyler's eyes.

"Russia is far away," he said.

"Not that far," she said. "It must be a golden land."

"From here, it may look like that," he said. "There is as much mud in Russia as anywhere else—maybe more."

Approaching the house, Anneke stopped at the barn and stared at the place on the splintered wall where she had felt the full thrust of the Russian prince. She was beginning to question now if it had ever happened.

In the house she saw everything was again in order—all restored before anyone had gone to bed. She stood on the floor planks where she and Menshikov had sat touching each other.

Looking up at the portraits of the lady and the gentleman painted almost forty years earlier, she then turned to the mirror at the room's end. There she stood framed with the image of the woman with the ostrich feather in the mirrored background on the wall behind her.

She positioned the streaked tulip in her hands as her grandmother had held the feather. Her own hair was a brighter gold. But she saw the yearning in her eyes mirroring those of the lady on the day she was painted, and died. Anneke touched the lace bow at her own neck. Aleksandr had seen that, too. Looking at her grandmother's downcast eyes, Anneke tilted her head and asked, "Tell me Grandmother Anneke, what is love? Tell me please, do men keep their promises?"

The lid of the harpsichord was still open. The sun slanting through the window warmed the floral scene of birds painted on its underside. Anneke stood tall, took a deep breath, faced the bare tables, bowed as to the public, and announced so those in the back row could hear, "*Elegy*, by Francois Couperin." Smoothing her dress under her, she sat and again her fingers raced across the keys of the harpsichord with all the passion her aching heart could express. After her performance, she bowed to the imagined audience. Then she heard clapping.

The sound came from Henryk's scarred and wearied hands.

"You were named for her, my dear." Her grandfather padded down the last few stairs from where he had been listening, unnoticed, as Anneke poured out her soul. He looked at the portrait of his beloved Anneke with the ostrich feather and shook his head in his eternal disbelief. "We were to be married in three days, on Saturday." He rubbed the back of his hand across his eyes. "But Saturday never came—not for her."

He shuffled into the center of the room. "She died in my arms, holding that feather. I should have gone in the carriage with her that night." A weak smile crossed his face. "She left me a jewel—your mother. Then came you, another Anneke like the first." He gave his granddaughter a lingering hug and kissed her cheek. "I can still hear her voice, *'Don't ever leave me,'* she said. I promised—but I failed to keep that promise."

"*We*, grandfather, *we* will never leave her," Anneke whispered, her hands on his. "Both of you will always be at home, *our* home—together. I promise you that—forever."

CHAPTER EIGHT

THE AUCTION

The Hague
August, 1760

"WE WILL BEGIN THE afternoon session," the auctioneer said, "at exactly three, as you see written in the catalog." Arnold Franken, proud of his reputation for punctuality and exactness, began the afternoon session the same way as he did in the morning. He was a tall man. The podium he commanded only came to his waist. From the sleeves of his black coat, buttoned even in the August heat, hung starched white cuffs soiled with grime.

The auction was in the large hall of the Ottho van Thol auction house on the Achterom Straat, a narrow, short, curved street in The Hague, the capital of the United Kingdom of the Netherlands. Franken was confident in his experience as a professional auctioneer. He was in charge of auctioning the collection of the eminent dealer Gerard Hoet II, recently deceased.

The smell of sweat mixed with the aroma of lunch—of herring, stewed lamb, mushroom soup and beer saturating the beards and mustaches of the buyers just returned for the afternoon session.

Thirty-seven screened dealers and collectors were there from all over the Netherlands and Belgium, even two from Paris, and, of course, the important one from Berlin. The sounds of mumbling and side-of-mouth whispers were interrupted by an occasional belch.

The clock in the St. Jacobskerk read four minutes to three.

Franken felt good about the potential success of that day's auction, for the famed Hoet collection contained art of the Italian, Dutch, and the Flemish schools including the work of Anthony van Dyck, Peter Paul Rubens, and Rembrandt. In fact, seven Rembrandts in the collection were on the list to be sold that day.

The church bells sounded the prelude to the hour, but Heer Franken did not strike his gavel to begin the afternoon auction. He sorted papers, looked about, glanced at the door, and repositioned two easels, stalling a few more moments for his major buyer to arrive.

The door onto the Achterom stood open to admit what little fresh air there was. The silhouette of a man filled the doorway. The auctioneer smiled and nodded, "Heer Gotzkowsky, welcome back." Then his hammer came down with a decisive knock.

Franken was now pleased. He smiled as he motioned Johan Ernst Gotzkowsky to his seat. He watched his frequent customer, a successful banker and collector, with his large paunch, bush of sand-colored hair, and tobacco-stained mustache that curled beyond his rolling jowls. In the morning session Gotzkowsky had bought, amongst others in the catalog, items 44 through 48, five Rembrandts including the famous *Joseph and Potiphar's Wife*, and *The Holy Family*.

Franken was pleased to see Gotzkowsky smile at his recognized importance as he pressed his way between the others to the seat held for him between his two partners. But then Franken's attention was diverted by the clatter of an arriving carriage in the street just outside the open door.

Turning onto the Achterom Straat was a carriage with a driver straining two exhausted horses to a halt, the carriage's iron-rimmed wheels sparking against the cobblestones. Achterom Straat was only two blocks long, and crowded with other carriages, the horses munching in their feedbags.

The bells of the St. Jacobskerk finished tolling three.

The driver of the late arrival jumped down and tied his horses at the far end of the street. He raced around to open a coach door, and smiled, saying, "We are here, finally." Simon knew they were three hours late due to the high water at the De Merwede crossing at Dordrecht.

A woman's white-cuffed wrinkled hand emerged through the door, handed him a small leather purse, and with a cracking voice said, "Don't fail us, Simon." He hesitated for a second while she settled back with a sigh, wiping her furrowed face with a cotton kerchief. He knew she worried they had missed the reason for the long trip from Tilburg, far to the south. He raced off toward the open door of the auction.

Simon stopped in the doorway, breathless, his eyes darting about in vain for a vacant seat. He noted the auctioneer's curious glance at him.

Franken paused at the sight of an unexpected silhouette of a man in the glare of the open doorway, but he was ready to begin as the jewels of this auction were now to be sold. Simon listened.

"Gentlemen," announced Franken, waving the auction catalog in the air, "we will begin this afternoon with items 49 and 50."

Four white-smocked assistants carried the covered portraits from a back room, and placed them on the two easels. "These are the two prized portraits by Rembrandt," Heer Franken continued, "considered by the artist to be his best." He leaned forward with both hands on the podium, squinting his eyes and imploring the buyers. "These paintings were acquired by Heer Hoet years ago from the collection of a successful Amsterdam fur-trader after his demise."

Franken saw that the new man had now stepped into the room and was standing against the wall. He didn't know this man. He could see the man was short, and had a young face, but long disheveled graying hair. He thought him perhaps to be a curious passer-by, but Franken was not going to interrupt his sale to find out.

Simon had no choice but to stand by the door and watch. The assistants lifted the covers from the portraits in their heavy gilt frames. The woman's portrait stood on the viewers' left, the portrait of the man on the right, and Heer Franken scowled and summoned his assistants to switch them. "Now," Franken stood back, admiring the portraits, "better," then turned to the buyers. "These are called simply *The Lady with an Ostrich-Feather Fan*, and *The Gentleman with Tall Hat and Gloves*. Otherwise the subjects are unknown."

"These two will be sold," the auctioneer took a handkerchief from where he had placed it on the podium and wiped his brow, "either separately or as a pair, whichever brings the best price."

He paused and drew a breath. "Gentlemen, will someone begin this sale at one hundred guilders for the pair?"

"Twenty-five guilders for the woman," a voice called out.

"The woman only, Heer Gotzkowsky?"

Gotzkowsky nodded, "Yes."

Franken knew Gotzkowsky well—as someone who was personally close to Emperor Frederick the Great. He was puzzled however, as it was rumored that the Prussian ruler did not favor Dutch paintings. He knew also that the emperor was in financial difficulties resulting from his war with the rest of Europe, and that presently the Russian Army occupied Berlin.

"Come now, gentlemen," Franken said, "while we Dutch are blessed with the art of many great painters, a man's collection is known by the Rembrandts that grace his walls. Who will bid fifty for this beautiful lady?"

Simon was shaken by the sight of these two portraits so famous in his family, which he had never seen. He shifted nervously from side to side, feeling Franken's impatient decision to finally acknowledge him, and he nodded in response. Other heads turned to study him also. He felt greatly out of place amongst all the collectors and buyers in this auction. However, the Rembrandts, the *Lady* and the *Gentleman* now facing him, stirred in him an inner courage to achieve his goal, the family's goal as so clearly outlined by his grandmother waiting in the heat of the coach. Still, it was all new to him. He listened carefully to what followed. He moved a bit forward so he could see the bidders.

"Thirty," a bald man with a black beard offered from the far corner of the room.

"Forty," Gotzkowsky raised his hand.

"Fifty," the bearded man offered.

"I have fifty guilders from Heer Kluge from Brussels," the auctioneer acknowledged. "This is an embarrassingly low price for a Rembrandt, gentlemen. Do I hear at least seventy-five?" Simon watched Franken raise his eyebrows at Gotzkowsky.

Simon could not remain quiet, he felt compelled. He held up his hand. A few buyers turned to see who it was. He stepped away from the wall to draw attention to himself. "One hundred—but for the pair," he said in a strong voice that surprised even him.

All heads turned to the side. Simon was conscious of the stares. His black suit was disheveled and dusty.

"Sir," Franken said, "we are bidding only on the woman's portrait now."

"Sir," Simon replied, "you announced you would take bids either separate or together." Simon realized his accent further set him apart. He was not of the city, but from the Southern Provinces and he felt conspicuous. "I bid on both portraits," he continued. "They are a pair. They belong together. I bid on both together."

Franken glanced about the room.

Gotzkowsky pulled his spectacles from his vest pocket, held them to his eyes, and frowned at the newcomer.

"Heer…" Franken raised his eyebrows at the new bidder.

"van Vleek, sir, Simon van Vleek."

"Heer van Vleek of …?" Franken persisted.

"The Nord Brabant, sir."

"Heer van Vleek of the Nord Brabant bids one hundred guilders for the Rembrandt pair." Franken bent forward and looked at Gotzkowsky and then at Kluge.

"One hundred guilders for the portrait of the woman, alone," said Gotzkowsky.

Franken held up his hand. "Gentleman, I must call a recess to consult with the heirs of the estate." Franken stepped away from his podium and moved to a woman in black with her escort seated at the end of the front row. They conversed to the side, then Franken stepped back. "On the advice of the heirs of the estate and their counsel, we will continue with the auction of the two Rembrandts as a pair only. My apologies, gentlemen."

Simon smiled. He was still standing on the aisle as there were no empty seats.

Gotzkowsky ran his hand through his bushy hair and looked side to side.

Franken pointed with the handle of his gavel at Simon van Vleek, "I have a bid of one hundred guilders for the pair. Do I hear one hundred twenty?" Franken looked at Gotzkowsky.

The offer came from the corner of the room, "One hundred twenty," said Kluge from Brussels.

"One hundred forty," said Simon.

The auctioneer gestured toward Gotzkowsky, "The gentleman from Berlin?"

"One hundred sixty." Gotzkowsky set his jaw and Simon felt his scowl.

"One hundred eighty," called Simon.

Kluge, the man from Brussels, shook his head. He was out of the bidding.

"Is there another bid on the two Rembrandts?" Franken gestured across the room. "What about the rest of you? I will tell you that Rembrandt himself said these two portraits were the best he had ever done. I can't understand why only three of you have shown an interest."

"Two hundred," said Gotzkowsky. He bent over and whispered in the ear of his partner.

"Thank you, Heer Gotzkowsky," Franken sighed. "You obviously know the value for these works of art, but even at these prices the Rembrandts are an exceptionally good buy for you."

The gentleman from Berlin smiled.

"Two hundred ten guilders," said Simon van Vleek, with a firmness in his voice that belied his age or stature. He shifted uncomfortably from side to side.

There was silence in the room.

"Would Heer van Vleek," the auctioneer looked to Simon, "please speak to the man at the desk, my cashier?"

Simon moved to the cashier and after a short conversation and an inspection of the contents of the leather purse, the cashier rose and conferred with the auctioneer who then returned to the podium.

"I have a confirmed bid of two hundred ten guilders for the Rembrandts. Do I hear a higher bid?" The other buyers looked to Gotzkowsky. He said nothing.

"Is that it then?" Auctioneer Franken looked hard at Gotzkowsky.

The Berliner shook his head. He was out.

"Hearing no other bids…" Simon watched Franken search the faces in the audience. "Hearing no other bids, the two Rembrandt portraits go to Heer van Vleek of the Nord Brabant." It was a shock to Simon. He felt it within.

Franken closed the bidding with a strike of his hammer. "We will recess for a few minutes as the bid was made subject to immediate possession, according to my cashier."

Simon watched as Arnold Franken dipped his quill in ink and recorded the price paid in the margin of his auction catalog.

Simon stepped up to the cashier, opened the brown leather bag, and counted out two hundred ten guilders value in gold coin. That emptied the purse.

The assistants brought the paintings, each wrapped in oiled paper over sturdy canvas and tied with a small rope. Simon insisted on opening each to verify they were what he had bought and waited while they were re-wrapped with care. "Follow me," he said.

Simon van Vleek led the four gray-smocked men carrying their precious cargo to the waiting coach. He opened the coach door, leaned inside, and said, "I have them, grandmother."

The woman slid herself over to the other side of the carriage seat, gathering up her long blue dress and white lace shawl. The assistants prepared to stand the paintings on the floor. The woman, well along in years, her white hair still streaked with gold, had a strong face, with bright brown eyes—and a smile.

"Wait," she said, and with trembling hands she opened a large robe from the seat beside her and placed it on the floor to cushion the heavy frames—a thick fur robe of soft sable pelts. The assistants lifted the heavy portraits onto the cushioning fur and wrapped it about the Rembrandts with care.

Simon handed her the empty purse. She smiled. "We can take them home now, Simon. At last they are at home. We are all family again." Anneke Voss was happy, satisfied.

Simon knew it had been over fifty years since his grandmother's home and the beloved Rembrandts had been sold to pay off the family debt. Now, her "family" was with her again and she was committed to their safety.

FRANCE

1788

THE THREAT

West of Paris
November, 1788

FROM THE CHATEAU DE MONTFORT'S grand dining room, shafts
of golden candlelight pierced the November night, reflecting
in the crystals of snow. The air was filled with the sweet smell of
burning oak and birch from the fires inside. Winter had arrived
in northern France.

For over four hundred years The Chateau de Montfort had
stood north of the Forest Rambouillet, a half-day's carriage drive
west of Paris. The historic de Montfort dynasty reached further
back still, to the time of the Normans. Built of the same pink-
ish Bretignac limestone used for the thirteenth-century Troyes
Cathedral, the chateau had only thirty-nine rooms and, by French
country standards, was not considered grand.

Henri Comte de Montfort was not the first to carry that title,
but he was the last of that famous family in France. The earlier
de Montforts had long since gone to Britain with William the
Conqueror.

Fires roared in the hearths at each end of the long dining room. The Comte de Montfort stood there, proud of his French noble lineage, inhaling the aroma of roast venison mingling with that of the fires.

Looking up at the fireplace wall, he smiled at the portrait of his wife, Annette, in her bejeweled bridal gown. He felt a shiver of his forever pride in this woman and her strength of conviction. He held her as beautiful today as when he met her twenty-five years before on his return from Amsterdam when stopping in the small Dutch town of Tilburg in the Nord Brabant, at an inn run by her mother.

He was grateful for his comfortable life, his Dutch wife, and their only offspring, young Annelle, age twelve. He was thankful for their servants who tended their personal needs, and the peasants who milked the cows and ploughed the rich soil that had supported the family de Montfort for centuries. But, now he felt the ground shaking with tremors of political uncertainty.

He looked to the wooden table that in better times was set with Sèvres china and Saint Louis crystal for sixty guests of the aristocracy. Tonight it was set for three, including the Russian prince.

"What do you make of the terror in your country?" asked Prince Nicolai Borisovich Yusupov.

"We fear the complete collapse of the Empire," answered the Comte de Montfort, "There is little bread in the homes and much anger in the streets."

"We have so much at risk," added the Comte's Dutch wife, Annette. "Blood and destruction, the king does nothing. What can we do?"

The soft glow of candles in the wall sconces, the chandelier with its hundred lights, and the four massive candlesticks on the table, illuminated the stone walls covered with Belgian tapestries and paintings by Dutch, Flemish, French, and Italian masters.

Annette Comtesse de Montfort sat across from the visiting prince. Her eyes, a warm shade of light-brown, sparkled in the candlelight.

"There is good reason for your concern," said the Russian. "My sources say things will get worse before a change for the better." Prince Yusupov traced his noble origins back to the days before there was a Russia, to the Prophet Ali, a nephew of Mohammed. Prince Yusupov was now the Ambassador for Empress Catherine II of Russia. Representing the empire in the highest circles of politics, letters, and art in Europe, he mingled with Voltaire, Diderot, and Beaumarchais. He usually dined with King Louis XVI when in Paris—but not this night.

Always a welcome guest at the de Montfort chateau, he continued with authority, "You must protect yourself."

The political speculations continued until they finished the five-course dinner, which, following the Portuguese chicken, included roast venison with gooseberries in a champagne cream sauce.

Annette motioned for the servant standing by the fireplace: "We will take our cognac in the salon, Bruno."

Annette, in a sky blue taffeta dress, her honey blond hair hanging loosely to the middle of her back, led the men away from the dinner. "This was always your favorite room, Prince Nikolai," she said of the salon, warmed by the flames in the massive fireplace. "But, there are new occupants since your last visit."

Prince Yusupov began his inspection. Framing the fireplace were several small portraits. On one sidewall was a large biblical scene by Sebastién Bourden and under it, on a polished rosewood table, a glistening bouquet of roses, the stems and leaves of silver, the flower petals an intricate swirl in pink gold.

On the opposite wall hung a landscape by Claude Lorrain. Yusupov inspected each picture with a knowledgeable eye, leaning over to study closely even the smaller paintings. Turning to the wall opposite the fireplace, the prince paused, stepped back, and took a deep breath before the two portraits, which hung alone in their gold-embossed frames.

"These are Annette's treasures, the Rembrandts," Henri said.

The prince, his arms crossed in tribute, continued to inspect them in silence, turning from one to the other.

"This is a wonderful surprise, Comtesse," Yusupov said. "How absolutely alive they are."

"They were passed to me by my mother before she died," Annette said. "The Lady and The Gentleman have been in our family for over a century."

He asked, "What do you think is in the lady's mind, Annette? Those eyes!" He moved up close, then backed off.

"She has seen much I think," Annette answered. "Much good and much travail. But, she has a strong mind and a determined will, don't you think so?"

"And what is she about to say?"

Annette replied, "I think if he were here, not even Rembrandt could tell us."

"And the man," said the prince, "his eyes are in the shadow. What do they hide? I wonder."

The servant Bruno, expressionless, brought three crystal glasses of golden cognac on a brass tray, placing it on a low table of carved walnut inlaid with aged red leather. The de Montforts and the prince sat down in chairs the size of thrones with cushions covered also in deep red leather, cracked with age.

"You are gracious to host us," the prince said, raising his glass in tribute. "We will burden you only two nights. Her Majesty in Petersburg is eager to hear news of the unrest in France and we must be on our way." His eyes were still on the Rembrandts as he spoke. "The woman, who is she?" he asked.

Annette paused. "She is family, both of them are family. My mother knew, but she never spoke of it until her last days. In fact, they are my great-grandparents."

"An absolute revelation of character," Yusupov said. "It rivals the Leonardo in the Louvre. It is the mouth. And the eyes, of course. What is her secret?"

Henri warmed his glass of cognac with his hands. "And what will Russia do," he asked, "if France erupts?"

"My dear husband…" Annette placed her drink on the table, "…I respect your confidence in the authorities, or even friends, to control this uprising, but we have a comfortable home and a daughter to protect." Annette looked to Prince Yusupov, "Will anyone's army protect us? I doubt it. They will look after themselves, yes?"

"Russia is far away," the prince answered. "It has other problems. But," and he took a sip of cognac, "who is to know?"

"I pray," said the Comte, "yes, I pray the king will resolve these issues that have for so long plagued our country." The Comte was a lean man with serious eyes, a pencil thin mustache, and gray curls that fell to his shoulders. Known as a firm but fair landowner, he could flash a quick smile with an entertaining sense of humor, even among his peasants. But, he was not smiling tonight.

"That is wishful thinking," the Comtesse said, shaking her head. "So far he has only pretended to be a king. We have much to protect," she motioned toward the Comte, "the nobility of your family name, our lives, and most of all, our daughter." She pointed upstairs where Annelle slept in her warm bed.

Henri picked up his meerschaum pipe, pinching some tobacco out of a cloisonné can. With his forefinger he tamped the leaves into the pipe's deep bowl. From a brass box by the fireplace, he took a long splinter, lit it in the fire and sucked the golden flame into his pipe, blowing a cloud of aromatic blue smoke toward the ceiling.

The clock, eight feet tall in a mahogany case darkened with age, stood like a sentinel against the wall to the left of the Rembrandts, and began striking the hour. It was eleven.

"You are right, my dear," said Henri, "but nothing will happen until the spring." He drew on his pipe, blew the smoke aside, and flipped the burning splinter into the fireplace. "Leaving France is not an easy consideration for a de Montfort, the few of us who are left. We have a little time."

"We have no control over the past, and now we find ourselves in the position of having no control over the future," Annette said. "The French nobility assumes that their throne will last forever, regardless of their inept kings, their spendthrift women, and their wasteful wars."

"You are too hard on us," Henri said, "But you are right."

"However," Annette arose from her red leather chair, "we have total control of this moment. I say now is the moment to retire, gentlemen."

Henri laughed. "I wonder," he said, "are all Dutch women so independent? A strong mind and a determined will—like the lady with the feather. It runs in the family, yes?"

The de Montforts were asleep upstairs in their canopied bed. The clock chimed half past one. Outside, the wind came up and with it the blowing snow. The heavy wooden shutters, each painted green with a black diagonal stripe, were loose on two windows and began to bang against the stone walls. Henri and Annette were used to this winter noise. It didn't waken them. But, the candle still burned in the prince's room where he poked the coals with an iron, laying on another log. Wrapping himself in a wool blanket, he returned to his desk, quill in hand to continue writing in his journal.

Prince Yusupov wondered about the accommodations and morale of his men. There were seven carriages parked outside the dark stables where the horses were fed and rubbed down. The attendants were quartered elsewhere in the chateau outbuildings. Fifteen of this retinue were tall men in the green uniforms of the empress's own Preobrazhensky Life Guards, each with a carefully curled mustache.

Two of the Guards, posted to keep a watch during the night, were playing cards in a small outbuilding. The fire warmed the men while their muskets with fixed bayonets leaned against the wall by the door. They listened for unusual sounds, but were confident the dogs would give the first alarm. Every French chateau had dogs, maybe six or eight of them, but the de Montforts had only two.

One of these mastiffs was said to be worth a platoon of the king's men. The Chateau de Montfort dogs were brindle brown, muscular *Dogue de Bordeaux*, with huge heads, square like the stones in the walls. They had slobbering mouths and jaws of iron. They were the weight of a man, but in height only came to a man's knees. That night the de Montfort dogs were asleep in the shed.

They had seen their day. They were old, with rotting teeth. They could bark, but not bite—quite like France at the moment.

After two o'clock, the banging of the shutters was drowned out by the pounding assault on the massive front door by the heavy boots and fists of men. Alerted, the guards in the adjacent building slipped on their coats, grabbed their muskets and, as they reached for the door latch, saw an envelope that had been slipped under the door. It was addressed to Prince Yusupov. As they hurried into the dark, a guard stuck the note into his waist pouch.

CHAPTER TEN

THE ESCAPE

West of Paris
November, 1788

PRINCE YUSUPOV PULLED ON his boots, grabbed his coat, belt, pistol and sword, and raced down the stairs to the entry hall. He heard the raucous voices of the brigands outside at the front door. "Open up you rich sons of whores!"

From their billets, the Russian soldiers saw shadows and forms in the flames of the torches. "Stop!" shouted the guards, their breath curling in the freezing air, their leather boots slipping on the wet cobblestones.

The wild Frenchmen, there were ten of them, paid no attention to the guards who were shouting in Russian. The light from their torches flashed like fireflies on the falling flakes of snow.

The Russians poked at the brigands with their bayonets, making them madder and louder, but they moved. More guards piled out of the buildings, rubbing their eyes, pulling up their pants, and slipping on their coats. At last, the dogs joined the commotion, snarling at soldiers and rebels alike. Soon the ten

Frenchmen, some drunk and shouting obscenities, were herded into a group by the front door, surrounded by fifteen impatient Russian soldiers armed with muskets and bayonets.

Now the Russians held the torches, and the snowflakes were getting larger, landing on their eyebrows and lashes and making it difficult to see.

The door opened and Prince Yusupov stood in his unbuttoned coat, a pistol in his left hand, a sword in his right. There was silence at last.

"What is this? Who are you?" the prince demanded in perfect French. "Who is your leader?"

The Frenchmen looked about for one. A fat man, coatless and wobbling, spoke in slurred speech and managed to say, "Time to go. You time to go! Bastards!" He pointed somewhere in space, then slipped and spun to the ground.

Another said in more audible tones, "We're in charge now. We demand equality!"

Behind Prince Yusupov came Henri and Annette in their nightcaps and robes, along with several servants holding candles. Behind the Russian guards, gathered against the outbuildings, were the stable boys and other peasants wrapped in their blankets.

"You want equality? You leave this place at once or you will all be equally dead," said the Russian. With his sword he carved an arc over their heads, pointing it down the road. "And never return here!"

The soldiers opened a path and the ruffians shuffled away mumbling, three of them carrying the unconscious drunk, his leg dragging in the deepening snow.

Yusupov turned to Henri and Annette and reached to close the door. But, before it clicked shut, a soldier stepped forward and said, "Sir," handing him the envelope.

"They will be back," the prince said to Henri and Annette. "If not them, then others. Think about it, my friends." The prince turned to go to his quarters. "You can sleep now. My men will stand guard tonight."

But, Annette did not sleep the rest of the night. By morning she had a plan. "Henri, my dear." She sat on the side of the bed as he awoke. "Henri, we must take action. I fear the worst."

Henri blinked his eyes, his night cap skewed to one side. Seeing the determination in his wife's bloodshot eyes, he listened to her plan.

Henri nodded his agreement, "We will do what is needed. We will protect our home."

"That is necessary, Henri. But we must do more than that."

The Comtesse opened the curtains onto the courtyard. The snow had stopped. The soft blanket of white faded into the morning ground fog. The rising sun was still hidden by thick gray clouds in the east. Annette and Henri dressed and descended the stairs to meet the prince in *le petite salle à manger*, the family dining room filled with the aroma of fresh baked breads and brewing Arabian coffee. On the table were sliced sausages and several cheeses. The fire crackled from the new logs placed on the embers from the night before.

After the morning greetings Annette said, "Nicolai Borisovich, my husband and I have a proposal to make to you." She laid her silver on the top of her plate. "What happened early this morning will happen again, we know."

Henri added, "We do hope King Louis will save the regime, but in case he fails, we must take precautions."

"Of course," said the prince.

"What we have decided to ask of you, Nicolai Borisovich," Annette continued with a pause, "is a great favor."

The prince raised his eyebrows and swallowed. "Indeed, you are wise to protect yourselves," he said. With his hand over his heart he said, "I am at your service."

"We ask you," Annette looked to her husband who nodded support, "to take our daughter, Annelle, with you to St. Petersburg."

Prince Yusupov set down his bread and knife and straightened in his chair.

Annette continued, "Henri does not want to leave our home under these conditions."

Her husband added, "If necessary, we will fight. We will form a militia to protect our property, and our lives, if there is serious trouble."

"The brigands last night," Annette continued, "were a nuisance, but it will get worse before France decides what it wants to be."

From under his thick eyebrows, the prince looked at her while he sipped his coffee.

"In Russia," she continued, "we know our daughter will be safe. It is an empire of strength. It will survive forever."

The prince said, "Indeed she will be safe with us, but…"

"It will only be for a time," Henri said.

"I understand," said Yusupov, "you honor me with this confidence. Have you told your daughter?"

"We will," said Henri.

The prince pushed back his chair and stood. He walked to the window, his boots clicking on the stone floor. He looked outside. He walked to the fireplace. The monk-like servant Bruno stood motionless against the wall, his hands behind his back. The prince observed the servant closely and noticed an inappropriate degree of attention to the family conversation, and how quickly his eyes snapped straight forward when noticed.

The prince walked back to the window and back to the breakfast table. "We will leave today," he said quietly. "Walk with me to inspect the horses, my friends." Henri and Annette pulled on their long fur coats, following the prince out the door toward the stables. The sun had appeared and the snow was melting.

Yusupov motioned to the Captain of the Guard, who stepped forward and saluted, then bowed to Annette and Henri, clicking his heels. Yusupov and the Captain spoke in Russian. The Captain nodded, turned, and left. Alone in the stable yards, the prince asked, "Do you trust your household?"

"Absolutely," answered Henri. "Many have been with this house for years, as have their fathers and grandfathers. Why do you ask?"

"Someone thinks you should not." Yusupov pulled the envelope and note from his coat pocket. "This note was addressed to me." He opened it. "I will read it to you."

> "To the Russian prince,
> We trust you. Dangerous things are happening in France. The Comte and Comtesse are good to us, but we cannot protect them in these days. There is a traitor in the house. Warn them carefully. We trust you."

"It is not signed," the prince added. Yusupov showed the note to Henri and Annette. "This note was from your loyal household. They know better than any of us about what is happening." The prince folded the note, putting it back in his pocket. "They are telling the truth, I fear."

Henri took Annette's hand, "Then we're doing the right thing, my dear." They walked back to their home without a word.

The windows of Annelle's room faced east and through them warm rays of the emerging sun slanted in. Annelle stood by her bed with her mother. Curled up in the center of the disheveled bed covers purred a golden Persian cat. A maid entered with a leather travel chest and placed it on the floor. She left the room and returned with two leather suitcases under her arms. She opened them on the long wooden chest at the end of the bed and began to pack Annelle's belongings.

"But Mamá," Annelle said in that small voice that always got results, "I don't know these people. Do they speak French?" She pulled the cat to her, cradling it in her arms, stroking its fur.

"Yes," the mother said, "many of them do. I am told it is the language spoken by the Empress herself." Annette straightened the girl's collar, kneeled down in front of her, and held her by the waist with both hands. She loved the clean smell of her daughter, fresh from her morning bath. "You will be safe. Besides, your father and I decided to send along with you Simon, your favorite."

The personal coachman of the de Montforts, old Simon van Vleek had been their servant since their marriage. In his late sixties now, he was with Annette's mother in Holland. Like a devoted grandfather to Annelle, he told funny stories to amuse her, always calling her *Princess*.

"When will I come back, Mamá?"

"Soon, we hope. When it is safe again. In Russia you will live in a palace. You know what is happening here." The mother felt an emptiness inside, like a hunger.

"I know, Mamá. I've heard the servants talking. But, I'm afraid for you and Papá, too. Don't do anything dangerous."

"You will be safe with the prince and his family. There is peace in Russia."

By noon the snow remained only in patches under the trees on the north side of the house. The Russian soldiers, the coachmen, and servants in Prince Yusupov's party were packing the last cases onto the carriages.

Inside, Annette met Prince Yusupov as he descended the stairs in his heavy canvas pants and black leather jacket, and carrying a fox-fur longcoat. "Prince Nicolai, may I speak with you in private?" Annette asked.

The prince placed his things on the floor and followed her into the salon.

With her back to the warming fireplace, Annette said, "You don't know how much this means to us, as painful as it is."

The prince nodded in understanding. "We will care for your daughter as one of the family. That may relieve your concern, but not your pain, I know."

"This is no holiday for Annelle." She forced her words. "And we don't know when she will return to us. We want to make sure that she is well cared for. We have prepared a purse of gold."

The prince held up both hands. "That is not needed, I assure you, Comtesse. The Yusupov family is never in need."

"We insist."

"Then it will be for her personal use."

"And not knowing how long will be this absence," Annette added, "we are sending with you something else."

The prince raised his eyebrows.

She nodded to the opposite wall.

He turned and saw there two blank spaces where the Rembrandts had hung the night before.

"I am sending my treasured portraits with you. They too are family, my family."

Yusupov waved his hand and shook his head, speechless.

"There is something I will tell you." She looked toward the door. "I am not sure if even my husband knows it all," she said. "In a way, our daughter is going home. You see, I grew up without a father, as did my mother. My mother never talked about it. She said her father was a naval officer who died at sea. A similar thing was actually true about my own father. We have not had much luck with men, it seems. Until now, of course."

Arms folded, Annette stood beside one of the red leather chairs. "Before my mother died," she continued, "she told me the truth. My grandfather was an Ambassador with Czar Peter the Great's party when he visited Holland almost a century ago. She never revealed his name."

The prince looked into her eyes, then into the fire. He shook his head and narrowed his eyes. "Amazing story, Annette."

"So I am one quarter Russian," she continued, "and Annelle is an eighth. These paintings are part of our family. They are of my great-grandparents, as I have said. We have a covenant with them to keep them safe and together. I want them with Annelle—just in case. She understands."

"Comtesse," and he bowed, "I am honored."

"Also, Prince Nicolai," Annette continued, reaching over to the chair, "I will send with you this leather valise. It contains the whole story—a journal with the thoughts of all the mothers of this family, including my thoughts of last night, and going back to…" and she nodded toward the blank wall, "…her." It is to be given to Annelle, to keep, when she is fourteen."

"Surely, Comtesse, you will be able to give it to her yourself. I will keep it safe."

"Maybe so, but if…," and the words caught in her throat, "…we are not in a position to see our daughter again, the portraits are to guarantee her safety and a happy life—and to protect as your own."

"You have my word before God, to fulfill your wishes," the prince said. With his right hand he crossed himself. "We pray to return your daughter and the paintings in the nearest future."

Henri stood in the doorway. Prince Yusupov motioned toward Annette. "Your wife…"

"I know, Nicolai, I know. She wanted to tell you herself. God bless you." The two men embraced.

"You, Henri, are a brave and noble man," the prince said. And Comtesse, you are a wise and loving mother."

The seven carriages were each harnessed to four horses, snorting, their hooves stamping the mud and crushed stone in the roadway. Annette watched as Simon struggled to the third carriage with Annelle's cases and chest, where the men secured them on the roof. Six of the Preobrazhensky Guards sat astride their horses ready to protect the procession. The others rode on or in the coaches.

It was two in the afternoon, late in the day to be leaving she knew, and the sun already low, but Annette trusted the Russians. The precious Rembrandts in their heavy, gilt frames were wrapped in layers of canvas cloth, oiled paper, and rope and placed inside the fourth coach.

Young Annelle stood with her bonnet tied under her chin, tears in her eyes. She was to ride with the prince. Her father squatted down, taking her by her hands.

"You will be safe there, my dear," the Comte said, "and you will return to us when it is safe here in France. Simon will be your friend as always. The prince will be your protector." Henri looked away to hide his heartache. "Always remember who you are, my dear little Comtesse. And be a good mother to our family portraits. God's love goes with you. Never forget that."

Annelle wiped her tears with the back of her hands. "I will remember who I am, Papá. Soon I will come back to you and Mamá, with my ancestors, the Rembrandts." She grabbed her father and held him tight.

Simon stood by and in one hand held the leather grip of a small wooden cage that contained the Persian cat. He took Annelle by the hand and said, "Come along, princess. We have a long way to go." The servants stood in their white uniforms, arms folded against the cold air. They waved and one servant rushed forth to kiss Annelle. Bruno, a crooked smile on his face, stood in the shadows behind the rest. Simon lifted Annelle into the coach and placed the wooden cage with the cat on the floor.

Annette reached back to a servant who was holding a large leather bag closed with straps. She took the bag, opened it, and handed the contents to her daughter, "Annelle, you will need this in Russia and on the trip there. It was your grandmother's." She unfolded the sable pelt robe and placed it over Annelle's lap, smoothing it, petting it with her hands as if it were alive. "Also, you have here the recipe book we have been working on. You can treat the Russians." She smiled.

"Take care of her, Simon," Henri said, "she is our jewel." There was a tear in the father's eye.

"Ah, yes, Monsieur," Simon said. "I am careful with jewels."

"And Prince Yusupov," said Annette, handing to the prince the leather valise, "please take this and guard it carefully. It is our heritage."

Prince Yusupov, now wrapped in his own furs, smiled and gave both Henri and Annette an embrace. "She is safe with us."

Looking him in the eyes, Annette said, "Dear Nicolai Borisovich, family and home are everything to us. Even the distance will not separate us in spirit. Home, we know, is not a place; it is where we belong to each other. We all will always be at home."

The coaches rattled off into the cold, darkening afternoon. The tearful girl under the sable robe was silent. The child, with mixed blood of the nobility and merchant classes of three kingdoms, would, after some weeks, land with her family portraits and cat in the Russian Empire—the largest and most powerful in all of Europe, stretching from the Arctic to the Black Sea, from the Baltic to The Pacific, and even into North America, if reports were to be believed.

With the largest army in Europe, Annelle felt assured, as her mother had told her, that the Russian Empire would last forever, and she and her family treasures, the Rembrandts, would be safe.

RUSSIA

1796–1919

CHAPTER ELEVEN

BECOMING RUSSIAN

The Fontanka Palace
St. Petersburg, Russia
December, 1790

ANNELLE WOULD NEVER FORGET the freezing, bone-shaking, trip east across France, Germany, and Poland into a safe land under the double-headed eagle flag of the powerful Russian Empire. Although that long and threatening journey was now two years in the past, on cold, dark, winter days it seemed like yesterday.

She remembered the times when she felt it was the end of her short life—and it might have been except for the kind and protecting soldiers who rode alongside her carriage through heavy snow and blowing storms. She loved the comforting companionship of old Simon who made sure she was heavily covered with furs, and who endured it all with kindness and respect. Her carriage's broken axle in the Polish blizzard seemed so final—until the guards fixed it. Annelle's freezing trip ended in the warmth of the palatial home of Prince Nicolai Borisovich Yusupov where she was treated as one of his famed family. She now walked down the Fontanka river embankment in the blowing snow toward that palace.

She pulled her sable fur more tightly about her neck, and thought about her changing life as she pressed along the path from beside the wide River Neva and Peter the Great's Summer Gardens, which she so loved even when buried in icy white snow. She loved the hundred marble statues of women in those gardens, each covered with a snow-capped wooden mantle. She knew they patiently awaited the spring to shine, as do all Russian women. Annelle's black, knee-length, fur-lined boots made these winter treks possible. It was a long walk in the freezing air, but a chance to think.

It was now her second winter since she arrived in St. Petersburg with *her family*, the Rembrandt portraits. She felt comfortable, happy, and safe in Russia, and even started to feel like a Russian, however she persisted in telling herself, *I will always be French*.

Annelle puzzled about Russian life and its contrasts. She questioned the nobility's preoccupation with itself, its dress and its jewelry, the gossip about who was dating whom, and their changing titles. The young men were taken up with their potential places in the royal regiments. However, she, too, enjoyed the long velvet dresses, the jewelry, even if borrowed, and the luxurious parties and French cuisine in gigantic homes where everyone spoke French to separate them from the common folk who were servicing the tables.

She even felt a distant identification with the revered Empress Catherine, who had ruled since long before Annelle was born—for Catherine the Great was a German, but educated in the French culture and language. St. Petersburg was Catherine's city. Annelle often heard the prince, the empress' confidant and protector, speak proudly of her.

For Annelle, the most important Russian was *her* protector, Prince Nicolai Yusupov himself—and her heart was grateful for his care. She learned, however, that the term *Russian* covered a wide variety of bloodlines, and that the Yusupov family was originally Tatar, that ancient clan from the southern Volga region, the land of Genghis Khan. She shivered. It was a very intercultural place, St. Petersburg—an amazing contrast to Paris. From what Annelle remembered of France, nothing in that country equaled the grandeur of these elegant Russian palaces, like the Anichkov and Sheremetev on The Fontanka.

Approaching the front entrance to the Yusupov Fontanka Palace with its six gigantic, marble columns, she questioned again her identity in this very different place. Was she really *home*? She did feel there were other, more distant and family things to consider. While living deep within the safety and comfort of the grand palace walls, what she saw in the streets was greatly at odds with the nobility.

She watched those new palaces and noble homes being built by slaves, called serfs, in their long and battered coats, freezing in the winter winds. She instinctively compared the injustice with the problems in France and the uprising against the privileged, such as her own family. There was a distinct distance between the bejeweled rich and the bedraggled poor. She wondered if an uprising like the one in France might occur someday in Russia.

Despite all the noble mentality, she found the young around her were much like her friends in France. They talked about their world, their parents, themselves, school, and each other. Annelle saw her similarity, and her difference. She had a responsibility, which she felt as she entered through the walnut doors opened by tall, loyal servants with their silver pointed hats. She was returning into her home, the Yusupov Palace on The Fontanka Embankment, warmed by a fire in every room.

She wandered through the rooms, filled wall to wall with great European art. She was now familiar with almost the entire Yusupov art collection. The palace's designer was Giacomo Quarenghi, the Empress Catherine's favorite architect, who also designed the famed Alexander Palace nearby. This newly built Yusupov palace and its already notable gardens were her home. The magnificent chandeliers were so big and so high that she could never count the candles.

The art was now on its high plaster walls and the precious Rembrandts, her family, hung proudly in the center of the North Wall in the grand ballroom. The art had to be *high* on the Fontanka walls as St. Petersburg was beset with constant floods that would, at times, reach into the lower floors of the palace.

She was proud to stand back and hear the prince when he told the visitors what he knew of the Rembrandt paintings, and how they happened to be in his palace. She loved to hear him introduce her—the French girl, who he explained, was related to the woman holding the ostrich feather fan.

In her room, she exchanged the fur for a black woolen skirt and a white linen blouse. A servant wiped the boots before placing them on a tin shelf with her other boots and shoes.

Then the servant answered a knock on the door. "We have been waiting for you," said the dark-skinned Maxim in his green and gold jacket. He was the prince's personal attendant. "Prince Nicolai would like to see you."

Annelle followed Maxim into the prince's private chamber. The prince motioned for her to sit in a high-winged red leather chair by a side table with a five-candle lamp. He opened a brown leather valise and positioned it under the lamp. She got a quick glimpse of the family journal that her mother had entrusted to Prince Yusupov upon leaving France. He lifted it out with two hands and handed it to her.

Annelle sat back and held it as if it were magic. She slowly opened it, her fingers turning each stained and fragile page. There was a smell, the smell of the ages past. The Dutch writing had been copied by someone in French. For Annelle, a broadening view of her own life began to emerge. She was part of a defined family heritage.

Prince Yusupov stood back and watched her for a time and then left her to her discovery. A servant brought her a cup of tea and a smile. The leather diary book contained the whole story—everything, which the mothers of the generations before had wished for their descendants to know. But, also it was on those weathered and torn pages that Annelle got a sobering view of her core purpose in life, and the reason why she was now in Russia instead of France.

From these pages she learned that her Russian great-grandfather was an ambassador with Czar Peter the Great's official party when he visited Holland so long before. She was disappointed the ambassador wasn't identified by name, but she had learned by now to accept unfulfilled expectations.

In this case she was nevertheless assured of her small portion of noble Russian blood. She already knew her heritage was recognized by Prince Yusupov and that, along with her French noble relations, enabled her to receive the title of Countess Annelle in The Russian Empire.

Annelle was most impressed when reading those first hand-scripted words of Anneke, the woman holding the ostrich feather fan and painted by Rembrandt. She began to feel the woman Anneke was also one who yearned to identify herself and her purpose, and this is what those mysterious eyes were trying to tell Annelle.

Annelle's view of the Rembrandts had sharpened after her rescue by Prince Yusupov. Now, in the faded pages of the family diary, she read consoling truths about home, a place Annelle was unsure of since leaving her loving parents in France. The faded script of Anneke reassured her, *Home, we know, is not a place; it is where we belong to each other.*

She closed the diary, touching it as if it were sacred, and returned it to the valise on the side table, and left the room. She felt a deep sense of familial identity inside, all the way back to the man and woman so immortalized by Rembrandt with his brush.

With the terrible news coming from Paris, the riots and damage to great buildings, and the bloody stories, Annelle was grateful for the love of her parents to have sent her to the safety of peaceful Russia. Letters from her parents sometimes mentioned the danger and destruction. But, they also reported on the blossoming roses, the tomatoes and melons, and the condition of the dogs. She longed for these letters that came only about once a month, but now it had been almost two months, and she worried. She prayed every night for her parents' safety.

She was comforted at times by Prince Yusupov, who had constant ties with the French King Louis XVI, and received assurances of safety from the king to pass on to the Empress Catherine. Although Annelle was treated like the nobility, she worked diligently as part of the Yusupov family, out of gratitude, out of her sense of dedication. A favorite place was in the Yusupov kitchen, where she worked with Julia, a French chef with whom she shared recipes from the cuisine book her mother had slipped into the baggage when she left Paris.

Annelle longed to return and help her parents, but she knew that was out of the question. It was her destiny to be here in St. Petersburg. She and the beloved Rembrandts were safe. Then, one day, when she was walking among the art, she was approached by her friend Kristina, a special assistant and relative to Prince Nicolai. Kristina handed her an envelope, and after a slight bow, backed off and waited for Annelle to open it. It was handwritten. Annelle read it and said, "He's asked me to meet with him?"

"Yes," said Kristina, "Please follow me."

Prince Nicolai greeted her with a particular kindness that caused a fear and quiver inside. He asked her to sit in that same red leather chair, and this time he sat beside her. "Dear Annelle," he said in a low voice as he held her hand, which was beginning to shake, "I have the sad duty to tell you that I have received news that your family home was attacked and burned," he paused and gently held her hands in both of his, "and that your dear parents died protecting their home and property."

CHAPTER TWELVE

THE GLORY OF
ST. PETERSBURG

The Fontanka Palace
St. Petersburg, Russia
November, 1796

WITH THE DEATH OF HER parents, Annelle's familial cord to France was cut. Even after eight years of concentrating on becoming a Russian, she sometimes went to sleep on a pillow wet with tears for France.

She had her place in the Yusupov palace organization. St. Petersburg was her home. Like all her friends and the Yusupov family, Annelle spoke Russian with the servants and French with the nobility.

She loved working with the massive art collection of Prince Nikolai Borisovich Yusupov, the largest in Russia. She also accepted that the treasured Rembrandts were now also at home in Russia, in that Yusupov collection, and were safe there.

Her beloved Simon, always her protector, had died the year before. She knew there was no going back. Yet, she was more determined than ever to stay close to her *family*, the Rembrandts, whatever might happen.

She sat in the Grand Ballroom, in a tall, black-and-white embroidered arm chair facing the portraits centered in the North Wall—the stately man in black, tall hat shading his face, with gloves in hand, pointing to the woman; and that woman, that mysterious woman, also in black with the crisp white collar covering her shoulders, her hand holding the ostrich feather pointing toward the man. Annelle remembered asking her mother, "Was she unhappy? What was my great-grandmother thinking? What was her secret?" Her mother always answered, "We'll never know."

Much was going on in the capital of The Russian Empire. Annelle listened to the stories, but much of it passed her over as it was mainly political, complicated, and beyond her understanding or responsibility. She heard that Empress Catherine was ill. The rumors about her successor were rampant and confusing.

Annelle was pleased with the marriage of Prince Yusupov to Tatiana Vasilievna von Engelhardt, a niece of the famed Prince Potemkin, hero of the Turkish war and favorite lover of Catherine the Great. Annelle became friends with Princess Tatiana Vasilievna, sharing her grief when the princess lost her first son at birth.

Annelle knew Prince Nicolai Yusupov was considered the richest man in Russia, with over twenty-thousand serfs on many estates. He was often away in Moscow where, Annelle heard, he lived in his seventeenth-century chambers on Kharitonyevsky Pereulok, given to Prince Nikolai's father by Peter the Great. Prince Yusupov had increasing responsibilities. He was now a Senator, the Private Counsel to the Empress, the Imperial Theater Director, and as Minister of State Properties, head of all the imperial porcelain and glass-making plants.

Annelle felt her responsibility even more strongly. For even with all the increased demands on the prince, still he personally attended to his own art collection of over five hundred paintings and hundreds of sculptures. She helped everywhere she could to maintain the collection, and wherever the prince and the family needed her. The fact that she heard whispers about the prince's other large collection—that of pretty young women, including even Catherine at an early age, did not lessen her gratitude for his protection and sponsorship.

Annelle, approaching twenty, made many friends—those who loved art, plus others to talk and laugh with. Of her palace academic tutors, she specially enjoyed one who was French, Adam Archambault, with whom she studied European history and French literature.

She also valued the opportunity to be part of the team of nobility and staff who helped in the common emergencies of the fall floods of the Neva, which were propelled by winds off the Baltic Sea. The Neva would rise sometimes four to five feet above normal, the waters backing up the Fontanka River to the Yusupov palace. The art had to be moved upstairs—a very big task for the palace staff.

It was a stormy November and she watched out the upstairs window at the advancing Fontanka River. "Come on everyone, it's coming," Annelle cried to the staff. She ran down the staircase, into the entry, and again she called, "Get everyone! The water is already coming under the front doors." She raced into the Grand Ballroom where staff were running in and grabbing the framed art that could be carried by one person.

"I know what you want," the young lieutenant said. He smiled and said, "Let's go. Ladies first!"

"Oh, thank you so much, Sergei."

They headed for the Rembrandts, each taking a side of the heavy frame of *The Lady*, lifting her up and off the hooks in the wall.

"We will be back for him soon," the lieutenant said as he nodded toward *The Gentleman,* and then headed for the central staircase with the Rembrandt portrait of Annelle's ancient relative. They waded in the water on the marble floor of the entrance, and wrestled the painting up the staircase to the second-floor hallway where they left it leaning, face against the wall. "Hurry," he said, "before it gets too deep."

Sergei Bazanin, a young lieutenant of the regal Preobrazhensky Regiment, was one of a dozen men assigned to the Yusupov Palace. The floods happened often during the fall and winter, and he was always helpful when they threatened the palace and its art. During the flood emergencies Annelle observed and respected Lieutenant Bazanin's official conduct, seeing him as firm, but courteous toward every one. At times she found him studying the art. With her, he was especially attentive and she felt good about that.

The water was to their booted ankles as they lifted the framed *Gentleman* off the wall and carried it up to the second floor to rest beside *The Lady. The* water rose until midnight.

"My deep thanks to you, Sergei. The Rembrandts are so large and heavy. They need a man."

"I am glad I was here and could help you," he said, "and not somewhere with my regiment."

Annelle felt special with Sergei. He was not like so many of the Russian young men. Their mutual bond extended beyond the recurring floods—with long walks in colorful St. Petersburg, with its evening entertainment, plays, concerts, and especially the Imperial Russian Ballet, which Annelle was proud to know was founded by a Frenchman.

Then the thing happened that all had feared. Catherine the Great died. Things changed.

Prince Nikolai played a major part in the contested changeover to Catherine's unpopular son, Paul. The prince was in charge of the coronation ceremonies of the new czar.

Annelle received advice from many that she would have to come to a decision about her deepening relationship with Sergei. He was soon to be marched out to some distant battlefield. They married in early 1797, with the understanding she would stay with the Rembrandts and help manage the art collection.

Sergei, an officer in Russia's top military regiment, was away from St. Petersburg much of the time. With Russia so increasingly at war, the men were in foreign lands more than in the safety and comforts of home. Sergei was called to Persia. He went with a deep commitment for returning to build a family. Sergei left Annelle with happy expectations of that–with a child inside.

CHAPTER THIRTEEN

THE FRENCH SURPRISE

Moscow
Arkhangelskoye Palace
1811–1812

AFTER THE CONSTANT THREATS of damaging floods in St.
Petersburg, Prince Yusupov committed to finding a dryer
place for the art. This place was Moscow.

The move south with the Yusupov family and their growing
staff was a trip, Annelle thought, more like being part of a moving army. The endless caravan of carriages full of servants and
serfs, and the carts of crated art and sculptures struggled through
the villages, and were often delayed for an exchange of horses. It
was a challenging voyage for Annelle, but she accepted her part
in the family.

She knew a minor part of the collection had been left in St.
Petersburg, in the residence reserved for Prince Yusupov's required
presence in the capital when performing his recurring duties as
a counselor to the czar.

Annelle thought about her glorious last years on the palatial Fontanka estate in St. Petersburg, the blossoming capital of Russia. She loved the golden summer evenings when the sun lazed over the Neva for hours around midnight, framing the majestic Peter and Paul Fortress and the elegant cathedral tower. The weather on those nights required only a light shawl. It all had passed quickly as she was now a mother, busy raising her daughter Alexandra, whom everyone called Sasha. It was always hard work, and now their job was in the big city of Moscow.

Sasha, now in the school for children of the nobility, was adapting to a new home and making new friends. Her mother, who liked being called Countess, was approaching her midthirties.

Annelle was comfortable with her increased duties which included more supervision over the service staff, the serfs, plus a shared obligation for more of the paintings and sculptures that had arrived from St. Petersburg.

When they first arrived, they lived on the Kharitonyevsky Pereulok in Moscow. The art was housed partly in the building's antique chambers. There, Prince Yusupov would take time from his busy schedule to tell stories to the children. Young Sasha loved the tales of Catherine the Great and the stories from Prince Yusupov's many trips around Europe. One of Sasha's story-time friends was the boy Aleksandr Pushkin.

Another move was in the plan as the prince had purchased a new estate, not far to the west of Moscow, from the widow of Prince Golitsyn. Annelle was happy with the new facility as it promised sufficient space for the art and sculpture collection, which she knew was too large for any other exhibit space in Russia. She was satisfied that the art would now be safe on the walls and in the halls of the magnificent Arkhangelskoye palace.

Annelle, with the art staff, worked amid constant construction while the prince upgraded the buildings and expanded the immense garden overlooking the River Moscow. Prince Yusupov made it clear he was building Arkhangelskoye as a palace for enjoyment of the arts, not for the nobility. Annelle particularly loved the gardens.

Arkhangelskoye was more than a palace, it was a palatial estate that included a theater, museums, and a seventeenth century church. It was a half-day's coach ride west of Moscow.

Wanting to preserve the close rapport with her now thirteen-year old daughter, Annelle sat silently with Sasha on the marble stairs in The Garden, between the ancient statues. She looked out toward the River Moscow, missing her husband and praying for his safe return. She had seen nothing of Sergei since their move to Moscow. He was serving with the Preobrazhensky Regiment in Austria and elsewhere in Europe. She was grateful for his occasional letters describing the green European countryside, the tidy homes, but also the pitiful war wreckage in some of the cities. Annelle so wanted to share with him her life and their growing daughter.

That daughter, Alexandra, or Sasha, was involved with her new friends in Moscow. Annelle welcomed this chance to sit with her in the summer sun, breathe in the sweet garden scent and talk about things.

"Do you feel a difference here, from St. Petersburg?" Annelle asked Sasha.

"Yes, Mother. St. Petersburg seems far away. To many of my friends, it's almost a different country," Sasha said.

"I understand," said Annelle, "St. Petersburg is about the present and the future, about European connections. Yes, the people think differently here in Moscow. St. Petersburg people think about their future, where as those in Moscow seem more concerned with their past. Moscow people think St. Petersburg is a temporary seaport connection with Europe, and that Moscow is *real Russia*."

"Moscow has its beauty, too," Annelle added. "I admire the ancient architecture and the beautiful Russian Orthodox cathedrals; a handsome city in its centuries of growth on the border of Asia. Things are changing, but the future is unknown. I do miss St. Petersburg."

"Yes," said Sasha, "but, friends are important. I have good friends here, too."

"To the prince," Annelle said, "Moscow is much closer to his homeland, to all the many Yusupov estates to the east and south. I have learned of Moscow's many-cultured history of conflict. It goes way back hundreds of years, when the Mongols and Tatars battled for control of a land much larger than we can imagine." She waved her arms toward the east.

"Prince Yusupov's family history," added Annelle, "goes back to the Muslim Khan of Kazan and before. I enjoy the story of Sumbecca, the Queen of Kazan, taken as a prisoner to Moscow by Czar Ivan the Terrible. I almost feel a relation of sorts with her."

"So much to learn," said Sasha, "and we have so much to be grateful for—our support, our safety."

Annelle was very aware of the continued confusion of the Russian leadership, which was in turmoil after the passing of Catherine the

Great. She knew Prince Yusupov was always involved somehow in the highest politics, but her thought was always focused on the art, on the love of her husband, and on her maturing daughter.

In that vast art collection, Annelle was also responsible for the display of two exotic Gobelin tapestries, a gift from Napoleon to Prince Yusupov on a recent trip to France.

Now, Annelle thought, Napoleon's tapestries were of minor concern compared with the troubling reports of Napoleon's march from the West, toward Russia, with over a half-million men. She heard everyone talking about it. When the French crossed the river Neman, from Prussia, she heard the Russians all claim it would be a disaster.

Annelle's life rapidly took on conflicting allegiances. She was both fearful and heart-stricken to learn that the Preobrazhensky Regiment with her husband Sergei, now Captain Bazanin, would be facing the French. It was hard to accept that her beloved husband would be killing Frenchmen. But, she had work to do since Arkhangelskoye was in Napoleon's direct path to Moscow. To quickly move the art out of that path was a challenge to all, but her prime personal responsibility was the safety of her teenage daughter.

Annelle had young Sasha by her side when Prince Yusupov's empty wagons began arriving at the palace for the art—scores of horse-drawn wagons. While she supervised much of the art being boxed and packed into the wagons, the sculptures were wrapped by the household staff, and then buried underground in the woods about the palace by soldiers. Much of the framed art, covered in cloth and hides, began the trip south during the last, hot summer days of August to the prince's palace in Astrakhan, that ancient city on the banks of the Volga where it enters the Caspian Sea.

Annelle was thankful for the dependable assistance of young Sasha, who personally assured her the Rembrandts were especially well protected, being wrapped in wool and animal skins.

The sounds of gunshots and breaking glass filled the air. Annelle met the French lieutenant in the grand oval room, the center of the main palace building. He was well dressed, polite, and looked like he was from a good family.

Annelle said to the officer, "Please tell your soldiers not to destroy this beautiful home."

The French officer hesitated, taken for a moment by the Russian woman with her Parisian French. "Who are you?" he said returning his sword to its sheath.

"Please," she repeated, "tell your men to respect this historic palace. It means so much to us." Annelle's hope was that the lieutenant might be responsive and have heart as well as authority.

"But," he asked again, "Who are you?"

"I am from Paris. The Russians have been kind to me. I ask you to remove your men."

"I have no control over that," he said. "This is war." He waved his left arm toward the west. "We are winning Borodino today and the main force will be here tomorrow."

Annelle turned to receive her daughter who whispered in her ear, "They are gone, mother, our Rembrandts. We're ready to go now, too."

The officer turned to respond to a soldier. Annelle and Sasha hurried out through the massive doors and into the waiting coaches.

Safely packed in the last of the wagons of art that left Arkhangelskoye, the Rembrandts were on their way to the south of Russia, out of sight of Napoleon's army. Countess Annelle, daughter Sasha, and others of the palace household squeezed into coaches hurrying north and east to a village out of the path of the French troops. They stayed safely as guests in country homes for all of that autumn, for which they deeply thanked the power and arrangements of Prince Yusupov.

The French, after the bloody battle of Borodino, entered Moscow destroying everything as they went. Arkhangelskoye was badly damaged. Windows were smashed, railings bent, walls shattered by the invading army. All of the destruction was on a beautiful palace under restoration. Even defaced was the sacred Church of Archangel Michael for which the palace was named.

Napoleon entered an empty Moscow, burned by its own people under the command of the one-eyed General Kutuzov. The French faced a disgraceful lack of victory, a city with no food or reward, a total defeat. They began their ignominious retreat in October, brutally pursued by the Cossacks and forced to take the same devastated path of their invasion. By December all of the starving French had retreated. Of the half-million armed men that followed Napoleon into Russia, only about twenty thousand famished stragglers limped back into Europe. They were pursued all the way to Paris.

After the French were gone, Annelle and Sasha returned to broken Arkhangelskoye to help restore its beauty, desperately hoping for the safe homecoming of the art. It was late winter before Annelle would greet the struggling wagons with the protected art as they came back in the horse-drawn carriages from the faraway security of Astrakhan. Over the approaching spring, the repair of the ravaged palace continued. Slowly, things returned to normal. Prince Yusupov spared no expense at rebeautifying his Arkhangelskoye. Sasha proudly reported to her mother, "See, the Rembrandts suffered only a few small scrapes to their frames. They will soon be secure on the replastered and silken walls." Annelle and Sasha were happy, confident the art collection was safe and well displayed again.

Annelle never saw her husband again. Sergei had survived the Battle of Borodino, but he was then lost in the spring of 1814 when the Russians, Austrians, and Poles finally entered Paris. She mourned his death, but at the same time felt gratitude for his love and fatherhood of their daughter, and for his heroic protection of his country. Life went on over the following years in the constantly expanding Russian palace.

All was relatively calm at Arkhangelskoye, except for young Sasha, now a tall nineteen. With her blues eyes, long brown hair and quick wit, she was popular with the young noblemen and officers. Sasha soon found a young officer of particular interest. Andrei was tall, good looking, and polite. He impressed Sasha, and her mother, as being anxious to be a good father. The wedding was a glorious affair which the Prince Yusupov sponsored in his home. As with her father, Sasha's husband was soon off fighting in foreign lands: Turkey and Persia. Before departing, he left her with a pair of twins: a girl and a boy, Ekaterina and Dimitri.

After Napoleon's destructive rampage through Russia, Prince Yusupov continued his prominent role in the Russian empire. He supervised the restoration of the Moscow Kremlin, presiding over the coronation of Czar Nicholas I in 1826. In 1830, he re-established his presence in the Russian capital of St. Petersburg with the purchase of a palace at Number 94 on the Moika canal. However, it was a relocation that Prince Nicolai Yusupov would not personally experience, for in 1831, the prince died at Arkhangelskoye, not from his age of eighty, but from cholera. He was a victim of a national epidemic that created riots against the uncaring czarist government, which then, in response, brutally suppressed the people.

Before leaving Moscow for St. Petersburg, Annelle sat with her daughter under a tree in the Arkhangelskoye garden by the River Moscow and discussed Prince Nicolai's passing.

"Life has many unexpected turns, as we know," she said to Sasha. "We are all shocked by the loss of Prince Nicolai."

"We owe our lives and well-being to this generous man. The Rembrandts would have burned in my parents' home if they had not been sent with the prince to the safety of Russia. He always was a powerful man, but I am convinced he was moved by a personal kindness to help in that dangerous case."

"Mother," Sasha responded, "I know what you say is true. He is respected among all. We owe him much. Russia owes him much. Whatever happens now, I will do my best to act in the best interest of his heritage and his magnificent art. Maybe we have not really lost him, if we follow his commitment in spirit and do a good job."

"Sasha dear, we are both committed to his memory and to our family, including the Rembrandts, *The Lady* and *The Gentleman*. To ensure their safety we are moving back to St. Petersburg to the Yusupov's new palace. It will be a lot of work again, but it will be good to be home."

CHAPTER FOURTEEN

THE MOIKA PALACE

1834–1916
St. Petersburg

COUNTESS ANNELLE SIGHED with contentment upon returning to St. Petersburg. She was coming home. It was a happier
place. Her granddaughter Ekaterina could begin her ballet training.

Working for Prince Nicolai Yusupov's surviving son, Prince
Boris Nikolaevich Yusupov, was a challenging experience for
Annelle and her family. Prince Boris was Marshall of the Imperial
Court, and at age forty-two the prince inherited the immense
family wealth that included thousands of acres in almost every
territory of Russia, sixteen palaces and estates, and forty-thousand
servants. He was not a lover of the arts as his father had been,
which, in fact, gave Annelle more control over the Yusupov art
collection. The prince was primarily concerned with the business
of the Yusupov vast holdings and investments.

Annelle found her work easier after Prince Boris expanded
the Yusupov estate on the Moika Canal. In a two-story extension
he added many rooms to accommodate the art collection. In its

classic chambers, the new Yusupov Palace was now home to over four hundred world-renowned works of art, including the two Rembrandts, and fifty-one marble statues.

The collection now contained the Antoine-Jean Gros painting of the youthful Prince Boris Yusupov with scimitar and flowing cape on a rearing stallion. In 1839 she helped with an official inventory of the collection.

Even amid the growing uncertainty in Russia, Annelle's family of women and daughters enjoyed the developing culture, the celebrated writers, including Chekhov, Dostoyevsky, and there was the popular Pushkin—who died in a duel over an extramarital affair. They enjoyed the music of Tchaikovsky and Borodin. Now in her fifties, Annelle felt blessed having at her side her daughter Alexandra with her fourteen-year-old twins, Dimitri and Ekaterina.

They were all happy and active members of the palace family, although Annelle found it was a more serious atmosphere under Prince Boris, the businessman. When he died, the great art collection lived on behind the thick walls of the Yusupov Palace on the Moika.

While Russia's fatal, foreign military exploits in the Mediterranean and Crimea shook the nation, the order within the Yusupov Palace remained devoted to the family and dedicated to its art.

With her daughter and granddaughter safe in the Yusupov estate, and in comfortable control of their responsibilities, Annelle reflected on her continually changing life. She never forgot the cold and sudden coach trip so long ago—from her happy family home in the French countryside into the cold aristocracy of a developing imperial St. Petersburg.

She constantly gave gratitude for her unplanned, but secure and interesting life of service, particularly to her generous Yusupov family, but also for her success in protecting her own family in their rich wooden frames; Rembrandt's *The Lady with an Ostrich-Feather Fan* and *The Gentleman with Tall Hat and Gloves*. They hung calmly on the gold-encrusted Moika walls, side by side, at home, gesturing their eternal love toward each other.

Annelle, while grateful for her comfortable life, was not without concern. Outside the shelter of the palace walls Russia wrestled with the foreign world, and with itself. Losing the Crimean War to an alliance of France, Britain, and the Ottoman Empire had a tragic, domestic effect. It was one of Russia's historical attempts to reach and command a warm water access to the world. They lost almost a million men, and that tragedy reached into the Moika Palace. Young Dimitri did not return from that disastrous conflict in 1854. The entire Moika household joined grandmother Annelle and mother Alexandra in that sadness.

Respected in her advancing years, Countess Annelle gathered the family to discuss their art-centered lives in the worrisome changing times. There was daughter Alexandra, granddaughter Ekaterina, great-granddaughter Alisa, plus the newest member, young Anya, age three. Anya was the child of Alisa and her French husband, a professor at the University of St. Petersburg.

The descendant women gathered in the *Preciosa Hall* under *The Lady* and *The Gentleman* who looked down on them with inquiring eyes.

"My dear family," Annelle began, "here we are, a lifetime away from my arrival with these two paintings of our beloved ancestors." She looked up to the portraits, blessing them with prayerful hands. "I will be leaving you one day," she said to her family of women, "but already you are doing your honorable familial task."

"I still consider myself French, but I know each of you is conscious of your Russian blood—and Russian life. Nevertheless, our family commitment is still to the safety of our beloved Dutch relatives." She rested her arm on the weathered leather valise on the table to her left.

"With young Anya, there," she pointed to the attentive young child, "we are an amazing five generations. We know Russia is going down an unknown road. Emperor Alexander has released the serfs. Where this leaves noble families like the Yusupovs with their great wealth," and she waved her hand about the gilded walls, "we do not know, but we must be prepared."

She paused, looking at their serious faces. "I know whoever has to take charge of the Rembrandts will do it well. It is our God-given destiny."

She reached for the leather valise, placing it on her lap. She turned the brass latch, folded back the fragile cover, and carefully pulled out the leather journal. "This is our history. You have all seen this. You know what *she*," and Annelle pointed to *The Lady* on the wall, "wrote in it—for us, and forever." She turned the yellowed pages filled with the faded script of different hands over the ages. Stopping at the original sheet dated December 12, 1660, and with a careful voice, she read the early Dutch to her children:

> "What is happiness, I ask, on this promising winter day?
> Surely, to know that I am loved and protected and that,
> come Saturday, the door will be closed on the painful

tricks of man and nature. We and our offspring will be forever safe under our roof and my secret will be forever silent. But, if destiny clouds the rays of hope and we leave this earth too soon, our souls will be captured on canvas by the Master's brush and if that is the closest we shall come to immortality, then it is still all worth it. After all, home, we know, is not a place; it is where we belong to each other."

She closed the journal and smiled. "We all belong to each other. God bless you all." Little Anya ran up and kissed her. The others followed.

After Annelle succumbed to old age a few years later, her descendants clung to those secure family roots, fulfilling their duties within the Yusupov family. They were shaken by the assassination of Alexander II. They knew their Russian world was coming apart. They wondered how and when it would affect them.

The Yusupov security tightened. Even Czar Alexander III, in order to see the Rembrandts, had to issue a command to Prince Felix Yusupov, originally the Count Felix Felixovitch, Count Sumarakov-Elston, now husband of the Princess Zenaida Nikolaievna Yusupova. Young Anya was pleased to help in this special event, especially when asked by the Princess Zenaida.

As Anya grew into adulthood, her responsibilities developed along with her relationship with the Princess Zenaida. Anya was impressed by the princess, as she was not only intelligent, but a leader in control of things. She was kind and respectful to all around her, using her vast fortune to assist struggling painters, sculptors, composers, and singers. Anya found her beautiful and sweet. As the last blood descendant of the Yusupov family, the Princess Zenaida was also considered the richest woman in Russia.

"I want to tell you something," said the Princess Zenaida. Anya, now in her responsible twenties, sat with the princess in her golden study in the Moika Palace, around a small round table with blue patterned Royal Doulton china cups of tea.

"We all know things are changing in Russia. It is no longer the safe place as when your brave ancestor, the Countess Annelle, arrived with the great Rembrandts, your family."

"We have felt," Anya replied, "part of the Yusupov family ever since then. You all are so kind to us. We are so grateful," Anya smiled.

Zenaida leaned forward, looking directly into Anya's eyes, saying, "I want you to know, dear Anya, that whatever happens, I personally share your family's commitment to protect these great works of art. I feel a part of your family for this purpose, just as you feel a part of ours. I will do my best to keep them safe, and together, as they want to be. I promise you that on behalf of all our Yusupov family."

Putting her hand on her heart Anya said, "Oh, thank you so very much, dear Princess Zenaida. True, we are all one family, one home. Home is where we belong to each other. God will tell us what to do in these doubtful times."

Zenaida and Anya hugged.

"But, I have more to tell you, Anya."

Anya settled back and listened.

"We have received a very special request. It is an official request from Amsterdam. A special exhibition of Rembrandt paintings is being held in September to celebrate the inauguration of Queen Wilhelmina of the Netherlands. We have the honor of sending our pride, *The Lady with an Ostrich-Feather Fan* and *The Gentleman with Tall Hat and Gloves.*"

"Oh," said Anya, "that is indeed an honor, Princess Zenaida, but..."

"I know your concerns, Anya," the princess smiled, taking Anya's hands in hers. "The paintings will be under guard the entire time. They will travel to and from the Netherlands in a special ship of our Emperor. All will be safe."

"This is wonderful news, Princess Zenaida," offered Anya. She knew she had to trust. "Can I help in any way?"

"Indeed you can. I am planning on it," said Zenaida. "I want you to help oversee the packing of these jewels and the preparation for the Rembrandts' visit."

Anya was still managing the conflict between her head, who knew this was a wonderful event in the life of the paintings, and her heart, for in her twenty-one years she had never been a day without the comfort of her framed relatives nearby on the silken palace walls. "They are going back to their birthplace for a visit," she quietly said.

The Princess Zenaida smiled and added, "Yes, they will be on a vacation and return to their home here in about sixty days."

"Thank you so much for sharing all of this with me, Your Highness." Anya bowed her head.

Again they hugged.

Anya helped in the preparation of the Rembrandts. She was impressed with the careful work of the staff who wrapped the framed paintings in soft quilting, then in tightly sealed, waterproof fabric, then padding them into the two wooden cases for the trip.

When finished, she returned to her studies and her work with the staff with the other paintings as needed.

The paintings returned as scheduled. Anya supervised their return to their proper place on the wall in the Moika palace.

Unpredictable and confusing events continued to occur in Russia. Czar Alexander III had died of internal disorders in 1881. Nicholas II was now the Emperor. There were aggressive political divisions. Czar Nicholas was clearly not in control of the country. Starting and then losing the war with far-off Japan in 1905 was a disaster for Nicholas, losing over fifty-thousand men, the entire Russian navy, and the respect of the Russian people, and the international community. In a polished corner of St. Petersburg, the fate of the Rembrandt portraits was a growing concern.

Princess Zenaida called for Anya one day to inform her, "We now have a new situation. A rich American will arrive soon, especially to see the Rembrandts. He saw them in the Amsterdam exhibit, and is coming here with hopes of buying them. Of course, we have no intent to sell them. But, how we handle this is important. I would like you to meet him and help him see the paintings. Then I will join you for a dinner, but I have no other time."

In 1909, in the midst of Russian national disorder, the rich American arrived. Peter A. B. Widener of Philadelphia motored his large steam yacht through the newly expanded Kaiser Wilhelm Kanal into the Baltic Sea, and then on into St. Petersburg—specifically to see and buy the Rembrandts. Mr. Widener was considered one of the hundred wealthiest Americans. An avid art collector, already with twelve Rembrandts in his collection, he wanted more.

The *Lady with an Ostrich-Feather Fan* and *A Gentleman with Tall Hat and Gloves* were, for a short time, in a rare display of the art of Russian palaces. Widener considered the two Yusupov portraits to be among Rembrandt's best. Anya accompanied him to the restricted display and took charge of the showing.

At the dinner in the Moika, Mr. Widener made an offer for the Rembrandts, which was promptly, but politely rejected by Princess Zenaida.

After the dinner, Princess Zenaida took Anya aside, saying, "We remain committed to the safety of your Rembrandt portraits. My personal attention to this is challenged by the present events. My son, Prince Felix, is committed to work with you as needed."

"Thank you, Princess Zenaida," said Anya. "Yes, I know he loves art. We will work together."

Even amid the growing chaos, the wild shouting in the streets and depressing reports of war in Europe, romance prevailed within the Yusupov's Moika Palace. Anya was surprised to receive a gold-embossed, sealed envelope from the Princess Zenaida. She sat down in her favorite, blue-velvet arm chair in her private sitting room and opened the envelope.

It was a formal invitation to the coming marriage ceremony of the Princess Irina Alexandrovna and Prince Felix Felixovich Yusupov, the remaining son of Princess Zenaida. The ceremony was planned for February 22, 1914, only six weeks away. She knew this rumored event was being accelerated in light of all the domestic and European unrest. She was excited to accept this invitation to a celebration she considered surely a national event, a Yusupov and a Romanov marrying.

On the wedding day, Anya watched the arriving coach, driven by four white horses, deliver Princess Irina and her parents to the Anichkoff Palace. Then, inside the palace, Anya, in her assigned seat, turned with all the others to focus on the entrance of Princess Irina on the secure arm of her uncle, the Czar Nicholas II.

Heads turned and eyes focused on the princess in her shining, white satin dress, embroidered in silver, with a train several meters long. The talk around the palace was that Irina's diamond and rock-crystal tiara was commissioned from Cartier, and that her face veil had belonged to Marie Antoinette. Princess Irina was delivered down the aisle on the arm of the czar, to the side of Prince Felix, and the elaborate ceremony began.

In June of that year, while on their honeymoon in Middle Eastern Europe, the Prince and Princess Yusupov fell into dangerous waters as war in Europe broke out while the newlyweds were there. Through all the confusion they were able to negotiate at the highest diplomatic levels, finally making their way through anti-Russian Germany, to Denmark, Finland, and back to St. Petersburg.

There was wild shouting in the streets of the Russian capital. The war was beginning in Europe. Anya was in the middle of the confusion of the Russian disorder. Inside the Yusupov palace it was pack and pray. There was no faith in the immediate future. The Yusupov private rail coach filled and left for the Crimea as quickly as it returned from that seaside haven of the nobility. Anya was reassured now that Irina and Felix were back in the Moika palace. The question of their shared responsibility for the Rembrandts dominated her thought.

Princess Zenaida was among the last to leave St. Petersburg, along with her new daughter-in-law Princess Irina. Anya had developed close relations with the prince and princess, even in the short time since the new couple had returned from their desperate European honeymoon. Among the men remaining in the Moika was Prince Felix.

Anya remembered what Mr. Widener had privately said to her a few years before about the Rembrandts he so badly wanted. "They will be safe in America," he had told her. She didn't know what he was talking about then, but now she remembered his words.

CHAPTER FIFTEEN

THE PLAN TO KILL

December 29, 1916
Petrograd (St. Petersburg),
Russia

FROM HER BEDROOM WINDOW high on the east side of the
palace on the Moika, Anya, squinting into the winter light,
could barely see over the snow-laden trees of the courtyard to the
embankment on the far side of the river. There, a young man in
an officer's brass-buttoned longcoat watched for something. Anya
knew why he was there, and for whom he waited. She knew he
watched for a car to turn off Fonarny Lane and head toward him.
She hoped the rumored plan would not happen, at least not in the
palace home where she had lived for over thirty years.

Anya turned away from the frosted window and stood warming herself by the fire, turning the plan over in her mind, and
wondering how it would affect her and her beloved Genrykh.
What was their responsibility under such circumstances? They
totally disapproved, yet had no control over what now seemed
certain to come to pass.

She thought of Annelle de Montfort, that courageous young countess, her great-great-grandmother who, over a century before, was rescued from the terror of the French Revolution with the Rembrandts and her cat, and became a woman of the nobility in the Russian court. Was Russia, like France, falling into the same unpredictable madness now?

After an hour of straining in the December cold, young Captain Sukhotin saw yellow car lights sweep across the darkened palace buildings on the far side of the frozen river. He waited a few moments to make sure it was Prince Felix and his scandalous passenger. Turning, the Captain raced across the footbridge and down the path along the canal, his boots slipping on the icy stones, his coat flying about his heels, his breath hanging in clouds behind him in the frigid air off the Gulf of Finland.

At Number 94 Moika, the young officer slid to a stop at the heavy carved door on the east end of the palace—the private entrance to the apartments of Prince Felix and Princess Irina Yusupov. Behind that door lived the wealthiest family in Russia—richer than the czar, it was said. He tried the door and found it locked. With his gloved fists, he pounded on the door. A hand inside moved aside a curtain on the small glass window of the door and a man's face appeared. "Who is it?" the voice called.

"It's Sukhotin, Genrykh. Let me in!"

"Already after twelve, Captain. I have locked up for the night. What do you want?"

"They're coming!" The officer pounded again. Serge Mikhailovich Sukhotin, jerked his head side to side, squinting through his spectacles, oval and silver-framed. "Don't you understand?" he said, "They're almost here!" A captain in the czar's own Preobrazhensky Life Guards, he had been an influenza patient in the hospital supported by Prince Felix Yusupov. It was there that he had met the prince. He heard the keys turn in the aged locks, and then Genrykh pulled open the solid mahogany door. Sukhotin ran though the entryway, brushing Genrykh aside, turning left, past the darkened ballroom with the crystal chandeliers, and into a small hexagonal room with eight, identical, mirrored doors for walls. One door on the left, barely perceptible in the dim light, was open. The captain bounded into Prince Felix's study.

Two men were waiting at an inlaid walnut table set for tea in a room filled with yellow lamp light and the smoke of Turkish cigarettes. A cut-glass decanter of cognac sat on the lace-edged tablecloth. A porcelain clock with golden nymphs stood on the side table. The clock read one minute until one. They listened for the approaching car. They knew it carried Gregori Rasputin.

Rasputin was considered by the masses to be the scourge, and by a very few, the savior, of Holy Russia. He was, in fact, a wandering *muzhik,* an illiterate peasant from the far Siberian bogs, a self-appointed monk, an embarrassment to the Russian Church, and a drunken, unwashed debaucher of women. The gossiping populace believed him to be a spy for Germany in The Great War now underway. Many blamed the devil for Rasputin's admission into the inner sanctums of the monarchy, the halls of the Russian court and, as rumored, the beds of its noble women.

His hypnotic influence on the impressionable Empress Alexandra convinced her that he was not only the savior of her hemophilic son, the heir to the throne, but that God had sent him to save Russia. State ministers were hired and fired not only by the decisions and command of the czar, but often at the suggestions of this mesmeric holy man. This night, five men were committed to ridding Russia of this cancer.

In the car, escorting the monk, was Prince Felix Felixovitch Yusupov, slight of build, with dreamy eyes and narrow, delicate features. His father, the Count Felix Sumarokov-Elston, of Prussian origins, a strict military man, was never close to his sons. Felix gained his title from his mother's side of the family after his older brother was killed in a duel over a married woman.

When younger, the partying prince was an embarrassment to family and friends when he dressed in his mother's gowns and pearls, and flirted with the officers in the cafés. Felix's immunity from the harsher realities of Russian life made him the very unlikely man to commit a murder. But, it was he who led the noble conspirators on that dark, cold night.

"Well?" shouted a man leaning forward from the edge of his chair, his hands gripping the carved tiger paws at the armrest ends. His eyes, blinking with excitement, were like two black marbles in a cannonball of a head. Vladimir Mitrofanovich Purishkevich was a member of the Duma and an outspoken leader of the Monarchists. It was said that "the only thing politically further to the right of him was the wall."

Captain Sukhotin drew in a sharp breath, "They're coming— Felix and the *starets*," he said. He pulled off his gloves, rubbing his hands together for warmth. "We have to do this right. This holy man is a threat to the empire." The captain doffed his coat, tossing it at Genrykh who was standing by the door.

Genrykh Kassatkin was Chief of Security at the palace. A tall man of fifty with a thin mustache, he had served as an officer in the Chevaliers Guards under Prince Felix's father. He knew how seriously they should take this man, especially since superstitions were flooding the land about his mystical powers.

Genrykh's face was drawn with fatigue, his dark eyes edged with red. He knew something of great consequence was threatening that night. He heard the wild rumors of spies in the czar's chambers and whole divisions of Russian soldiers massacred on the front. He hoped it was not true. He was motioned away with the flick of the Grand Duke's hand.

The Grand Duke Dimitri Pavlovich Romanov sat sideways at the table with his cup of vodka, drawing on a long, thin cigarette, cocking back his head, blowing smoke rings the size of dinner plates. He was in his twenties, tall, thin, with close-set eyes in a sensitive white face, and compared by the servants to the elite Borzoi hunting dogs of the czar. Grand Duke Dimitri led an undistinguished and unhappy life. It was an open secret that he still brooded over the fact that beautiful Irina, niece of the czar, chose Felix instead of him for a husband.

Sukhotin separated the white window swags, his face catching the yellow flash from the headlamps of an approaching car. He called, "They have turned into the courtyard."

Dimitri, Purishkevich, and Sukhotin hurried into the octagonal room and cracked open another of the eight mirrored doors. It was the door to the secret staircase down to the basement room that Prince Felix had spent weeks preparing for this occasion—for the murder of Gregori Rasputin.

Genrykh raced upstairs. When he reached Anya's bedroom he gave the usual code; one knock…two knocks…one knock. She was wrapped in the down quilt pulled from her bed. Her blond locks spread like a fan across her back, reaching her waist.

"I saw everything," she whispered and shivered. "Prince Felix's car, and that horrible man. It's really *him*. They entered by the new door."

Genrykh pulled her close, leaned over, and gave her a kiss on the corner of her mouth where her smile usually was. To Genrykh, Anya Kaganova was the most perfect blend of womanhood; combining the charm and mystery of a Russian woman with the culture of the French, and the determination of her Dutch ancestors. "Those beautiful feet must be cold, Anychka," Genrykh said, "even on the bearskin rug."

"There is so much at stake," she said. "This country, this estate, this art."

"But not our love, Anychka." He hugged her closer. "That is not threatened. We will be as one when this is over. The Grand Duke," said Genrykh, "that detestable man Purishkevich, and Sukhotin, they are waiting for him."

She stepped away from her post at the window, shaking her head. "Then the rumors are right. This is terrible, Genrykh. If Rasputin is to be killed, let it be in a dark alley, not here. This respectable home, and every treasure in it, will be a target."

"We will do what we can," he said. "But, it is in the hands of the men in the room below."

"More is expected from the nobility than vengeful acts of childish men," she said. She reached toward an onyx box on the lower shelf of her commode, pulled up her family journal, and holding it to her eye level, said, "I know who I am."

Anya glanced down into the courtyard and saw Felix's silver Rolls, the lights on, the doors standing open. She pulled the down quilt tighter about her as the embers in the grated fireplace darkened and she whispered, "It is the end of the Russian Empire."

Genrykh embraced her from the back. She felt his hands through the quilt and his kiss on her neck. She hugged those hands. She warmed to his embrace and promise of protection.

"I will be needed before the night is over," he said.

"I'm coming with you," she said.

Anya hurriedly dressed. In felt boots and fur coats, they slipped through the hallway, through the darkened galleries, their gilded walls lined with the works of Raphael, LeBrun, Bol, Fragonard. The Yusupovs had eight paintings by Rembrandt, but it was the Master's portraits *The Lady* and *The Gentleman* that were the most treasured. "Do you realize what will happen to this collection if the mobs take over? They will tear this house apart," she said. "The Countess Annelle escaped the French with these Rembrandts. Now it is my duty."

The portraits of the Dutch couple hung in the center of the silver wall of the *Preciosa Hall* along with Velasquez, van Dyck, Rubens. On long-held instructions, she always placed the two Rembrandts out of sight when certain guests were present.

Anya stopped, facing *The Lady* and *The Gentleman*. "You will be protected as you have always been," she whispered to them. "Trust us." She hurried on.

"I don't want it to end," Anya said. "I am proud of being a Russian." Anya's father, Count Kaganov, a colonel in the Imperial Army, fought the Turks, never returning, like so many other fathers and sons whose severed heads were piled before the Sultan. In spite of her French and Dutch heritage, Anya was a loyal part of the Yusupov household, the only family she had ever known. "Yes," she said, "we'll do what we have to."

Genrykh and Anya huddled together unnoticed on the staircase, where they could hear everything and see much.

In the octagonal room, the faces of Dimitri, Purishkevich and Sukhotin strained, like peeking children, to see down the stairs through the crack in the doorway; but they closed it without a sound as the voices of Prince Yusupov and his victim drifted up the stairs from the room below.

Dimitri turned. "The music, start the music! We are having a party—remember?"

Sukhotin opened yet another mirrored door in the room. Behind it, on a table, sat a wind-up gramophone with a lily-shaped wooden sound-horn. Sukhotin turned the crank, moved the lever that engaged the turntable, lifted the arm, and placed the needle on the turning record. It scratched out *Yankee Doodle*.

"What a day of honor," Purishkevich straightened his stubby body and smiled showing three gold teeth. "With that evil monk removed, the dignity of our czar will be preserved—the Russian Empire will stand forever!"

> *Yankee Doodle went to town,*
> *Riding on a pony.*

Only Dimitri spoke English. The others did not understand the words of the song from the American Revolution. Dimitri lit another cigarette.

> *He stuck a feather in his hat*
> *And called it macaroni.*

The staircase door opened. It was not Felix, but Doctor Lazovert who came in, throwing on the floor the chauffeur's hat and the coat he had used to drive Felix and his victim.

"I had to wait," Lazovert said. "They are down there now, in the room."

"Did you lock the courtyard door?" the Grand Duke asked.

"Of course," said the doctor. Dr. Stanislav Lazovert, a quiet man, a devoted doctor, was a Pole, the Senior Doctor for the Red Cross unit on the hospital train provided by Purishkevich's riches.

Purishkevich paced about, wiping his shiny head, "It's now thirty minutes already," he said.

"It must be soon," Sukhotin said. "Is everything ready?"

"Naturally!" said Dimitri, "my car," and pointing into the study, "the canvas, the chains in the sack on the floor there. Everything."

"Then I wish he would do it," Purishkevich added, shifting from foot to foot.

"These things take time," Dimitri shrugged, turning to Doctor Lazovert. "Are you sure the poison will work immediately, Doctor? He has powers, it is said."

"There is enough in one cake to kill a horse," Lazovert answered. Beads of sweat appeared on the doctor's brow. "The cyanide came from the hospital's locked vault," he said.

"The music, Sukhotin. It's your job."

"Isn't there anything else?" Purishkevich asked. "A march, maybe?"

"No. Irina took the rest with her to The Crimea. It won't take long."

"Then keep it going."

Sukhotin opened the closet door and wound up the gramophone for the third time.

"Yankee Doodle, keep it up,
Yankee Doodle dandy;
Mind the music and the step,
And with the girls be handy."

Sukhotin stood by the window, peering into the dimly lit night.

Dimitri sat in silence, flipping an unlit cigarette in his fingers and tapping the table.

The doctor paced with his hands behind his back, his eyes following the symmetrical designs in the blood-red Persian rug.

Purishkevich sat bent with his elbows on the tiger paws, his head in his hands, but would jerk up like a nervous dog at the slightest sound, search the room, blink his eyes, and drop his head again.

Genrykh leaned over from his watch post on the stairs. He heard only the impatient sighs from the study. Yankee Doodle had stopped again, the needle clicking in the last groove.

Anya shivered. Genrykh wrapped his robe about her. "Listen!" Genrykh cupped his ear and pointed to the staircase door. "That's Felix! He's playing the guitar and singing a song! What is going on down there?"

It was two o'clock.

They then heard loud banging sounds coming from the study. "I guess they are remembering they were supposed to be having a party," Genrykh said, as the conspirators stomped their boots on the parquet floor, laughing like drunken peasants, dancing with locked arms into the octagonal room. Dimitri feigned a woman's giggle.

"Absurd," said Anya, "absolutely absurd!"

The mirrored door to the basement room burst open. The frivolity stopped as if switched off. It was Felix.

Anya tightened her grip on Genrykh's arm. They leaned forward to hear the news.

Felix shut the door behind him and stood there, silent, in a fearful trance, with his hands behind his back on the doorknob. "The cyanide!" Felix hesitated. "It isn't working."

They all leaned toward Felix, squinting in disbelief.

"That's impossible," said the grand duke.

Purishkevich inched forward, blinking his eyes. "But the dose was enormous. Did he take the whole lot?"

"Every bit." Felix trembled. "It's not working." Felix turned, looking over his shoulder at the door behind him as if he expected to be followed. "The cyanide," said Felix. "He ate two cakes and drank two glasses of Madeira. He only groaned and kept drinking, saying the cakes are tasty. He wants to see Irina!" Felix threw up his arms in despair. "He says I promised. Or to go see the Gypsies—can you imagine?"

"We must go down, all together," Purishkevich said, "and finish it now." He pulled his revolver from its holster on his belt and pushed it at the prince. "You will have to shoot him, Felix."

Felix raised his hands, "No, I can't shoot a man. I've never shot anything, not even a rabbit. My father will tell you that."

"You must shoot him," Purishkevich demanded. "This is *your* plan."

"Poison or a bullet, dead is dead!" said Sukhotin, "What is the difference?"

Genrykh shook his head. "They are getting reckless," he said.

The dark hallway was cold. He whispered, "What would the princess say of this?"

"She is a clear thinker," said Anya. "Before she left I heard her say to Felix, 'Please take care. Do not get mixed up in any shady business.' No, the princess would not approve."

"Russia must be rid of Rasputin, they say," said Genrykh.

"Maybe so, but not here. In the end it will only make things worse," she said.

Purishkevich approached the door to the basement. "Then *I* will do it," he said, holding his pistol with one hand, reaching for the doorknob with the other. "Let's finish it." He motioned for the others to follow.

"Wait," Felix insisted. He raced to put his back against the door, spreading his arms. "Who knows what that devil would do if he saw all of us coming down the stairs—with guns?"

"Then *you* must shoot him, Felix, like I said!" Purishkevich blinked.

"Calm down," Dimitri interrupted, "We had a plan. We did not agree to shoot him."

"I'll try more cakes, but," Felix said," I'm afraid of that man, I tell you. The devil protects him."

It was now past two-thirty.

"Take my pistol," Dimitri said. Felix hesitated, then took the revolver, opened the door and vanished down the stairs into the basement, the gun held behind his back. The door clicked shut.

CHAPTER SIXTEEN
THE MURDER

December 30, 1916
Petrograd (St. Petersburg)

T HE SHOT SPLIT THE AIR like an immense crack in the thawing river ice. The waiting men in the octagonal room jerked as if the bullet had struck each of them.

Still on the stairs, Anya grabbed Genrykh's arm so tightly that he winced.

A wild scream rolled up from the basement room below. Dimitri and Purishkevich rushed for the door to the stairway, but neither touched the doorknob. They heard heavy steps ascending the stairs from below. Purishkevich drew his pistol.

The footsteps stopped. The doorknob turned. The door opened. It was Felix. He said nothing at first. His face was pale.

"He's dead," whispered Felix, the revolver in his shaking hand. "No question—in the heart."

"That's it then," said Dimitri, retrieving his revolver from Felix. "I'll get the car. Sukhotin, you put on Rasputin's coat and hat." He looked to the doctor, "Lazovert, put on your chauffeur's coat and hat. If anyone is watching, they will see Rasputin returning home."

Just then, a horrible scream curled up the stairway and through the open door.

"He's, he's alive," Felix cried looking down the staircase. "He's at the bottom of the stairs!" Felix grabbed a rubber club, but could not move.

Anya tightened her grasp on Genrykh's arm. "*Listen* to him! It's like the cry of a wounded animal!"

Rasputin roared, "I am going...to tell...the empress!"

Purishkevich drew his gun from its holster, held it above his head, and led the conspirators down, their boots booming like an avalanche on the wooden stairs.

Genrykh and Anya raced to the open stairway door.

"He's out here!" Sukhotin yelled as he ran into the courtyard. Purishkevich and Sukhotin, pistols in hand, stumbled after the faltering hulk that was the bleeding monk. Only weak shafts of light from the streetlamp and the open door of the house penetrated the dark.

"Don't let him get away!" Felix shouted from the doorway.

"The door was *locked*!" Lazovert said, shaking his head. "I don't understand how he got out."

Rasputin groped toward the open gate in the courtyard fence. "The empress!" His voice weakened. "I'm going...to tell... the empress!"

Felix fled past Genrykh and Anya and out through the front door to head Rasputin off from the street, just in case.

"I must help!" shouted Genrykh as he raced into the courtyard where he saw Purishkevich rushing toward the staggering

Rasputin, pointing his pistol at the dark image of the swaying man. The politician fired a shot into Rasputin's chest. The monk fell onto one knee, bent double and rolled over into the snow. Purishkevich kicked him in the head and stood back. "He *is* dead now. My god...." But, Rasputin continued to twitch, face up into the freezing dark, his arm groping the air.

Then Genrykh saw another man running through the open courtyard fence, gun in hand. The man aimed point-blank at Rasputin's forehead, firing a shot. The man stood, looked around, turned, and ran back out the open gate. Genrykh realized he knew who the man was.

Felix was now outside the wrought-iron fence. Ignoring the fleeing visitor, he ran to greet an unexpected policeman racing down the Moika embankment toward the sounds.

The officer recognized the prince. "I heard revolver shots." He looked into the courtyard.

Felix moved to block his view.

"What has happened, Your Highness?"

Felix put his arm on the policeman's shoulder and turned him away from the body on the courtyard ground. "Nothing of consequence," Felix answered, "just a little horseplay. One of my friends drank too much and fired his revolver into the air. No harm done."

The policeman stretched to see into the courtyard, but the prince moved again to block his view. The policeman gave up. "Thank you, Your Highness," the policeman said and shuffled away in the snow, looking back twice.

"Come help!" Dimitri called to Genrykh. Blackish blood flowed from the holes in the holy man's silk blouse.

Felix wiped his brow. "I feel faint!" he said, and staggered toward the house brushing against Genrykh in the dark.

Genrykh and Lazovert dragged Rasputin's body into the house. Purishkevich followed, kicking at the snow to cover the blood.

"Go lie down, Felix," Purishkevich said, seeing the prince's condition, "We'll take care of things now."

Felix made his way to his studio and sank into a deep comforting chair, closing his eyes.

Anya was waiting in the hall outside the mirrored room. "You have blood on your coat, Genrykh. Where is the body?"

"On the stairs," he said.

They heard the purr of the grand duke's Rolls Royce as it sped away. "They will come back for the body. That's their plan."

"Anya, it was the Englishman. That last shot. It was Rayner, that English secret agent friend of Felix," Genrykh said. "He was outside, ready when needed." Genrykh pointed to the center of his forehead. "Right between the eyes."

"Genrykh," Anya gripped his arms firmly with her two hands and set her jaw. "If anything works tonight, it will not be the plan of Prince Yusupov. As usual," she said, "whatever the intended result, the outcome will be exactly the opposite. We have so little time."

"They have returned," Purishkevich said to the semi-conscious Felix. "They said I must stay with you. They are wrapping the body now."

Dimitri, Sukhotin, and Lazovert dragged the body down the stairs into the basement room and wrapped it in the canvas. They called for Genrykh's help. The four men struggled with the body, moving it through the side door into the dark, and lifting it onto the black leather back seat of Dimitri's Rolls Royce. Dimitri started the engine; they droned away, leaving Genrykh standing in the snow with bloodstained hands.

The silver Rolls followed a wandering route through the back streets of Petrograd crossing the Neva at the Troitsky Bridge. Within thirty minutes they reached their destination, the Petrovsky Bridge over the Little Neva between Petrovsky and Krestovsky Islands. The sky was overcast; most street lamps were dark. Dimitri turned out the car lights as they passed the pensioners' home, and drove onto the bridge without waking the sleeping bridge guard in the frost-covered shack. At the middle of the two-lane bridge they stopped.

The cold wind off the Gulf of Finland nipped their cheeks and stung their ears. Dimitri had no gloves on. Dr. Lazovert had ridden in the back seat with the corpse and its deathly stench of alcohol and blood. Lazovert opened the door and they dragged the canvas bundle onto the snow-covered bridge. The three men struggled to lift it over the four-foot railing. Lazovert had the head end of the canvassed body. It slipped out of his hands and onto the bridge floor with a thump.

"Sorry," said the doctor.

"Let's set him down, get a better grip," Sukhotin said. He had the other end of their victim.

"Get the chains," said Dimitri, "we need to weigh him down."

"What chains?" asked Lazovert.

"The chains to wrap him so he sinks."

Sukhotin looked in the back seat of the car. "There are no chains."

"No chains?"

"We forgot them."

"Oh my god," said Dimitri. He took a deep breath and exhaled a cloud. "Dump him anyway."

"Is the tide going in or out?" asked the doctor.

"Dump him! All lift together, *now*," said Dimitri, who had the middle. They got the body to the top of the railing. "Now push," ordered Dimitri. The body flipped over head first, hurtling the twenty feet onto the ice with a thud.

"It's frozen."

"Of course it's frozen, Doctor," said Dimitri. "But he will slip down the hole by the pilings. That is the plan."

But, the body lay there on the solid ice, a foot away from the water around the pilings.

From behind them a voice called out of the dark. "You fishing?"

They jerked around to see who it was.

"Can't fish tonight, no—no moon." The drunk carried a kerosene lantern, which lit their faces with its golden glow.

Dimitri took a breath, "You are right, my friend, bad night for fishing." He squinted to see the man's face. "Had you not be home?"

"Yes. Wife is waiting. Big trouble." He stumbled on.

"The body is gone," said Sukhotin. The others hung over the bridge to see if it was true. The weight of the body had broken through the thinner ice by the pilings and Rasputin had disappeared into the dark waters of the Neva.

"Maybe we didn't need the chains," Lazovert said.

"We've done it," said Sukhotin. They drove to the end of the bridge, backed and turned the long car around to return. The guard still slept, but even had he been awake, the windows on his little guardhouse were so covered with frost that he could not see outside in any case.

Felix was awake in his studio when Dimitri and his helpers returned to the Moika Palace.

"Well?" Purishkevich asked.

"It's over," Dimitri answered.

Prince Felix straightened. He took a deep breath. "That is that, then," he said. He began to feel the blood returning to his face. Then he pointed to a burlap bag in the corner of the room. "Dimitri! The *chains*!"

"Forgotten, Felix."

"*Forgotten?* That was the *plan!*" Felix began to shake. "How can he sink to the bottom of the river without the chains?" He wiped his face with a kerchief. "What am I going to tell Irina? She said something will go wrong and the world will know. What am I going to tell her if they find the body?"

"The body slipped beneath the ice," Sukhotin said. "The current will carry him away. He won't be found until spring."

"This is terrible news. Can't..." Felix slapped his forehead with the heel of his hand, "...can't we do anything right in this country?"

"This is not England, Felix. And you are not at Oxford now."

CHAPTER SEVENTEEN
THE DISGUISE

The Moika Palace
Petrograd (St. Petersburg)
April 1917

A NYA HAD ALWAYS LOOKED FORWARD to late April. The temperature was above freezing during the day, the sun warm, the wind still. She remembered the familiar saying, "With the sun always comes hope." But, there was little sign of hope in the streets of now-called Petrograd, or inside the halls of the Moika Palace. She shook her head in dismay.

She felt that the finale of the Rasputin murder played out like the end of a Chekhov play: everything going wrong. The murderers forgot the chains to sink Rasputin's body in the Neva. It resurfaced in a few days with water in its lungs, and like Chekhov's despondent Platonov who could not drown himself in the shallow river, she heard the blame placed on "poor Russia."

Prince Felix Yusupov and his accomplices had been dispatched to the far corners of the empire by Czar Nicolas a few days after the discovery of the body. The prince had promised to return, but when that would be, Anya had no idea.

The Murder of Rasputin was a bold, but singular act in the blood-soaked drama of the fall of the Russian Empire. The czar and family had fled to Tsarskoye Selo, a country estate twenty-five kilometers away. With the people starving, the army dissolving, and guns at the palace doors, Czar Nicolas II had no option, but to resign. The announcement of the czar's abdication was greeted with a variety of emotions, including delight, relief, fear, anger, and total confusion.

The street chaos worsened. The Yusupov Palace itself was now threatened, protected from the disorganized rabble only by the few remaining, loyal, household servants. The largest art collection in Russia was still intact, and a plan was in place to save at least the Rembrandts.

Anya was pleased that after his absence, and as promised, Prince Felix Yusupov slid back into Petrograd from *Rakitnoe*, the family estate near Kursk in Central Russia to which he was banished by the czar. Genrykh and Anya met Felix in his study, which was unchanged since the night three months prior when the bearded monk was poisoned and shot in the room below.

"It sickens me," said Prince Felix, "to see the empire disintegrate into bloody anarchy. Thank God the princess and the other Romanovs are still safe in The Crimea.

"I wonder how long it will last." He pulled his French bulldog *Gugusse* onto his lap. It licked the prince's cheek.

"As Pushkin warned," Anya added, "'God defend you from the sight of a Russian Rebellion in all its ruthless stupidity.'" She paused. "It may outlast us."

"The madness keeps growing," said Genrykh. "There is no law, the police side with the rabble. Nobility and generals are beaten in the streets."

"Bread rations are fifty grams per day," said Anya to Prince Felix as he stroked his dog, "but there is no bread. You must stay out of sight, Your Highness."

Genrykh and Anya recognized that the bloody affair in the Moika Palace the previous December had accelerated Russia's disintegration. The man in front of them was a contributor to the downfall of the monarchy he was trying to save. But, that was of little consequence to her now. Anya's priority was protecting her family Rembrandts.

The knocks on the heavy main doors of the palace were loud and impatient. "Who knocks with such impertinence?" a servant grumbled as she hurried from her dusting in the music room.

The main entrance to the Yusupov Palace consisted of three heavy, carved doors forming two vestibules. The servant pulled open the first door. In the outside vestibule, stood a woman wearing a red armband on her oversized, stained, brown coat. A torn canvas bag hung from her shoulder.

"We are here from the People's Committee on Culture by authority of The Petrograd Soviet," said the woman, her voice hoarse from yelling. Two sullen-faced men stood behind her.

Upstairs, a security guard, one of the few left, interrupted the privacy of Felix, Anya, and Genrykh. "Excuse me sir, but there are some unpleasant people at the main door. Olga is detaining them."

Genrykh hurried to check. Anya moved to a corner of the grand staircase landing where she could peek and listen undetected.

Olga, the family servant at the entrance said to the visitors, "And what do you want?"

"Let us in!" commanded the shaggy-headed woman. She was built like a box, standing with her stout legs braced apart, her feet crammed into frayed, gray socks slopping over the tops of battered boots. Her clenched fists were cemented on her hips.

Olga stood defiant in her starched apron, her hands also on her hips. Her hair was pulled back into a neat bun. Wincing at the intruding woman's foul breath, she spread her arms further to block the door, demanding, "I asked what do you want!"

The two men on the steps were silent, but the tall one had the stern look of authority on his face. The shorter one held a notebook in his arms, watching the street like an expectant dog, looking up to his master for reassurance.

The woman took a deliberate step with her dirty boots into the inside vestibule. The others pressed behind her, filling the small space. "We came to inventory the art," she said.

"This is a private home," Olga said. "The estate of the Prince and Princess Yusupov. Who are you anyway?"

"Don't you understand? We are from the Petrograd Soviet. No private property anymore."

"What you ask is out of the question. I cannot allow that without permission from the prince."

"Permission is no longer necessary," the shaggy woman insisted, inching forward so the Bolshevik and the servant stood chest to chest in the doorway. "Besides, your prince is not in Petrograd, we know that."

A man's voice came from the inside. "What is the problem here? I am Chief of Security on this property."

Olga stepped back into the entry hall to let Genrykh speak. "You want to inventory the art in this collection?" Genrykh said. "Are you out of your mind? It is private."

The woman put her hand into her canvas bag. "There is nothing private any more. Everything belongs to the people." She pulled out a short-nosed revolver and crossed her arms. "Is there a question?"

Genrykh did not flinch or appear to notice the gun. "No question if you have proper authority. Show me your documents."

The woman with the gun stopped short, turned, and looked at the tall man behind who stepped forward.

"That is a reasonable request, Comrade," the tall man said. "Of course I can bring you documents. But there will be more than three of us at that time, you understand." He flashed a one-sided smile. Holding his eyes on Genrykh, he ordered the woman, "Go wait in the car, Masha." His eyes flashed beyond Genrykh into the foyer with its grand red-carpeted staircase lined with Roman statuary. "This will not take long. We will not disturb a thing, Comrade Chief of Security. It will happen sooner or later, you understand. Better now."

Anya, listening on the staircase landing that led to the upper living quarters and the galleries, turned and crept away as the intruders entered the foyer. She then raced two stairs at a time, running straight to the galleries to do what she and Genrykh had decided to do when the revolution reached the palace.

The tall man from the Petrograd Soviet took the marble stairs with a stiff gait, his assistant following like a shadow. When the man came to the first landing, where the life-sized statues of *La Venus de Medicis*, *L'Europe*, *L'Asie*, and *L'Afrique* watched down on him from its corners, he turned to the left, marching up the next flight. He paused only to take notice of the immense gold and crystal chandelier and stared, as if counting the candle lights. Genrykh was at his side.

Paintings hung everywhere, in the halls, in the reception room, the dining room and other rooms on the way to the galleries. The tall man and his assistant entered the first gallery, the *Nicolas Hall* with its red damask walls and eight electrified chandeliers. The assistant opened his notebook, holding the stub of a yellow pencil in readiness, licking its tip. But, the tall man did not speak.

Anya watched him walk bent over like an inspector with his hands clasped behind his back, stopping in front of the Velasquez, then in front of the Greuze, then the painting of the *Interior of the Church of St. Jean de Latran* by Pannini. He muttered something Anya and Genrykh could not hear.

He stepped into the next gallery, the *Preciosa Hall*, with its green papered walls, and was confronted by the grand work of Jacques David, *Sappho and Phaeon*. Genrykh stayed close by his side as they all moved into the largest gallery, the *Salle des Antiques*, with its silver silk walls. The little assistant was always a shuffle behind, pencil poised, head cocked awaiting an order.

"Close the book," the man said to his assistant. He turned to Anya, who was waiting, silent. "Too many to list now I can see. What is your name, woman?"

Anya stood, her arms folded, studying the Bolshevik's face. It was not hard like his words. She felt a tinge of sincerity in his eyes. She wondered what was behind his revolutionary insistence.

"Kaganova, Anna," she said.

"Well, Comrade Kaganova," his hands still clasped behind his back, "you will list the paintings, tapestries, and sculpture for me and have it ready in five days. I will call back."

"I only take directions from the prince or the princess. What is *your* name, please?"

The man pulled back, stunned by her impertinence. "I see some paintings are removed," he said. He nodded toward two obvious spaces on the walls.

A chill went down her back. "For cleaning perhaps. I don't know," said Anya.

"The prince has of late acquired some modern paintings—Kandinskys, yes?"

She did not answer.

"Why do you want to know my name?" he asked.

"So I can tell the prince and princess of your visit."

"You may tell your prince when, or if, he returns from his exile, that Boris Stepanov, Chief of Cultural Affairs for the Petrograd Peoples Soviet will return for the inventory of art. If the list has not been prepared, you can explain to him why the art was removed to a safer place for inventory." He shook a long finger in the air. "And this is not just an interest on my part, Comrade, it is a command."

Petrograd Soviet Chief of Cultural Affairs Stepanov, trailed by his shadow with the notebook, marched back through the galleries and halls toward the Grand Staircase. He then turned to face Anya once again. His voice was calm, but stern. "You can also tell the prince and princess that we know much about their collection. There was an inventory before, you know. We are not uninformed." With that, he descended the stairs, leaving the Yusupov Palace through the three, heavy, carved doors, the servant closing them behind the visitors with a loud crash of finality.

"Five days," Anya said, "Five days, Genrykh, for us to execute our plan. Thank God, the prince has returned."

Later that day, Anya, Genrykh and Prince Felix, his dog in his arms, stood on the parquet floor in the Salle des Antiques. The paintings of the largest private collection in Russia looked down on them from the silver walls. They reached agreement on which ones could be saved, taking into account size and weight. Older items painted on wood panels were too heavy so only those on canvas were considered. Anya listed first *The Lady* and *The Gentleman*.

Before the Soviet official had ascended to the top of the stairs earlier that day, Anya and a maid had lifted the Rembrandts off their hooks and slid them into the service room.

"These Rembrandts, Your Highness, are our family," said Anya. "We have a two-centuries-old promise to uphold."

Felix nodded. "We know they are your family. Irina wants them saved above all others in any case," he said. "They have lived here as part of our family as well."

"If the czar," Anya said, "had to make an appointment with the old prince in order to see the Rembrandts, some self-important commoner with dirty boots will not have that privilege. They survived before, they will survive again."

The prince put Gugusse on the floor. "It will be the Rembrandts on this first trip. That is final. I will return for others."

"Gregori has set up your studio, Prince Felix, where you can work in peace. The canvases are there."

Anya slipped into the service room. The Rembrandts stood on the floor against the wall. She looked them in the eyes. "You must take another trip, my dear family. It may not be easy. God willing, you will reach your new home." She reached forward and kissed the woman on her forehead, the man on his cheek.

Gregori, the estate manager, had everything ready for the prince: the canvas, the paints, the oil, the brushes.

"I must work quickly," said Felix. They all squeezed into the painter's converted studio. It had no natural light, but was well lit with electric lamps. Two easels stood each with a new canvas stretched and mounted on a frame.

Felix donned a canvas smock. "In art school...," he raised his eyebrows, "...they said I had talent." He tied his smock. "This will be the true test," he said.

"But first," said Anya, "We must remove the lady and the gentleman from their frames."

They stood with their eyes fixed on the paintings; no one wanted to make the first move.

"Do you realize," said Genrykh, "that Rembrandt himself mounted these portraits in these frames?

"The woman looks tired," said Gregori.

"She has suffered," said Anya. "I feel that for her."

"And survived—as we will," added Genrykh.

"And the man," said Anya, "he is her strength. Keep them together, Prince Felix."

"Let's start," said the prince. "The paint takes days to dry," He reached for the sharpened knife Gregori had taken from the medical closet. Felix looked exhausted. He had not shaved for days.

Anya bent over to watch the surgical operation as the men disassembled the back of the frame, removing the portrait of the woman from its wooden backing.

"They are simply going for a holiday," said Felix.

While Genrykh and Gregori held the portrait, Felix took the surgeon's scalpel and began to cut the canvas about the edges.

Anya winced as if she feared bleeding.

"Like a battlefield amputation," said Genrykh, "I have seen a few." Then they repeated the cutting on the portrait of *The Gentleman*. The unframed Rembrandts were laid on a table side-by-side like wounded nobles, covered with a white damask tablecloth.

Anya held her hands over her mouth.

"I begin," said Felix. "If you will please leave now."

In the secrecy of the unvented room, Prince Felix began his art of deception. With a wide brush, he covered each new canvas with a base of white and yellow in a random mix. He even made sketches as he had learned in art school. Then he turned to the canvas, adding a blue wash in the lower right corner with large blotches of it in other places. He followed with the vermillion, azurite, and yellow ocher, smearing each of those colors in large spots about the canvas. He worked on both canvases at the same time. His priority was speed.

Then he took the burnt umber, snaking a major curve from top right toward the center. It looked like a leather whip with a fat handle. Blue again followed the whip like a shadow. This process took Felix eight hours in total. He stood back and smiled with relief.

Gregori checked on the prince after midnight, delivering a bowl of hot turtle soup and bread.

Anya and Genrykh hurried to see what was done. "They are almost too good," said Anya. "They might want to take them, also."

Anya nodded toward the gallery, "I have begun rehanging the art so the two won't be missed. We will be ready for Comrade Stepanov."

However, Chief of Cultural Affairs Stepanov did not come as promised, in five days. He came at noon on the fourth day. Olga, in her starched white apron, again answered the door. Comrade Stepanov was alone. He pushed his way into the hall before she could stop him.

"Is the Kaganova woman here?" he demanded. This time he was dressed in a brown uniform complete with red armband, a black belt with a pistol snapped into its holster at his waist.

"I will get our Chief of Security."

"We hear that the prince has returned," Stepanov called after her.

Genrykh arrived from a side room. "That is right," he said. There are no secrets anymore, he thought.

"Then he understands my task," Stepanov said.

Anya descended from the Grand Staircase landing, welcoming the Bolshevik with an insincere smile. "We expected you tomorrow."

"Perhaps you have it ready now," Stepanov said. "We hear the Yusupov private coach is at the Nikolayevsky Station. We thought the prince might be leaving us."

"We are not privy to his plans."

Stepanov started toward the staircase without further invitation.

"This is an inconvenient time," Anya said as she and Genrykh backed up the stairs slowing Stepanov. "We are cleaning."

Remembering where to go, Stepanov arrived in the *Salle des Antiques* standing without a word for a few moments then said, "The paintings are rearranged."

"We hope to have your inventory tomorrow or the next day, Comrade."

"There were two empty spaces right here," he said, pointing to two country scenes of nude women and cupids where the Rembrandts had hung. "What is that smell?"

Anya raised her eyebrows in ignorance.

"Is it linseed oil?" he asked.

Anya gasped. They had kept the door to the service room closed trying to hide the smell of the paints.

Prince Felix stepped into the gallery dressed in his uniform. "It is fresh varnish for several paintings," he said. It was the same uniform with brown belts he wore the night of the murder. "Who are you, sir?" Felix asked.

"I am an official of the Petrograd Soviet."

"I am Prince Felix Felixovitch Yusupov." He stood erect. "And you are also a lover of art I see."

"Is this, Prince Yusupov, and the art in the other galleries I saw before, the entirety of your collection?"

"You have seen it all." Felix spread his arms in opposite directions toward the other galleries.

"And the ones with the fresh varnish?"

Again, a shiver went through Anya's body.

"I want to see them," said Stepanov.

"In that room at the end of the hall. Nothing special," shrugged Felix.

Hesitating, Anya opened the door to the service room. The brooms and buckets stood in the corner. The two paintings by Felix leaned against the wall in their frames. The easels and paints were gone.

"Ah," said Stepanov, "Two more."

"These are student paintings. We support the Conservatory," Felix said.

An hour before, Prince Felix's modernist scenes were secured on top of *The Lady* and *The Gentleman* with a wheat paste from the kitchen. Gregori had hidden everything when the Chief of Cultural Affairs showed up.

Stepanov stepped over to the paintings and started to pick one up.

"Please don't touch," Felix said calmly. "The varnish is still wet."

Stepanov backed away.

"These are of little value," Felix said, "and should not be in the inventory I think."

Anya nodded.

Stepanov's eyes fixed on the paintings. "I agree," he said after a pause, "I think maybe these two paintings should be kept out of sight, off the inventory list."

The Bolshevik folded his arms, his face in a half-smile. "Yes, keep them in this room." He returned to the gallery, walking in a figure eight about the floor. He waved his hand saying, "You realize, Citizens, these great works will now be displayed for all to enjoy, not hidden on silk walls for only the rich who have even forgotten them in their quest for more riches. They will go into The Hermitage for all, including you, to see." He spread his arms in a gesture of possession. "Don't you agree?"

Anya said nothing, realizing that despite whatever sincerity the man might feel inside, the people would, in fact, be the last to benefit from the revolution. The Hermitage had already been ransacked.

"Except for the student's art," Stepanov looked around as if someone would overhear, "I will pick up the student's art myself."

Still no one spoke.

"And, why not," Stepanov looked around for agreement, "as you say they have no value."

"When would that be?" asked Anya.

"Tomorrow afternoon, I think." He turned and with his crooked grin walked away.

Genrykh escorted Stepanov down the stairs to the front door. In the vestibule, Stepanov turned to Genrykh and said, "You must know, Comrade Chief of Security, you have not fooled me. Your prince calling those paintings the work of a student—I have a degree in art. Who does he think I am?"

Genrykh held firm.

"I do not hold this position for nothing," Stepanov continued, "Have those paintings ready for me tomorrow. Inform the prince not to expect to travel in his private rail car soon. I saw photos of the exhibit in Stockholm. I know Kandinskys when I see them."

CHAPTER EIGHTEEN

THE TRICK

The Moika Palace
Petrograd
April 1917

THE REMBRANDT RESCUE PLAN designed by Anya and Genrykh involved a deception. Anya had recommended Slava Barakov, a close friend of the Yusupov family. They needed someone with the prince's height and build. The Barakov family lived down the Moika from the Yusupov Palace, on the *Kolomensky Ostrov* past the New Holland Gate. Slava traced his heritage back to the Kievan princes, but was not considered nobility.

Slava knew Felix from an art class they took together before Felix was forced to quit it by his father who thought it unmanly. Slava never participated in Felix's scandalous parties where the prince dressed as a woman and winked at the officers, but out of respect, he was willing to help the Yusupov family in this crisis. He had agreed to help, but how and when was not discussed.

Now, after two people were shot on his front doorstep and vandals broke his street-level windows, Slava felt it was time to return to his Ukrainian roots. As was true for many of those active at various levels of the Holy Russian Empire, the fact that his family's origin was in this ancient birthplace of Russia was a cultural anchor. His breathless arrival at the palace was unexpected.

Running all the way from St. Isaac's Cathedral, Slava rushed into the palace through the private doors of the prince's apartment at the same time that Comrade Stepanov left through the main door at the center of the long palace on the Moika Embankment. A servant, one of the remaining Tatars in the Yusupov household, led Slava into Felix's study where Genrykh came to meet him.

"Genrykh!" Slava struggled to speak. "There is fighting in front of the Mariinsky Palace. Mobs are coming this way. Massacred bodies everywhere, even children."

The sounds of gunfire and shouting men came from the direction of the monument to Nicolas I, only a few blocks away. Still panting, Slava added, "I will never make it home for tea. There was no other place."

"You couldn't have come at a more perfect time, Slava," said Genrykh.

"What?" Slava cocked his head.

"It is today. We have to do it today."

"Today?" said Slava. "We agreed on tomorrow or later."

"The Bolshevik will come for the paintings tomorrow," Genrykh said. "I'll send a messenger for your things."

Slava asked, "Where's Felix?"

In the service room, Anya and Genrykh removed the paintings from their new stretchers. Cloth was layered between the two paintings. "Slowly," she said. "The paint is so thick in places, roll them slowly."

"If it cracks, it can be repaired," said Genrykh. "It is our only hope."

On the Moika Embankment, Chief of Cultural Affairs Stepanov ran from the palace to the safety of his car. Glass bits flew as a bullet shattered the windshield of the black Ford Model-T touring sedan he had earlier liberated from some merchant's garage. His driver, wiping blood from his cheek, backed the car up and turned it around. A boy with a red armband crouched in the back seat, unscathed.

The driver drove across the bridge to the other side of the river where he stopped and Stepanov left the car. He gave instructions to the driver to stay and watch both front doors of the Yusupov Palace until he returned. He then ran down a side street.

Genrykh carefully rolled the paintings and placed them in a long canvas bag, binding it with heavy cotton cording in two places. It was now nine o'clock and darkening under a leaden sky and spitting snow.

Genrykh, the canvas bag under his arm, descended the dark staircase with Anya and approached the octagonal room.

"Is the man in the car still there?" asked Anya.

"He's where Stepanov left him," said Genrykh peeking through the curtains.

"When does the train leave?" she asked.

"It's scheduled for eleven as usual. But who can tell?"

Anya knocked on Prince Felix's study door. "Are you ready?"

"Not yet," the voice answered. They waited, inquiring three more times, and the answer finally came, "Ready."

"Hurry, Prince Felix," she urged. "The train leaves at eleven."

"The Rolls is ready in front?" the prince asked.

"Of course; Gregori will drive. The paintings are rolled and packed for you," Anya pointed to the canvas bag with a strap of twine. She anticipated his next question, "And in the rear is the other car," she said.

Felix's fur coat reached from the sable fur *shapka* on his head to the top of his black boots. He carried a large, saddle-leather case. It was the one from Felix's Oxford days, a meter long and twenty-two centimeters deep, closed by two wide harness-leather straps and heavy brass buckles. Its best feature was it was big enough to hold the paintings.

Pulling up the collar around his face, the man with his suitcase walked out the front door of the palace private apartments and stepped into the waiting Rolls.

From the window of Felix's study, Anya waved to the departing car and pulled the curtains tight and doused the lamps.

Petrograd was dark, but light from the surviving street lamps was enough for the driver in the black Ford to note the exit of the man dressed and packed for a long trip. The boy sitting with the driver scurried off with a message to Stepanov. The Ford, with shards of glass for a windshield, crossed the bridge and chugged along after the purring Rolls.

The *Nikolayevsky Voksal* smelled of cinders, sweat, and fear. The rail station teemed with jostling people; disheveled revolutionaries, despondent mothers with hungry children crying in their arms, and soldiers running from the war.

Trains on the tracks were scheduled for Murmansk, three to Moscow for transfer to Crimea and Central Asia, but some were standing cold, the crews shouting in revolt. The express Russian

Imperial Train No. 1 to Moscow was on Track 4. The man in the long fur coat with the saddle-leather case exited the Rolls and vanished into the crowd.

At curbside the black Ford and a bakery truck arrived. Out of the bakery truck jumped four uniformed guards, rifles slung over their shoulders. They muscled into the crowd followed by Boris Stepanov in a determined stride. With a blazing look in his black eyes, he pressed forward, pushing people aside as if they were stray dogs.

The men rushed straight to the Yusupov coach, connected next to last onto the train to Moscow. This car, even in all the riot damage, stood out. Its yellow curtains and green leather seats could be seen though the cracked and dirty windows—a glimpse of past elegance. The soldier hired to guard the coach door was brushed aside by Stepanov's henchmen, and they stomped up the steel stairs into the plush interior with its mirrors and crystal. The coach was empty.

Returning to the platform the men spread themselves along the train, waiting for its passenger. Stepanov pulled his watch from his inside jacket. It was now five minutes after eleven. The train made no sounds of moving. The uniformed men and their leader waited, watching for the man in the fur coat.

Out of sight, disguised in ragged coats, Anya, under a faded shawl, and Genrykh with a piece of red felt in his cap, watched from behind a pillar across the empty adjacent tracks, their hearts pounding.

The crowd never thinned. It was filled with women wearing scarves on their heads, clutching twine-wrapped bundles in their arms. Confused men struggled with bulging suitcases tied together with rope. Strolling, self-appointed police with red armbands and suspicious looks had nowhere to go, but made trouble by stopping people and demanding nonexistent documents.

Through this struggling horde the guards saw their target and moved to cut him off at the coach door. The man had his hand on the chromed assist bar by the lowered steps.

"Prince Yusupov!" a voice called. The man with the large leather case did not respond. "Stop in the name of the Revolution."

The train whistled its first warning for departure.

One of the guards grabbed an arm and another grabbed the leather case and pulled the man off the train.

"Now, my prince," said Boris Stepanov while he leaned forward, his hands clasped behind his back and his eyes glaring with accusation. "Where are you going and what are you taking with you?"

The suitcase was thrown onto the cement platform. Two guards unbuckled its straps and threw it open.

The fur-coated man turned to Stepanov saying, "Yes, who are you addressing?" He pulled back his collar and scowled.

The guards yelled, "Here is what's in the case, Comrade. Trousers, shirts, underwear, a bag of sugar, and three pamphlets by…" they squinted their eyes in the dim light, "…Vladimir Ilyich Lenin."

Stepanov caught a breath. "You," he said, "you are not Prince Felix Yusupov!"

"Someone," Stepanov stepped back, narrowed his eyes and said, searching up and down the platform, "…someone will pay for this deception."

The guards closed the leather case, first removing the bag of sugar and tussling over it until the paper tore and the precious contents spilled on the dirty cement. The train's whistle blew again.

The trainman yelled at the hordes still clamoring to get on board. Slava Barakov gathered his things into his suitcase and rebuckled the straps. He stepped into the coach that would take him, and the others now forcing themselves on board the Yusupov railcar, to Moscow, to Kiev, and beyond to the Black Sea. The train gave a lurch, and the first steaming puffs of forward motion shuddered along the line of cars.

From their vantage point, Anya and Genrykh, turned, watching a man in a long canvas coat, a black Bolshevik cap, and a four-day face stubble, muscle his way on board, three cars forward, pushing his battered suitcase ahead while protecting the heavy canvas cylinder slung over his shoulder on a home-made strap of twine. Felix and the Rembrandts were on their way out of Petrograd.

Anya and Genrykh trod home arm-in-arm through the unshoveled snow along *Nevsky Prospect,* Petrograd's main street, the windows of its fashionable shops now but broken splinters and emptied by the looters. Over her shoulder, Anya carried a large canvas bag, like those hefted by the old women on the train heading for a safer place.

The snow continued to flurry in large damp flakes. It was warm, only three degrees below freezing. The snow sloshed, it didn't squeak. It was quiet—no shouting, no shooting. The street was dark, no electricity.

"The prince said he will return," said Genrykh.

"Maybe he will," said Anya, "and maybe he will not."

"But, it worked, Anya." Genrykh smiled. "Our plan worked."

She kissed him on the cheek. "*The Lady* and *The Gentleman* are gone," she said. "They have survived this madness." Anya loved the smell of his stubbled cheek, sweaty, the smell of success, at least for this night.

"Maybe they will come back, let's hope," he said.

Anya paused. "The Russia we knew is over, Genrykh. It's a wild pack of starving dogs now."

They crossed over the Fontanka River, turning left on Sadovaya Ulitsa, past the empty market stalls of Gostiny Dvor, across Sennaya Square and along the Ekaterininski Canal toward the rear entrance of the Moika Palace of the Yusupovs.

She kicked the slush. "*The Lady* and *The Gentleman*," she said, "they will find a new home—together, somewhere. They always have." She opened her shoulder bag and pulled out a fur stole, a warm sable stole that had warmed the women in her family for generations and wrapped it about her shoulders. "We will meet them again, I pray. They are in the hands of Princess Irina and Prince Felix now."

In the gutter blocking their path was a snow covered dead horse. They crossed the street. Anya shivered.

"When I was young," Anya said, "I used to sit in front of the paintings and treat them as if they were my wise grandparents. I talked to them as if they were real. I promised them my care and asked them to tell me their secrets. They spoke with their eyes. I felt good. But," she paused, "I never learned their secrets."

When they turned off the *Ofitserskaya* into the service yard behind the Moika Palace, Genrykh suddenly stopped blocking Anya's progress with his arm. "Look," he said pointing at the snow. "Three sets of tracks."

"The old ones are ours from earlier, the next are Gregori's return. But these," he pointed to the fresh narrow tracks, "are Stepanov's car."

They peered around the wall. They saw the black Ford with the shattered windshield and three men forcing Gregori against the fender of the Rolls, speaking in intimidating tones. The tall one was shouting and shaking his fist.

"Stepanov," said Genrykh, "and he is not happy."

The Bolshevik turned, looking in their direction, but saw nothing in the dark.

"Come this way," said Genrykh. "He didn't recognize us." They scurried up the private pathway, dark and shielded from the angry Bolshevik's view by the cars, past the outbuildings, and through a servant's door into the palace. "Pack a suitcase, Anya. One suitcase, that is all."

"I've already done that," she said.

"We are marked. There is nothing left for us to do here." He then outlined their route of escape. Out the side door he told her, the door where the dying Rasputin had fled, then across the Moika, down the back streets to the Nikolaevsky Bridge on the Neva. "We will follow *The Lady* and *The Gentleman*," said Genrykh, "but on a different path. I have a friend, Anychka. He is a Finn. He has a boat. God willing, he will be waiting for us when we need him."

CHAPTER NINETEEN
THE FAREWELL

The Crimea
April, 1919

Princess Irina was the last of the Romanovs. The Romanov family had ruled the Empire for three hundred years, and she was the last of that great family. Leaving Russia was a sad event.

Tears especially ran when she thought of her cousin, Czar Nicolas II, the Czarina Alexandra, their five children, their doctor, and three servants—all lined up against a basement wall and shot dead the year before in the Ural city of Yekaterinburg.

She knew The Crimea was the exit gate from this now precarious land. She trusted that any day the gate would open for the survivors of the bloody revolution to press through it to safety somewhere.

Irina said to her husband, "These are terrible times. We don't know what is next. But, we have to be brave, to show our strength." She and Felix, with their five-year-old daughter, also named Irina, were at Koriez, the Yusupov's Crimean villa. She knew she had duties now; the Rembrandts. Where would she take them?

Irina felt it a comfort that her mother, the Grand Duchess Xenia Alexandrovna, and her father-in-law Prince Felix Sumarakov-Elston, were with them in the family estate. This was especially so when her husband so bravely risked his life for the family's welfare.

"We have lost all we are going to lose," said Prince Felix to his wife. Since his escape with the Rembrandts, Felix had snuck back into Petrograd twice to retrieve jewels and other valuables from the family estate on The Moika. On one trip, to save his life, it was necessary to hide the jewels under the stairs in their Moscow estate for a planned later rescue.

The Bolsheviks, sweeping down through Russia were advancing fast—their approach like the constant booming of distant thunder.

She was not surprised that, even amid all the tension, the remaining Romanovs, young and old, were celebrating the birthday of her mother, the Grand Duchess Xenia. It was a relief from the fearful uncertainty.

In the middle of the celebration, a servant stood in the entrance and made a loud announcement. "I present Captain Charles Johnson, Captain of the British dreadnought HMS Marlborough." The frivolity calmed and heads turned at the arrival of the tall British officer in gold-braided blue uniform, white shirt and tie, his hat neatly tucked under his left arm. He was not unexpected.

Bowing and addressing the Dowager Empress Marie Feodorovna, the British officer said, "My apologies, Your Majesty." The Dowager Empress, wife of the late Alexander III and mother of Czar Nicolas II, bowed her head in recognition. The captain continued, "I am here to deliver an offer of asylum from our

King, and an appeal from Queen Alexandra, and to receive Your Majesty's decision."

Irina and Felix had seen the telegram that advised of Britain's King George V's order for the giant battleship to arrive at Yalta for the evacuation of the King's aunt, the Dowager Empress, and her immediate party, to Malta and on to safe exile in England. In addition, the letter from Queen Alexandra, wife of Edward VII, was a sisterly plea to take this chance to escape sure death as had befallen the czar and family.

Captain Johnson was there to determine their readiness to leave Russia in the face of the present Bolshevik advance on The Crimea. The royals had been increasingly imprisoned in their own palaces. Time was up. It was the end of the world as they knew it. Still, some refused to believe the facts. The Empress announced her refusal to leave.

In The Crimea, there remained of the Russian Imperial royalty, in addition to the Dowager Empress, only her daughter Grand Duchess Xenia Alexandrovna, sister to Czar Nicholas, her daughter Irina, five of the Grand Duchess's six sons ranging from twelve to twenty years, the Grand Dukes Nicolas and Peter, other Romanov family members, plus their servants and cooks.

Irina kept quiet in the confusion and looked to her husband in disbelief.

"The Empire is over," Felix said. "They are in denial. I will talk to the captain. We all must leave Russia now."

Captain Johnson left with the Empress' conviction that she would not leave, but as he was being escorted out by Prince Felix, he was assured that she would be persuaded to accept the offer and would leave on the British ship. By the end of the birthday party,

Empress Marie agreed to leave, but only if everyone in her party and an undetermined number of loyal others would be included.

The Bolshevik thunder in the distance grew louder.

Irina and Felix had always stayed at the ready. The valuables were packed in common cases along with the Rembrandts in a concealed vault on the second floor of the Crimean villa. A total of twenty leather cases were ready to accompany the Yusupov family to England.

The next days were a Russian test of British order. Many more people than the captain expected appeared on the pier for evacuation on the battleship. The Empress Marie insisted that all who wanted to leave would be taken. The captain had to make room.

"Where are the promised French ships?" the Empress asked Captain Johnson.

"I am sorry, Your Majesty, the French sailors rebelled, and their ships turned around," he said, "But never fear, all of your family will be accommodated on board." The captain's orders were to provide an escape, a safe passage from Russia, for The Empress Marie and her immediate family, maybe four or five persons. The battleship had no accommodations for the scores of others; it was a warship. The captain did not realize that even the cooks were counted as family by the royalty, as the royals had no intention of existing on English puddings. Servants, also, were like family.

The ship's officers provided their quarters for the Romanovs and their families. The captain moved out of his own cabin for Empress Marie. In the end, while expecting five or a dozen people, the Marlborough took aboard fifty persons, of whom thirty-eight were women—four generations of the murdered czar's family. It took days.

With empty hearts, the Princess and Prince Yusupov stood on the steel deck of the HMS Marlborough watching the panic on the piers in Yalta. Hundreds had raced to the beach when the ship arrived. They were struggling to get out to the ship, some leaving cars with doors open and engines running. Luggage was strewn across the beach.

"We have to look out for ourselves," Irina said to Felix. They wrestled their way into the ship's dark hold, through the mountains of luggage all crammed between guns and ammunition. They secured their twenty suitcases, including the rolled up Rembrandts, well-disguised in their canvas wrappings.

In the afternoon of April 11, 1919, Irina stood among the others on the rear deck of the departing British warship. With gratitude for their safe escape, she watched the beautiful Crimean coast fade from her view as the HMS Marlborough drifted silently into the mist of the Black Sea.

On the side deck Irina watched a little lone figure, the Empress Marie, standing in her heavy dark furs. Several hundred White Army Imperial Guards in a British sloop slowed alongside to honor the Empress, the men singing the Russian Imperial Anthem in their harmonious deep voices. The men, almost all officers, saluted the Empress, before heading toward shore on their way to their fight with the Revolutionaries—and certain death.

Irina clutched both hands to her heart and breathed deeply as the Russian shoreline slipped out of her sight. She reflected on her identity. "In Russia," she said, "I considered myself a European. Now, on my way to Europe, maybe never to see my home again, I know I am a Russian."

She thought of her responsibility, the two Rembrandts packed away in the ship's hold. She asked, "Will any of us on this British ship ever see Russia again?"

ENGLAND
AND
FRANCE

1919–1922

CHAPTER TWENTY

THE EXILE

London
September 1919

IRINA WAS ON FOREIGN GROUND, but it was obvious to her that for Felix, the flat at Number 15 Parkside, Knightsbridge, London, felt like home. The party was at the London flat the prince had retained since his years at Oxford.

The war was over. Irina felt the darkness of London. She felt the mourning for the loss of the millions in the bloody trenches of France. On the trip from Yalta, she witnessed Europe's devastation everywhere. The upbeat and cordial tone of the London party this evening was puzzling.

Tesphé, the demure Abyssinian servant, was not to Princess Irina's liking, but he was her husband's choice. Prince Felix employed the man as his valet after rescuing him from a mob in Jerusalem when Irina and the prince were on their honeymoon. The servant added a brilliant splash of Oriental color and charm to the room, swishing about in his azure silk robe, Turkish slippers, and white turban. A six-inch silver cross on a massive chain hung to his waist. Tesphé served drinks on a cloisonné tray.

From a wind-up RCA gramophone in the corner sang the scratchy words, "I wish I could shimmy like my sister Kate."

Irina sat quietly in a dark red velvet chair. She had little to offer in response to the glowing greetings of Felix's London admirers. She thought she knew quite a bit about Felix's past, but tonight she realized she had more to learn. She watched a woman approach Prince Felix. She turned to hear the conversation.

"These hands of yours," the starry blue-eyed woman said to Felix, "do not feel like the hands of a murderer." She spoke with the seductive voice and a disarming look of innocence that seemed to please the prince.

"You know?" the prince replied with a smile.

She straightened with a start of surprise, but kept his hands in hers, even after he had, with Russian panache, kissed hers. "What do you mean, Felix dear?"

"Do you know what a murderer's hands feel like?"

"Don't be absurd, darling, of course I don't," she said, "But your hands are soft, unlined by guilt."

He looked at his palms.

"Dear Felix," said Lady Diana, "how absolutely sweet of you to invite us."

Diana was tall. Her golden curls peeked from under a blue silk hat shaped like a matador's. Lady Diana Manners, heralded in the society press as *the most beautiful woman of her generation*, had gathered together *The Greats*, as they called themselves, from the prewar days, to attend this welcome-back party.

With her sparkling eyes she swept the room to gather interest. The room, familiar to most from their college days, still reminded his old acquaintances of something occult with its black walls and lavender carpet.

"We are dying to hear the whole story," she said so all would hear. "Every detail."

"The press, dear Felix," Diana said, "have milked this disgusting Rasputin story and your daring escape from those horrible Bolsheviks. Disguised like an art student they said—how thrilling." She took a sip of wine. "With the Rembrandts in a bag over your shoulder and the jewels about your body. How clever, Felix. Did you really?"

"The Greats" all wanted to hear the notorious story from the celebrated murderer himself—and he enjoyed telling it.

"And we are with such agreeable friends," Diana said as she cast her smile about the room. They were all waiting: Eileen Sutherland in her trademark mauve, and Sheila Loughborough in her ubiquitous, décolleté black silk; Freda Ward with a Fatima cigarette propped in her long silver holder, and Terence Phillips, whose family had owned department stores in Moscow and St. Petersburg, all now lost. Some of the old crowd were missing, those who had died in the mud of France. No one mentioned them. Society was trying to forget.

"We are fortunate, darling Felix," said Diana, "to have you safely back in London." With a silken voice she added, "But it would be preferable under different circumstances."

Princess Irina, listening to all the English talk, straightened in her chair.

Before the war, Felix spent three years at University College, Oxford. Diana then thought him exotic, telling her friends he had gypsy eyes. Eight years later they were now together again. Much had changed. There had been a war and both had married.

"May I introduce my wife?" Felix said to his guests. Diana released his hands as he gestured toward Irina.

Princess Irina was in white chiffon that set off her gray-eyed, dark-haired beauty. She wore a double strand of black pearls that reached below her waist. They had once hung from the neck of Marie Antoinette.

The "dears" and "darlings" of her English guests bemused Irina. The English, to her thinking, were the nicest people, not as insincere and passionless as they may first appear. But, she wondered why they went to such lengths to impress. All form and little substance, she thought, where the Russians, she admitted, often erred in the other direction.

Irina was a Romanov, after all, the only child of Grand Duke Alexander and the Grand Duchess Xenia, sister of Czar Nicholas II. The Empire was gone. Her title meant little now except in a confused throng of Russian émigrés, but Princess Irina Yusupova carried herself with the natural grace to which she was bred. It troubled her to know that the Russian nobility, including what was left of the Romanovs, were in fact refugees without a home, not to mention an empire.

"You have suffered so much," Lady Diana said. She spoke slowly to be understood.

"Not as much as many others," said Irina.

"I am sure you are right, Your Highness," said Lady Diana who showed surprise when the princess replied in perfect English with only a trace of accent. "But, really," Diana said, "you had so much more to lose."

"I am talking about lives, Lady Diana," Irina answered. "The rest really doesn't matter." She stood, clasped her hands, and moved to Felix's side. "In our case, we have your brave Navy to thank for our own safe deliverance."

Lady Diana, for once, did not have a response.

"We have our lives," Irina added with a smile, "and our Rembrandts. We intend to keep them."

"May I," Diana said, "introduce my husband?" She turned and with a smile called over to her escort who wore a gray pinstripe suit, red tie, and mirror-polished wing-tips. "Duff is aspiring to the House of Commons," she said.

Duff Cooper, tall, with a studious look and a short mustache, was a decorated Lieutenant in the Grenadier Guards in the war just ended.

"How d'you do?" Duff said, snapping a bow, clicking his heels, and looking about.

"Dear Felix," said Diana, "now do tell us your story. How did this terrible thing come to happen? Why were you mixed up in it?"

Lady Diana remembered Felix Yusupov as a gentle soul who at times was wild and unpredictable. She remembered he would appear at a ball dressed like Genghis Kahn, and chase about the Oxford yard at two in the morning, shouting bloody war cries, waving his jeweled scimitar. She thought perhaps he was irresponsible, but never malicious. Now standing before her in a black cut-away coat, a blue and red repp tie on a white shirt, he was dressed like a sober English gentleman, looking like every other man in the room. He parted his hair on the left and combed it over his balding pate.

"Turn off the music," said Diana, waving her hand in the air.

"Please do, Felix," Irina motioned toward the gathering audience.

The prince paced in front of the mahogany sideboard in the crowded parlor of his Knightsbridge flat.

"It had to happen," the prince began. He raised his hand as if blessing the crowd and they hushed.

Princess Irina knew how he enjoyed telling the tale that became more dramatic in its details each time.

"It was all because of the Czarevich's bleeding," he said, "and the Empress Alexandra's guilt and superstitions." He soothed the crowd with his hands, his voice softened. "She felt responsible for his sickness," he said. "Hemophilia is passed on through the mother's side, you know." He paused, raising his finger like a professor. "And, of course it was the czar. That quiet, gentle man had no control of his government from the start—quite like Louis XVI." He paused for effect. "The czarina was mesmerized by the mystics," he said. "Nicolas and Alexandra—they were like two cooing doves that fly away at the first bark of a dog."

Then his voice rose and he gestured his hand in mystery. "Rasputin!" he said. He let the name float in the air, the room so quiet not a breath was heard. "Rasputin! I felt a coldness when he entered the room—as if my soul drifted out of my body—into his cold and evil hands." Felix brushed away the offer of a glass of wine from Tesphé's tray.

"Rasputin," Felix chanted, his hands swaying, "he was a serpent. As the serpent beguiled Eve, Rasputin cast a spell on the empress. Through her he corrupted the czar's court and Mother Russia herself."

The guests, some sitting on the edge of their red velvet chairs, some standing on the lavender carpet, were spellbound by the prince's practiced narration.

"Did he really, as they say," asked Sheila Loughborough, her blue eyes big with curiosity, "sleep with the empress?"

Irina was quick to interject. "Absolutely not! That is mere conjecture by malicious minds—black rumors."

Felix nodded agreement and continued, "I enticed him to visit us on the pretense that he was to see Irina." His eyes shone as he described the visit to Rasputin's apartment. "It had the smell of cheap soap," Felix added. "The filthy man seemed to have washed for once." He placed his hand on his wife's shoulder. "Irina, my beloved wife, was one of the few who had not fallen under his spell."

Irina had many times heard this prelude to the murder. It no longer embarrassed her. "I was not even there," she said. "I was at our family estate in The Crimea. Continue, Felix."

Felix's voice lowered again as if telling a child's tale. "I led him to the special basement room I had prepared," he said, "and fed him wine and then poisoned cakes." Felix looked about the room. He paused. "But he wouldn't die." He paused again and glanced up as if at something supernatural. "He was protected by some magic power."

He spoke faster, waving his hands like a Frenchman. "He wanted to pray." The prince crossed himself. "I sent him to the crucifix on the wall. I told him he should pray for Russia." Felix paused. "Then I shot him." Felix shaped his hand like a pistol. "Right in the heart! The blood splattered on the white bearskin rug." He paused. "It was black—the blood was black."

Eileen Sutherland shuddered.

"In the back?" asked Duff Cooper.

"In the back!" said Felix.

"Damn awful!" said Duff.

"Oh!" Diana Manners shivered and interrupted. "But didn't he heal the czar's son of his hemophilia? We read that in the newspapers."

"The empress believed so," Felix answered. "She believed everything he said."

"The man," added Irina, "told Empress Alexandra what she wanted to hear. The boy's healing was never permanent. The bleeding shortly came again," she said. "We believe the dirty *muzhik* was a German spy. He had his secret 'advisors', we knew."

"He had evil powers—no doubt," said Felix. He shook his shoulders. "I felt them." He focused on the listeners. "The piercing eyes. Gray-blue. They drilled right through you. The women gave him everything he wanted." Felix shuddered. His hand became a pistol again. He looked at Duff. "It *had* to be in the back, you see." Felix paused, lowered his voice, continuing as in a trance, "Powers like an animal. Magnetism. Animal magnetism wrapped in filthy holy robes."

"But he didn't die, as we hear," said Duff.

"Exactly," said Felix. "We shot him again. Then we packed him off to the river and dumped him into the freezing water." Felix waited for a response, but added, "Then they found him the next day, with water in his lungs."

Felix's knowledge of the British Agent Oswald Rayner and his finalizing shot to Rasputin's forehead remained a secret.

"Damn awful," said Duff again. "But here you are."

"Indeed," said Felix. He looked into the eyes of his friends, "And what good did it do?" There was a hush in the room.

"Well, that is for time to tell," said Duff Cooper, reaching for a drink.

In a sad whisper, Felix said, "But our czar is dead."

"And your art collection, dear man," said Lady Diana. "Your precious Rembrandts! You saved them. What a clever and courageous act."

"Yes," added Irina. "We have them here."

Tesphé left the room to bring the paintings. There was a clinking of glasses on the serving table against one wall where drinks were being poured—Scotch, wine, and vodka. There was a spread of canapés, assorted cheeses, blinis with caviar, cold salmon, and hot cups of a rich Georgian beef soup with cherry plum purée.

"Place the paintings on the sideboard, Tesphé," Irina said. Tesphé placed one, then the other against the wall, both covered with white sheets.

"I'm ecstatic!" said Lady Diana.

Tesphé opened a window to vent the smoke filling the air from the American cigarettes and the Cuban *Romeo y Julieta* cigars.

All was quiet as Felix gently lifted the wraps. The portraits were placed like they had hung on the silver walls of the *Preciosa Hall* in their Russian palace. Tesphé arranged the floor lamps to better illuminate the paintings that had darkened over the centuries. There was a collective gasp. Irina smiled.

The paintings now on temporary stretchers were clean, the disguising masks removed, the hardened flour paste washed away. *The Lady* and *The Gentleman*, now two hundred fifty-nine years old, were again revealed to gaze, in their silent and knowing way, at the room of admirers.

Duff Cooper shook his head in amazement. He was the first to finally speak. "Breathtaking, Prince Felix. I can see why you have saved these amongst the many."

"I must give credit," Felix said, "to devoted members of the household for making it possible, the Countess Anna and Genrykh, our Chief of Security."

Irina added, "I hope they are safe."

"And this man and woman in the paintings, what do they say?" asked Freda Ward.

"Only the artist might know," said Irina. "And maybe not even him."

Lady Diana added, "Rather like the Mona Lisa, I'd say."

"And, we look forward," Irina responded, "to returning them to their home someday, in Russia. That is our goal."

"Yes, of course," replied Duff, knowing there was no longer a home for the Yusupovs or the Rembrandts in St. Petersburg.

Felix added, "Once the center of the world's largest empire, it is now called Petrograd. It is a bleeding city, which history has ground to a halt."

Before The Revolution, the Yusupovs were the wealthiest family in Russia. They had estates and palaces in every province, many factories and farms, and twenty thousand serfs. Now they had only empty titles, an old apartment, a few jewels and two Rembrandts. And, as Prince Felix said, "What good did it all do?"

Someone put the needle back on a record. The scratchy song was, *There'll be some changes made.*

CHAPTER TWENTY-ONE

THE PRICE

London
July, 1921

"**D**O YOU THINK HE'LL COME?" Prince Felix asked his wife. "Why would he *not* come?" Princess Irina answered. "He and his father before him have always wanted the Rembrandts. He will come."

The prince, impeccable in his morning coat and striped, gray trousers, paced the floor in the guest suite of the London home of his Belgian friend, the diplomat Baron Egmont de Zuylan de Nyevelt, at 8 Carlos Place, Mayfair. It was an elegant, red brick Victorian townhouse between Grosvenor and Berkeley Squares. Finances had forced Felix to sell his apartment in Knightsbridge. He could no longer afford the price of a suite at the Ritz, where Maziroff had gone to fetch Mr. Joseph Early Widener.

They waited for Widener, the son of the Philadelphia traction-car king Peter A. B. Widener. He had inherited Lynnewood Hall, a 110-room American Versailles, just outside Philadelphia, on whose silken walls hung one of America's largest and richest collections of European art, including ten Rembrandts. Joseph Widener wanted two more—the Yusupov Rembrandts, which his father had seen on his trip to Russia in 1909. He would then have more of The Master's paintings than the tycoon Andrew Mellon. After all, it was known that a man's collection was measured by his Rembrandts.

"It's after three," Felix said. "Maziroff planned to arrive with Widener by two."

"Maziroff, in this case," she said, "is not in control." She reached out and caught Felix by the hand. "Be patient, dear."

The princess sat in the blue velvet armchair by a gold-draped window overlooking the garden and was poring over the latest news copy about *The Lady*. The Baron's gray and white Persian cat lay curled up in her lap. "The rain is so determined in London," she said. "It's tiresome." The faint scent of her *Guerlain Bleu* filled the air. She sipped tea from a small Minton cup.

"It's humiliating to present ourselves from another's residence," she said.

"We'll be back in Paris soon," Felix said. They both longed for their Paris flat where they could speak Russian and French with friends of like tastes.

"In a way, I hope he doesn't come," said Felix. "Why should we give up the Rembrandts to this common American businessman? They belong with us. They are nobility, like our family." He sat down in the Queen Anne side chair next to his wife, his head in his hands, his elbows on his knees.

"We're not *giving* them to anyone, I hope," said Irina. She placed her hand on his shoulder. "The money from the family jewels has kept us at an endurable level." She looked out the rain-streaked window again. "We are only going to borrow a reasonable sum against the art. I know we agree on that."

The Yusupovs were known for their generosity to many of the refugees fleeing the horrors of the Russian Civil War. "Your workshops and care centers," Irina asked, "how much do we still have left for those charities? I read there are over a quarter-million poor souls in London alone."

"I've no idea. That is Maziroff's business. But, we have to do something soon," he said, "sell the Rembrandts or borrow again against them."

"Not sell, borrow," she reminded.

Irina knew that Captain Maziroff, who acted as Felix's business agent, had little experience in business. Nevertheless, with a stature honed from his service in the Imperial Guards, the captain was a gentleman, trustworthy, with steel-gray eyes and a thin, curled mustache. He managed Felix's money. He was a friend in a foreign land.

"I know we've already borrowed against them," Irina answered.

"But, we must get more," Felix said. "Or, I'll be driving a taxi like the other Russian nobility. You will be doing what—waiting tables in a Russian restaurant serving *Uzbekskii Plov* to tourists from the West Country? What the bank loaned, £44,000, is insulting, the interest usurious."

"We," the princess said, "are not accustomed to dealing with money, where it comes from, or where it goes. We must now learn."

Irina wrestled with her situation. To Felix, it was all about money. She respected that priority. But, what about the Rembrandts? They had to find security. What were the choices?

Felix stood, watching the rivulets of rain snaking down the long, glass windowpanes. "How did this all happen? It was such a good life." Looking out at the gray day he said, "I am told Widener would do almost anything to get the Rembrandts into his gallery."

"We will see," she said, "what this American will offer." She stood, moved beside her husband, and putting her hand behind his neck, kissed him on the cheek. "We will do what we have to do."

"When Maziroff met Widener last month," Felix shook his head, "it came to nothing. It all had to do with price. Why does such a rich man argue about price?" He raised his hands in wonder.

"But you wrote him the letter," she said.

Felix shrugged, "I gave him two choices—a loan against the portraits, or a conditional sale with a repurchase agreement. In either case we would have an opportunity to get them back. But he turned those down." He raised both hands in exasperation. "It still is a matter of price." He shook his head in disbelief, "Impossible!"

"But he is *here*," Irina said. "I am sure you will fare better than Maziroff."

There was a knock downstairs, and the de Zuylen maid pulled open the heavy, mahogany door. There stood Captain Maziroff— alone, the water trickling off his umbrella.

Felix called down the stairs, "Where is Widener?"

"He is waiting in the car," said Maziroff. "I told him the paintings were in the bank's storage. He is not a man to waste time, Felix. No time for tea. He wants to be sure you are here."

Joseph Early Widener opened the door of the Rolls Royce Silver Ghost at the curb. He bent over, emerged from the car, and hurried bareheaded, heedless of the rain, through the wrought iron gate to the front door of the de Zuylen home. A tall, gaunt man who walked in a stoop, he was in his early fifties with dark blue eyes in a long face uncreased from smiling. Pulling a handkerchief from his coat pocket, he wiped the rain off his balding head.

The prince and princess descended the stairs. She was wearing her mauve moiré dress, and holding the gray-and-white Persian cat, which batted at the strands of black pearls.

"We finally meet, Prince Yusupov." Widener made a slight bow and offered his hand. "Your Highness," Widener nodded toward Irina. "Your story has circled the globe, Prince Yusupov," Widener said. "My father visited your St. Petersburg palace in 1909."

"I was at Oxford at the time," said Felix.

"I met your father. Very nice," added Irina.

"He told everyone," Widener added, "that his visit to your estate and seeing the Rembrandts was the highlight of his trip. My condolences for your recent misfortune."

"I hope," Felix said, "to host you in St. Petersburg on a future date. We plan to return."

Widener turned to Irina. "It must be difficult for you—my coming to see you about your favorite Rembrandts." His words were polite, his voice unemotional. "Under these conditions, it isn't easy for either of us, I assure you."

Irina straightened and stroked the cat. "Exactly, Mr. Widener, it is not easy. But I expect you and the prince will come to a satisfactory agreement—under these conditions."

"Well, yes." Widener again wiped his head. "Then shall we go see the paintings?"

Irina turned to ascend the stairs, but first whispered in her husband's ear, "Remember who we are, Felix." She squeezed his hand. "He has a certain charm," she added. "But, don't be taken by it."

On the way to the car, Widener said, "I respect your suspicions about dealers, Your Highness. But, I have invited along my agent, Mr. Arthur J. Sulley—for advice."

Felix knew well of the famous London art dealer. But, he distrusted dealers and purposely intended to make this exchange, if there was to be one, quietly and without the cost of an intermediary. But, on both counts he would be disappointed. The portly Sulley smiled, giving Felix a feeling of discomfort, the prince knowing the cost of that smile would, one way or another, come out of his pocket.

The white-gloved chauffer hurried to open the car door. Widener and the prince slipped into the carpeted rear seats while Maziroff joined Sulley on the fold-down seats facing them.

"And what of Russia, Prince Yusupov? What do you expect?"

"It will no doubt get worse, Mr. Widener. But, things will return to normal—in time."

Maziroff looked out the window as if he didn't want to be involved. The driver's hands were busy, operating the windscreen wipers by a small crank on the ceiling, shifting gears, and steering through the traffic. The Rolls crept through the rain and congestion dominated by the new, red, double-decker buses with their goggled drivers, rain-drenched in their Mackintoshes and caps in the open cabs. They inched down the Strand into Fleet Street.

"The fact that your father was even shown the Rembrandts," Felix said, "was remarkable because, except for that one exhibit, the paintings were never seen outside the family collection while they were in Russia."

Widener nodded agreement, casting a glance toward Sulley. "We heard that even the Czar had to order an audience."

They passed St. Paul's Cathedral and Maziroff said, "I believe we are here, gentlemen."

The private banking firm of Thomas M. Sutton was on a narrow street off Cheapside in The City, the financial center of London.

The firm's name on the brass wall plate was almost unreadable from decades of polishing. The visitors hurried in the front door under one umbrella.

It was a dark place with one high window facing the shaded street. Inside, two bare desks on an open mezzanine watched over an unmanned, glass-walled, teller's counter. Dusty, cut-glass chandeliers glowed yellow. Mr. Sutton, an unsmiling man of about fifty with a puffy face, shuffled out of his office in the rear, trailed by two assistants.

"Good day, Your Highness, gentlemen," Mr. Sutton addressed the visitors. The two gray-smocked clerks stood behind him, expressionless, hands behind their backs. "Right, you want to see the Rembrandts," the banker said. "Mr. Witherspoon and Mr. Smith, here, will take care of you. Let me know if you need my assistance." He bowed, turned, and retreated to his office and closed the door.

The visitors followed the gray smocks down the narrow stairway into the vault. The clerks, both balding and wearing identical round spectacles in black frames, looked strangely alike, Widener thought, even though one was shorter by a head and fatter than the other. The short one took a ring of keys off his belt and unlocked the two padlocks.

Felix held his ears as the steel door scraped open in an ancient groove in the stone floor. The tall clerk pulled a crooked cord for light. Over a heavy, wooden table in the middle of the room glowed one electric lamp in a dirty glass globe with five dead moths in the bottom.

Gray metal padlocked boxes of various sizes were stacked against three walls. Each carried a label with a number and name printed in heavy black ink with an artistic script. Larger wooden document boxes, stained with age, were stacked against a fourth wall, and there on the top was a newly made wooden box. It was a yard wide, over a yard long, and eight inches deep with a hinged top secured by two hasps with black locks. The label pasted on the side read "8576-5 Yusupov." The clerks strained to lift the box off the stack and placed it on the table.

They unlocked and opened the top, then unlatched an inside metal container and there, wrapped in soft cotton bunting were the Rembrandts on their temporary stretchers. The men stood in silence as if an Egyptian tomb had been opened. A clerk pulled aside part of the bunting from the top painting. The Lady peeked out of the tomb, the dim light falling on her gazing face, the gold jewelry glittering as if real.

Finally, Widener said, "May we take these to a room with better light?"

The clerks looked at each other, sighed, and closed the case. With the short one in front, they struggled with the case up the stairs like pallbearers, bumping their elbows on the walls.

"This is the best we can do, Mr. Widener, sir," said the tall clerk. "These are our Director's Chambers." The room had one high window for natural light, four electric wall sconces, and a chandelier over the center table on which were two ashtrays, and a cut-glass vase of wilted flowers. Scowling down on them was a portrait in an overlarge gold frame of a bearded man from an earlier age. "Thomas Sutton, the grandfather," the tall clerk said.

The clerks lifted the Rembrandts from the box, uncovered them, and set them on a sideboard against the wall.

"Mmmm," said Arthur Sulley, finally. "Rembrandt's Lady and Gentleman." Widener cleared his throat. Sulley then remained silent, but continued to inspect the paintings. Arthur J. Sulley was one of the most respected London art dealers and had helped Widener on earlier occasions with some acquisitions, including Rembrandt's celebrated, *The Mill*.

"I think you can see," said Felix, "why they are considered the finest portraits the Master ever painted."

Widener moved between Felix and Sulley.

"Mmmm," Sulley repeated, bending over. He took a looking glass from his pocket. With narrowed eyes he examined in detail the lace bow at the woman's neck, her sculpted jewelry, and then the man's eyes in the shadow of his hat. He looked up at Widener, raising his eyebrows and nodding his astonishment. Sulley handed the magnifying glass to Widener, but the American shook his head *no*, saying nothing.

"We still consider them," Prince Felix said, "as the best in the Yusupov collection. That is why I risked my life to save them. We want only a loan against them, as I have said."

Widener remembered his father's lament after he had sailed his yacht across the Atlantic only sixteen years before, through the new Kiel Canal, up to St. Petersburg to buy these very paintings, and failed. He did not intend for a Widener to fail again. "It is an unfortunate turn of events," Widener said, "that the great collections of Russia are no longer in the safety of private hands."

Felix blanched. "It's more than unfortunate, Mr. Widener, it is criminal. It's like feeding caviar to cats. Those common people have no respect for art."

Widener shook his head in silence, perceiving that the likely termination of the Russian Empire was something the last namesake of Russia's wealthiest family could not comprehend, nor accept.

"However, we are fortunate, sir," said Sulley, "that there are a few private collectors today, after that devastating war, who are ready to acquire, and preserve, these immortal works for posterity."

"The value of these masterpieces," said Felix, "increases by the day."

"Indeed they have great intrinsic value," added Widener. Turning, he pulled out a brocaded side chair from the walnut table in the room's center and sat down. "That's why I am here," Widener said. "But, these are difficult times for all of us. You should not hold an exaggerated view on this subject."

Arthur Sulley added his expert opinion. "In fact, Your Highness, there is almost no market for art in these postwar days."

Felix suspected Sulley was right, but it was well known that the Americans were buying. The London art dealers with their Canalettos and Cézannes camped on the lawns of the American mansions. They hoped, like Oriental rug merchants, that the rich Yankees would buy what they had earlier left on approval to hang in their galleries. Sulley, and others, fought hard to retain their American buyers. He was determined to deliver these Rembrandts to the Widener walls.

"I offered to Captain Maziroff," began Widener, "a fair price before. The market has not improved, Prince Yusupov. That offer still stands."

Felix turned, folded his arms, and faced the Rembrandts. In a low voice he said to himself, "I remember, when I was small, asking my mother why their eyes looked aside and not at me. She said they held a secret and were afraid if they looked at me, I would talk them out of it." He turned to Sulley standing by. "They still hold the secret, don't you think?"

Sully turned to Widener who raised his eyebrows and shrugged. Widener kept his silence. Felix wondered why. He noticed Maziroff still standing erect in the corner, twisting his mustache with one hand, holding the other behind his back. Felix started to perspire. He unbuttoned his coat.

He watched the clerks leave the room.

"I appreciate that offer," said Felix, "but now as then, the value of these portraits is well over £200,000, which I am ready to consider today."

Widener, still silent, sat down, looking at the portraits. In his mind he tried to place them on the walls of the Petersburg Palace he never saw, thinking of his father's disappointment in leaving without them. He now saw them in the red-walled room in Pennsylvania, which his wife planned as a special home for all his Rembrandts.

Watching the American's face, Sulley knew the richest man in Philadelphia could afford any responsible price. Really it was not a matter of money, Sulley knew. It was a matter of successful negotiation, and of pride.

Taking a cigar from his vest pocket, Widener said, "Their value is not questioned." He removed a silver match holder from another pocket. "Price is the issue here, not value." He opened the match holder, inserted the tip of the cigar into the hole in the cap and snipped it off. "Is that then your price, Prince Yusupov? £200,000?" he said. Widener took a match from the holder, struck it under the table, and held the burning match in his fingers.

"Yes, that is my price, Mr. Widener" said Felix, "as Captain Maziroff quoted before."

"I would venture," said Widener, "they are worth even more than that in better times. But, not today." The match still burned. "We can discuss the sale another time."

Sulley was quick to interject. "Mr. Widener is here, Your Highness," he said, "and ready to transfer the money." Sulley also knew other dealers would jump on this opportunity if the deal was not closed that day.

"I know the worth of these paintings, Mr. Sulley," Felix said, "I have turned down £150,000 from your competitor, Sir Joseph Duveen. I am firm. I waited for Mr. Widener, since in my opinion, he has presently the option."

Wincing as the burning match touched his finger, Widener blew out the match. He pulled out another, striking it under the table. "You should have taken the offer of £150,000," Widener said, "for you must know, Prince Yusupov, that no Rembrandt portrait, even in good times, has sold for over £45,000." He held the match to the end of the cigar and sucked in the flame, blowing clouds of blue smoke out the other side of his mouth. He shook out the match and dropped it in the ashtray.

"The prospect of parting with these paintings," Felix addressed both Widener and Sully, "as Mr. Widener recognized in his remarks to my wife, is a sensitive issue, gentlemen."

"We all realize that," Sulley said.

Widener turned the cigar in his hand, examining it.

"They are part of our family collection," continued the prince, "and have been for 133 years. If they are to now leave our walls, there must be more than ample compensation. It's that simple, gentlemen."

Widener pulled on his cigar, blowing out more smoke and said, "They have already left your walls, Your Highness."

"On the issue of price, maybe," Sulley added, "there could be a compro…"

Widener raised his hand, stopping his agent, "Mr. Sulley, we discussed this before," he said. "I am a fair man. I'm more than willing to pay full market price. I do not haggle like a tomato seller. One hundred thousand pounds sterling is more than fair."

Widener stood, and walked about the room, cigar in one hand, stroking his chin with the other. He turned to Felix, "Well?"

"Mr. Widener," Felix said, "in my letter I suggested a loan against the portraits. They would grace your gallery walls until I could redeem them, maybe after three or four years, with interest of course. Does that arrangement appeal to you, sir?"

"No," Widener was quick to say, "I'm a collector, Your Highness, not a pawnbroker. That is not an alternative."

Felix remembered the words of his wife, "I am sure you will fare better than Maziroff," also, "Remember who we are." His eyes were smarting from the cigar smoke. He rubbed one eye with his finger. He turned to focus on the American. "Mr. Widener, your offer today is the same as your father offered to my mother for these invaluable paintings, and was turned down, fifteen years ago. How could I accept such a price today?"

"Prince Yusupov," Widener said, "your mother did not place the same value on money as you must do today."

Felix blinked.

Widener leaned forward, looking at Felix out of the top of his eyes like a lecturing father, "And one more thing, Prince Yusupov: In this world, nothing is priceless."

Felix braced, "In that you are wrong, sir."

"Then what, sir?"

"My honor."

A silence filled the room.

"Maziroff," Felix said, "call the clerks to put the Rembrandts back in their box." Maziroff moved toward the door.

"Your Highness," said Widener, "I truly appreciate the personal value you place on these Rembrandts." He pulled a handkerchief from his coat pocket and wiped his hands. "They are indeed special, or I would not have come to London to talk to you." Widener looked again at the Rembrandts.

Grinding his cigar in the ashtray, Widener exchanged looks with Sulley and said, "Then we'll leave it at that." He turned to Felix, "I am truly disappointed we couldn't come to a conclusion today, Prince Yusupov—truly and sincerely disappointed."

Felix paused for a moment, then said, "So am I, Mr. Widener."

THE OFFER

London
July, 1921

L ITTLE WAS SAID IN THE CAR returning to the Ritz. Maziroff suggested continuing the meeting in Widener's suite, but Felix declined, claiming another appointment. However, Widener invited Maziroff to his rooms and they continued to talk in the American's parlor.

"The prince," Maziroff said, "is in a very embarrassing situation, Mr. Widener."

"That I know, Captain. I sympathize with him," said Widener, his face expressionless.

"There ought to be a way," Maziroff added, "for you to add these great paintings to your collection."

"I offered a fair price."

"Because the paintings," said Maziroff, "are so precious to the prince and his wife, he would like to have a chance to get them back when he can afford to do so."

"You mean a loan, Captain, and I've told you I am not a pawnbroker."

"Of course, Mr. Widener, but you know he will most probably never be able to buy them back. He will never see Russia again—none of us will."

Then Maziroff put a hand into his pocket and pulled out a pair of diamond earrings. He held them in his two hands before Widener's eyes. "We have been offered £4000 for these," the Russian said, "but they are worth much more, don't you think?"

Widener wrinkled his brow and stared at the unexpected offer.

"The loan interest," said Maziroff, "is due. It is my responsibility to pay it, or the Rembrandts will be the property of Mr. Sutton, the banker, and then, at a good profit, Joseph Duveen, and then, at a higher profit, some other Americans."

Widener winced, since that was a prospect he could not tolerate.

There were seven diamonds in each gold earring totaling, Widener thought, at least several carats. "But, Captain, I am not a buyer of diamonds."

"And these, Mr. Widener." As Maziroff replaced the earrings in one pocket, he pulled out of the other a broach containing a pearl half the size of a pigeon's egg circled with three rows of diamonds, with a pear-shaped pearl pendant hanging from it. "This broach was valued at £10,000 and..."

Widener held up his hands in protest. He shook his head. "*Please!* I don't buy jewelry. Now if you'll stop talking, I have an idea." He sat at the writing desk. "First of all, Captain, you must understand money is hard to get in these postwar days, especially for art."

The American paused, narrowed his eyes, and looking aside at Maziroff, pulled a sheet of ivory-colored bond from the desk drawer. "If I can raise the money when I return to America...," and he began to write. "What is his address?"

With a fountain pen from the desk holder Widener wrote only one long sentence on the Ritz Hotel letterhead.

> *8, Carlos Place*
> *London W.*

> *I the undersigned Prince F. Yusupov agree upon receipt of one hundred thousand pounds from Mr. Joseph Widener within one month from today to sell to him my two well-known Rembrandt portraits—reserving the option of purchasing them back from him, on, or, any time before January first 1924, for the same sum, plus eight percent interest from date of purchase.*

> _____

> *Prince Felix Yusupov*
> *July 12th*
> *1921*

"This is what I purpose, Mr. Maziroff." He blew on the ink and handed him the paper. "Take this to the prince," Widener said, "and see what he says." Widener replaced the pen, ran his hand over his thinning hair, and stood.

The rain still hammered on the window panes of the Baron de Zuylen's home. The prince and princess heard the excited knocking on the door continue until the maid opened it. Maziroff, dripping wet, called up the stairs, "We have a deal, Felix." He took the stairs two at a time.

"Quit waving the paper so I can read it," Felix said.

Maziroff laid the paper in front of the prince. "It is a loan of £100,000 and the right to buy them back."

The prince held the paper with both hands. "It looks that way." Felix smiled. "Look at this," Felix called to Baron de Zuylan who was home from his duties as Second Secretary of the Belgian Embassy.

"Well, that is going to help things a bit," de Zuylan said.

"It is not what I asked for, is it?" said the prince.

Irina entered, took the paper from her husband and read it. "Felix, it is not what you wanted. But, it is a good thing for now, and you have time to get them back. We won't lose the Rembrandts, which is most important to me."

Irina was not told that Mr. Sutton had called for repayment of the £44,000 held against the portraits. The interest of twelve and a half percent was due in advance every six months, and now overdue if they intended to renew the loan. Felix didn't have it. He knew Irina now was right.

Maziroff said, "Widener was quite sympathetic to your situation. He has a month to reply. He leaves tomorrow."

Felix asked Maziroff to type out the handwritten option document. He signed it. He instructed Maziroff, "Take this back to Mr. Widener tonight. Thank him for me."

The prince and princess stayed in London. Exactly thirty days later, at 9:52 p.m., August 9th, a cable arrived for the prince at the home of Baron de Zuylan.

PLEASE COMMUNICATE WITH MY AGENT
SULLEY WHO HAS MONEY TO TAKE DELIVERY
WIDENER

Felix jumped over a chair with happiness. He hugged his wife. She hugged Maziroff. Maziroff hugged the Baron, and was told by Felix to start writing checks. Felix responded to Widener that night by cabling one word: "Agreed."

But—that was not the *last* word.

The first thing Joseph Widener did in July upon arriving back in Philadelphia was to kiss his wife, Ella, and tell her, "We got them, the Yusupov Rembrandts."

Ella smiled, saying, "Now I will arrange for the Rembrandt Room. They will all be together—their home."

Widener said, "Father would be proud."

The next thing he did was to have his attorney draw up a proper Agreement of Sale. Horses were Widener's main interest. The money was made by his father, but Joseph inherited the entire Widener fortune after the Titanic tragedy took his older brother George.

The art collection was to Joseph as much a matter of size as anything else. Snatching the famous Yusupov Rembrandts out from under the nose of the Russians, the Europeans, the infamous dealer Sir Joseph Duveen, and most importantly, Andrew Mellon, should bring him attention and respect. The price would remain a secret. He wanted a sales contract that would keep the Rembrandts in Lynnewood Hall, forever.

While Widener was in Saratoga for the races, his lawyers created the sales contract. On July 25, 1921, two copies of the contract, signed by Widener, went into the mail in the Philadelphia Post Office at five p.m. One was addressed to Prince Yusupov, 8 Carlos Place, and the other to Widener's agent Arthur Sulley, 159 Bond Street, London. The mailing was timed to reach the steamship *America* before it sailed from New York for England the next day.

"Look at this, Irina!" Felix, red-faced and shouting, waved the document in the air, "This new paper from Widener! It is full of things we did not agree on or even discuss!"

Felix rushed to his London attorney and shook the papers in his face. "What does this say?" he demanded.

"It says exactly," the attorney read, "that your repurchase privilege, Prince Yusupov, is not assignable nor will it inure to the benefit of your heirs, or representatives, and that you, Prince Yusupov, represent that this privilege of repurchase will be exercised only in the case you find yourself in a position again to keep and personally enjoy these works of art."

"That is totally unacceptable!" Felix shouted. He felt faint. He braced his arm on the marble side table. He took his handkerchief and wiped his brow. "What kind of man is this American? This is despicable!"

"In addition," the attorney said, "should you wish to dispose of or sell the paintings within ten years, Prince Felix, it gives Joseph Widener or his representatives the sole right to repurchase them from you at the same price of £100,000."

"That is," Irina said, "absolutely an impossible, dishonest demand."

"Exactly, princess," said the attorney. "In as much as this transaction is clearly in law a chattel mortgage, a loan against the paintings, these restrictions cannot be upheld in a court of equity, which governs in this case in both England and the United States."

Felix again wiped his brow and looked to Maziroff for advice. "So what should I do?"

"You have already signed checks on the full proceeds from this sale, Felix. Sutton is pressing for payment of the overdue interest or he will take possession of the paintings. It would appear you have no choice."

Felix steadied himself. He wiped his brow again and dabbed his cheeks.

"Clearly," the attorney added, "the first contract, Your Highness, the simple one of July 12, is what governs."

"So," Felix asked, "I can ignore this restrictive language?"

"Yes," said the attorney. "Arguably, you can."

The next day, August 12, was the last day of the option period. Arthur Sulley already had the money. Felix had already spent it. Felix signed.

CHAPTER TWENTY-THREE

THE CONSPIRACY

Paris
April, 1922

WHILE THE REMBRANDTS hung on the red silk walls of the
Widener's signature room in Lynnewood Hall outside of
Philadelphia, a conspiracy was developing in Paris that would
change their lives forever. Two giants in the art world met on a
bright, spring day in Paris, each determined to bring the portraits
back to Europe.

Calouste Gulbenkian and Sir Joseph Duveen met first in
the lobby of the Buci, an ancient little hotel on a corner in Saint-
Germain des Prés. Gulbenkian refused to meet Sir Joseph in the
Ritz, where the Englishman kept a suite, and where inquiring
eyes would raise questions and draw conclusions.

"I have wonderful news for you, Mr. Gulbenkian," Duveen said.

Calouste Sarkis Gulbenkian, one of the most prolific art collectors in Europe, was as exacting in his business dealings as in his
dress. At fifty-three, he had already made his wealth in oil, being
a founder of the Royal Dutch-Shell Group. An Armenian, born in

Istanbul, a resident of Paris and London, he spoke six languages and was, in the lean years after The Great War, considered the only one who could bid against the Americans who were hungry for European art.

"Last time we met," said Duveen with his usual dimpled smile, "I reminded you that in losing the Yusupov Rembrandts, you had lost the best the Master ever created."

From his museum showrooms in London, Paris, and New York, Sir Joseph Duveen controlled the movement of most of those cities' art as well as their prices. For over fifty years, Duveen had been said to be the richest art dealer in the world. He protected his territory with biblical determination. A questioning word or a raised eyebrow from the imperious Sir Joseph Duveen about the attribution of the painting or sculpture of a competitor's sale could ruin their value for years to come, if not forever, often without him even seeing the target of his derision. The driving force behind the growing collections of the Americans—Mellon, Frick, Kress, Hearst, Huntington, Rockefeller, and others—was not to be ignored.

"I remember that too well," said Gulbenkian. "I was pressed with other matters at the time. I didn't like Ruck's idea." Arthur Ruck of London considered Gulbenkian a treasured client and had presented a devious plan to acquire the Rembrandts for the Armenian.

"Adjemov introduced me to Yusupov in 1919," Gulbenkian said, "when the prince wanted £300,000 for his Rembrandts. They were dirty and rolled up. I laughed at him. You know that, of course." Adjemov, a former monarchist Duma member, was a Russian lawyer and had his finger in everything to do within the Russian exile community in Paris. "Besides," Gulbenkian added, "I also told Ruck £200,000 was high." He paused, knowing there were no secrets in the underworld of art. "I was right, wasn't I?" he said. "What has changed?"

Gulbenkian, a private man, lived in a palace-like home on *Avenue d'Iena* where he kept his collection. Seldom inviting anyone there, he conducted his private life with the same oriental secrecy as he did his business. "Perhaps I made a mistake," said Gulbenkian. "It would not be the first."

"Well, this is my wonderful news, my friend," said Duveen. "I can now tell you," he said, "an opportunity to acquire the Rembrandts is once more at hand." Duveen had worked on obtaining this audience for months. He could not allow Arthur Sulley's involvement in the Rembrandt sale to Widener to go unchallenged.

"Shall we take a walk?" Gulbenkian said. "What people don't hear, they invent."

It was a short walk to Jardin du Luxembourg. Crossing Boulevard Saint Germain and entering the garden pathways gave Gulbenkian time to think. No one but the Americans trust Duveen, he thought. They call him Sir Joseph and seem to gain stature by paying more than a piece is worth. Yet, he pondered, Duveen controls the market.

"There is nothing like spring in Paris, is there, Mr. Duveen?" the Armenian said. The air was filled with the scent of lilacs, and the women strolled with their parasols and smiles under the greening chestnut trees as if there had never been a war.

"Indeed," Duveen answered and slowed to watch the collector's face.

"Go on, sir," Gulbenkian said. "What is your proposal?" Gulbenkian was a stocky man, with a short-trimmed beard, a curling mustache, and thick eyebrows, all turning gray under a black fedora. It was a warm day, but he did not loosen his foulard.

"You are fortunate to live in such an agreeable city," Duveen said. He lowered his voice, moving closer. "I have it on good authority, Mr. Gulbenkian, that the Widener sale included a conditional clause under which Prince Yusupov may repurchase the paintings."

"Conditions? What conditions?" Gulbenkian slowed his pace looking back at Duveen. "The Rembrandts," Gulbenkian said, "they hang in Mr. Widener's gallery in America, do they not?"

Duveen had all the appearance of a conservative English businessman, burly with a ruddy complexion, in a morning coat and a white, high-collared shirt, and white tie. His eyebrows moved up and down as he spoke, and he always seemed to be suggesting agreement—with him. A wispy mustache spread under an arching nose, and he walked with a military posture that gave him a deceptive impression of integrity.

"The condition is," said Duveen, squinting through his round spectacles, "that if the prince is able to resume his former life, the paintings may be repurchased at the selling price plus 8 percent. By a certain date. Soon."

Duveen's arrogance was legendary. It was said that after being dressed by his valet, he would wait at the elevator for his servant to push the button. In a restaurant he was known to clap his hands like an Oriental potentate when he wanted service.

"Widener. Isn't he one of your clients?" asked Gulbenkian.

A passing pair of women smiled at the Armenian. He tipped his hat and with closed eyes inhaled the seductive scent in their wake.

"Not on this transaction," Duveen said.

"So does the prince have the money to resume his former life style?" Gulbenkian asked.

"Of course not; he is desperate. That is your opportunity."

"I see. You want me to advance him the money?"

"The market is returning, Mr. Gulbenkian. The Rembrandts are worth more now than when I offered them to you earlier at £200,000."

Gulbenkian was silent. They continued to walk. They passed the Medici fountain, the pond, and more strolling ladies with their parasols. The air was filled with the fragrance of women and flowers.

"They are undoubtedly worth more than that now," Duveen continued, "but as a courtesy to you I can still get them at that price. That is approximately one million in United States dollars." The dealer lifted his gray fedora, ran his hand over his receding hairline and, like a cat eyeing a bird, watched the collector's eyes.

Gulbenkian stopped, folded his arms, and focused on Duveen. "You see, Mr. Duveen, I don't believe you. In the first place, Mr. Ruck has already approached me on this issue. I told him no. If they couldn't be had for £200,000 when the market was dead, how can you get them at that same price today, when the market has improved as you say?"

Duveen laughed, raising his hands to make a point. "That, Mr. Gulbenkian, is what makes this such an opportunity. I do owe it to you, sir." He held the smile, tilting his head. "That is why I brought this to you first." His voice lowered and his steel gray eyes sparkled. "You would not make a mistake this time."

Gulbenkian didn't know if he was the first or the last to hear of this, but he knew that if he said no, the dealer would send cables to others before the sun was down. "Only the best," Gulbenkian reminded himself, these portraits are the best. Rembrandt, he knew, was the measure of a man's collection.

"So," asked Gulbenkian, "how much is the advance?"

"A little over half of the final price—in dollars about $550,000, maybe a bit more."

Gulbenkian turned, continuing to walk. "And, what security would I have for that amount?"

"The portraits of course."

Gulbenkian stopped and turned. "But the portraits, Mr. Duveen, are in America. Do you think the prince's paper is worth more than Widener's possession?"

"The conditional clause," said Duveen, "assures that under law."

"Have you read the clause? Can you get a copy? Do you have a legal opinion?"

"Unfortunately, no," Duveen said, "but I have this information from one who was present at the negotiations. The prince confirms it. There is no doubt."

"What if you are misinformed, Mr. Duveen?"

"That is the risk."

"Indeed it is, sir!"

"I am seldom misinformed," Duveen added.

"I am often so," said Gulbenkian. "And I mark he who misinforms me."

Neither spoke as they crossed the park onto a returning path.

"I have an appointment for tea," said Gulbenkian.

"That is the risk we take," said Duveen, "to move the finest pair of Rembrandt portraits from Philadelphia to Paris, closer to their home."

"*We?* What risk do you take, Mr. Duveen?"

"My reputation, sir. It is priceless."

"And, what do you get out of this?"

"I said I do owe it to you, Mr. Gulbenkian. I will reduce my fee to only five percent. I am mostly concerned in doing the right thing."

"Of course." Gulbenkian became silent, looking straight ahead as his pace increased.

Duveen matched him and quickly added, "After deduction of the prince's expenses, of course."

Gulbenkian distrusted Sir Joseph Duveen who had, in his opinion, purchased his title through self-serving philanthropy. But, he wanted the Rembrandts—now more than ever, especially since they, like many other masterpieces, had gone to another provincial American.

"I will think about it, Mr. Duveen."

"You are wise to do so," Duveen responded. "Unfortunately," he then added, "this opportunity is not as confidential as I would prefer." He narrowed his eyes and lowered his voice. "Others, especially other dealers, will know about this soon. I cannot guarantee to keep the offer exclusive. I cannot keep the Russians from talking. You know timing is everything."

"As I said," Gulbenkian flashed a perfunctory smile, "I will think about it." Duveen knew that ended the conversation.

Calouste Gulbenkian was known as a calm and humble man, except when he lost his temper. Then it was like a terrible storm that comes out of nowhere and no one escapes unscathed.

Gulbenkian was shrewd, but known to keep his word, and to never forgive those who did not.

Joseph Duveen knew this—and still he persisted.

AMERICA

1923–1942

CHAPTER TWENTY-FOUR

THE ATTEMPT

New York
1923

I RINA SAT DOWN ON the blue velvet sofa in their room in New York's Vanderbilt Hotel. She spread the pages of the New York Times out across her lap. "We made the front page, Felix."

She pointed to the top left-hand column of the front page of the newspaper of November 24, 1923. "See," she said, and read, "The arrival in America of the Prince and Princess Yusupov." She went on to point out that in the second column was the second most important news of the day, the opening of the tomb of King Tutankhamen in Egypt. "We are in good company, Felix."

"But, I don't like what comes next," and she read, "They brought a million dollars' worth of jewels, including the famous black pearl necklace of Marie Antoinette; and they came to redeem the Rembrandts they claim as rightfully theirs; and that as murderer of Rasputin, the prince would not have been admitted to the US if it were not for his czarist passport." She threw the paper down on the sofa.

Their ship from London, the *RMS Berengaria*, was met by Mrs. William K. Vanderbilt II, well-known for helping the Russian refugees in Paris. It was to the Hotel Vanderbilt that the prince and princess had come for their stay, to wait for a reply from Joseph Widener. After meetings with Gulbenkian's attorneys, the collector's $570,000 was locked safe in a New York bank.

After two weeks the Yusupovs were still waiting. "We're in this hotel now too long, Felix," Irina said, "and still we hear nothing from the attorney." The hotel maid placed the tray with morning tea on the lace-covered table.

They were not idle in their waiting for they were also welcomed by the Russian émigré community: Rachmaninoff played his Prelude in D Minor for them, Baron and Baroness Soloviev treated them to *côtelettes Pojarsky* at their Catskill estate, Igor Sikorsky proudly hosted them at his new aviation works on Long Island, and Gleb Derujinsky began to sculpt busts of them both.

"We have been treated quite well," Felix said.

"We have done our best to show our gratitude," said Irina, "but we are no longer rich royalty. We only have Gulbenkian's investment in our getting the paintings back. Of course, Mrs. Vanderbilt was so kind in persuading the US Customs to release some of the jewels they impounded on the rumor they were stolen from the czar."

"I was told," Prince Felix said to his wife, "the attorney received an answer from Widener. It came late yesterday."

"And?"

"Widener said *no*."

Shocked, Irina said, "How can it be *no*? You have an agreement. You cabled him you were coming with the money." She set her teacup down hard in its saucer.

"It seems Mr. Widener reads the agreement only through his own eyes," Felix said.

"But, you can pay him back!"

"I know, my dear. The attorney said to let him work on it."

"I hope you are right, Felix. It is not our money, you know."

"But, it is important to Widener," he said, "that we appear to have resumed our former way of life."

"Do you think he really cares?" Irina added, shaking her head. "He only wants the Rembrandts."

Lynnewood Hall, the Widener estate, poised on 170 acres in Elkins Park, Cheltenham, in northwest Philadelphia, proudly displayed over two hundred of the best works of Titian, Hals, El Greco, Velasquez, Manet, Vermeer, and many others in its gallery halls. One room held seven van Dycks. The center of Widener's pride, however, was another room which at one time had held only *Portrait of a Lady with an Ostrich-Feather Fan* and *Portrait of a Gentleman with Tall Hat and Gloves,* but now had twelve other Rembrandts.

"Good morning, sir. A telegram arrived for you."

"Put it by the coffee, Edward," Joseph Widener said to his servant. In his silk morning robe, Widener glanced over his reading glasses at the Western Union envelope, then continued scanning the Philadelphia Inquirer, sipping his coffee. It was Sunday morning and the racing news from Belmont was fresh.

There were stables at Lynnewood Hall, and a racetrack for the thoroughbreds. The neoclassical estate was a grand statement of aristocratic pretense. When approaching the estate, one would first pass through a formal French garden with a fountain surrounded by Greek-style statuaries before setting foot on the front portico, which was supported by six Corinthian columns.

"Good morning, dear," greeted Ella Pancoast Widener. She was still a beauty at forty-eight, after twenty-nine years of marriage. Aside from their thirty-seven servants, the Wideners were alone among their 110 rooms. Although the richest family in 'The City of Brotherly Love,' the Wideners, being the descendants of German bricklayers and butchers, were unwelcome within the elite East Coast circles of social respectability. Their only son, called Arrell after the patriarch Peter Arrell Brown Widener, was married and gone. After Arrell's front-line service in The Great War he had broadened his view of humanity, narrowing his opinion of wealth. Pretty daughter Fifi, the girl without a pedigree, now had one, having married into society.

Ella leaned over and kissed her husband's balding head. "What is the telegram about, dear?" she asked. Ella's blue silk dressing gown matched her eyes. Her brown hair was curled up on top as if she was ready for a tea party with the ladies.

"Nice tribute here to Sinclair's Zev," said Widener still buried in the Inquirer. "A great horse. What I would give to have a Zev," he added, laying the paper aside. He sipped his coffee and picked up the yellow Western Union envelope. He saw it was from New York, and ripped it open with his finger.

She watched his face as he read it. "Yes?" she asked.

He shook his head. "I can't believe this!" He threw the telegram on the table. "It's that Russian prince again. He still wants the Rembrandts back."

"That's impossible," she said.

"I don't have time for this," he said.

"Just tell him *no*, Joseph."

"I did. But, his attorney now says he's coming here with the money."

"That's impossible," she said. "We are leaving for Florida."

Joseph Widener rolled the newspaper and slammed it on the table making the silverware jingle. "I have no time for indigent Russian princes. Especially not this one."

"You made a deal, Joseph, that is that—isn't it?" Ella said.

"Damn well be!" he said. "Has the czar risen from the dead? I think not."

Ella asked, "Where did he get the money?"

"I'll find out," he said. "His lawyer talks of pursuing the issue in the courts."

"Lawyers always say that, Joseph. As you yourself know."

"We are going to Florida," Widener said, "and will not discuss this further with the prince, or his lawyer." Widener again slapped the rolled-up paper on the table. "He's good counsel, though. Buckner is respected."

Widener decided to wait a few days, though, just in case something changed concerning the art.

"Are they here, Edward?" Widener sighed. "Damn! Show them into the library. Ask their attorney to come here to the study."

After a night in Philadelphia's Bellevue-Stratford, the Prince and Princess Yusupov arrived along with their attorney, Emory Buckner. It was exactly ten on Thursday morning, December 13, as scheduled. The lawyer sat in Widener's study.

"You understand, Mr. Buckner," Widener began, "I've agreed to this meeting as a courtesy to you only. I see no purpose in arguing the finer points of a signed contract that is clear." He shook his hands and paced about. "And, it is especially irksome to delay any further Mrs. Widener's and my trip to Florida. We are already three days late."

"Mr. Widener," Buckner said, "we do appreciate very much your receiving us. We understand your train leaves at two. But, sir, we do insist..."

"The contract is clear," interrupted Widener, "and the sale stands since the preconditions to a repurchase are clearly unmet by the prince."

"I was saying," Buckner cleared his throat and continued, "that we do insist on a different view of this transaction than yours. We are ready to pursue the issue, if necessary. The prince is here to hand you the draft for the full amount including interest—$520,334 exactly, sir. It would avoid a lot of cost and inconvenience, if you would accept it."

"Insist all you want, Mr. Buckner. We are talking about Rembrandts here, not some common commodity."

"Indeed, Mr. Widener," Buckner said, "We are not talking about products at all, but Rembrandts. And, what is correct under the law."

Felix and Irina remained in the library. They sat in large, Victorian wing chairs with embroidered, ornately carved crests, and covered in tufted velvet of a golden color that harmonized with the faded leather on the shelves. The princess quietly looked about the library, a room of cherry-paneled walls with cases of books. On the Sarouk and Mishkian rugs stood mahogany tables. The room smelled of old paper and leather. They were served tea in blue and white Spode cups.

"Welcome to Lynnewood Hall, Your Highnesses." Ella Pancoast Widener entered, stood straight, and held out her hand to Prince Felix and Princess Irina.

Irina smiled. "Your home is beautiful, Mrs. Widener," she said. "It is like an English manor."

The Attempt

"Precisely," Ella said. "It is based on a Georgian estate in Bath. Sorry you won't be able to stay longer. We leave for Florida this afternoon." She steadied herself on a chair. "My husband is planning a new racetrack there. He raises thoroughbreds, you know. He loves racing."

They sat, sipping tea and chatting about horses, palaces, and princes. Ella Widener was too polite to bring up the recent events in Russia, though, in fact, she knew little about them.

Widener and Buckner entered with forced cordiality. Widener said, "We meet again, Prince Yusupov."

There was a moment of awkward silence.

"Indeed, sir," said Felix, his voice subdued.

"I suppose," Ella said, "you would like to see where we have the Rembrandts displayed."

"Yes, thank you, Mrs. Widener," said Irina.

"You can see," said Ella as she led them down the halls, "that the galleries extend for the length of this wing of the house."

Irina was impressed with the galleries. From where she stood she could see the doors of each gallery room symmetrically framing the doors of the next room, on down the way. It was as in the Moika Palace where she could, through the door of the Ballroom, frame the doors in the Green, Red, and Blue Rooms. Such happy memories in that ballroom.

They passed by Manet's *Dead Toreador*, the room of van Dykes, El Greco's *St. Martin and the Beggar*, and into the room of Rembrandts.

Widener gestured with opened arms, "Well, here we are. It is my favorite room."

Irina gasped. In the center of one wall hung Rembrandt's celebrated *The Mill*. Widener pointed to a red leather armchair saying, "I sit in that chair to just look." The brooding windmill on the hill was framed in heavy, gilt walnut.

The princess turned. A chill shot through her body. Gazing from their new gilded carved frames were *The Lady* with her mystery, her secret, and *The Gentleman* with his kind knowing, his shadowed strength. Irina's words caught in her throat. She loved that couple as if they were of her own blood. She wanted to talk to them, comfort them, and tell them it was going to be all right. The portraits were hanging exactly as they had in St. Petersburg. She blocked out the other paintings, and for a chilling moment it was as if nothing had changed. It distressed her that the Dutch couple looked so comfortably at home in this American room, as though amongst old friends.

"I keep thinking of them, Felix."

"Who?" asked Felix.

"Anya and her dear mother. That whole line of women." She looked up to *The Lady* and quietly said to Felix, "All her family! Such devotion, loyalty, commitment. Will they ever see these treasures again? I am so glad I agreed to look after them. I hope I don't fail."

Elsewhere on the dark red walls was the beautiful young *Saskia*, painted by Rembrandt just before he married her in 1634. There was the ruminating *The Apostle Paul*, the dark *Philemon and Baucus*, a colorful Rembrandt self-portrait, *The Descent from the Cross*, *St. Matthew*, and others.

Felix struggled for the words, then said, "I am overwhelmed, Mr. Widener." For one precious moment the Yusupovs and the Wideners were not adversaries, but of one mind in awe of the old Master.

Felix turned slowly from *The Lady* and *The Gentleman* and surveyed the other paintings. "Your gallery sir, it equals the best in Europe, even in Russia." Felix scanned The Rembrandt Room, with fourteen of the master's best works. Felix was impressed, thinking that in the world of art, perhaps Joseph Widener was himself a prince. "And this room in particular, sir—you are to be congratulated."

It was hard for the Yusupovs to take leave of the Rembrandts, but it was approaching noon and attorney Buckner said in Felix's ear, "We must move along."

"Exactly," said Felix with a sigh. They returned to the library.

Widener took his wife by the arm and left the room leaving Buckner to speak with his clients in private.

"Prince Felix," began Buckner, "Mr. Widener and I had a few words in his study. I must report that he is immovable in his refusal to accept our view and release the paintings for the money we have brought today."

Irina sat down.

Buckner continued, "We can bring this to a court of law as we have discussed. But, you can see, the Wideners are a rich and powerful family. The outcome is not predictable."

"I made a decision in Paris," Felix said. "I have given my word to others; I must proceed. It is a matter of honor."

"Believe me," said Buckner, "you have no obligation to Gulbenkian, except for the amount you borrowed. His collateral is worthless until you have actual possession of the art. It is a risk he accepted."

"We will have to repay the loan for sure," said Irina, "even if we fail to retrieve the Rembrandts."

Buckner turned to Irina, "That is between you and the lender. But, I think you should, especially if you intend to live in Paris society."

"Then, Mr. Buckner," said Felix, "we must proceed with the courts. Hope dies last."

"Mr. Widener," said Buckner as their hosts returned to the Library, "my client understands your position and confirms that we will continue to press our view in court, unless you change your position."

"Well, then that's that," said Widener. "I expected as much. I assume you know my attorneys, Miller & Otis."

Irina took Felix's arm. She felt as though a loved one had been pronounced terminally ill.

"Prince Felix and Your Highness," said Ella Widener, "Mr. Widener and I both feel for your losses. We could see this in your eyes in the Rembrandt Room. I wish it could be different." She glanced at her husband who appeared about to interrupt, but he didn't. "The tragic events are... I mean an entire country, a gallant country, disintegrating. Such a loss. Americans cannot grasp that loss. But, the Wideners have had our losses, too."

Irina put her hand on her heart. "We do understand your tragedy, Mr. and Mrs. Widener, and please accept our sympathy."

Felix and Irina both remembered what Buckner had told them on the train before arriving in Philadelphia. Widener's brother, George, and George's son, Harry Elkins Widener, were both lost on the ill-fated *Titanic*. That loss, which still haunted the family, was all the more troubling, Buckner had explained, since their father, Peter A.B. Widener, along with other Americans, were the owners of the ship and had financed its building. That tragic event, along with the persistent refusal of the Philadelphia elite to accept the Wideners and their children into society, toughened

Joseph Widener's heart. "Joseph Widener," Buckner warned Felix and Irina, "is a hardened and intransigent man."

After celebrating both the Western and the Russian Christmas in New York with their friends, the Yusupovs took a flat to save money, and without servants, near Gramercy Park.

Buckner assured them, "In my opinion, according to New York and Pennsylvania law, your contract is, and should be considered a mortgage. In a court of equity you should be able to redeem your portraits. It will not be an inexpensive affair," the attorney warned, "but it should get your Rembrandts back."

"Should?" Felix asked.

"Nothing is for sure in the courts," said Buckner.

"We still have the jewels to sell, Felix," Irina said, taking his hand. "We must try harder to do that."

"I am ready to file," said Buckner, "and we will provide the best trial lawyer."

Felix and Irina had discussed the issue before the lawyer had arrived in their two-bedroom flat. It was a risk they were willing to take. The Gulbenkian money was being used at a faster rate than expected. They could not return to Paris with nothing to show for it.

"Yes, it is what we want you to do, Mr. Buckner," Felix said.

"May I serve you tea, Mr. Buckner?" asked Irina.

Buckner nodded and smiled.

The princess went into the kitchen to boil the water.

CHAPTER TWENTY-FIVE

THE PEARLS

New York,
1924

"NEW YORK," SAID PRINCE FELIX, "is a city where the worth of a man is measured by the money in his pocket, not the value of his calling in life." He stood before the rain-stained window in their fifth-floor flat overlooking 19th Street, which was bustling with people holding their hats, speaking to no one. "I do not feel like myself in this place," said Felix.

"I can't believe it's March already," said Irina, "I miss our daughter, our home, our family, our friends."

"Buckner tells me," Felix said, "the pretrial process will take time. It may not come to the courts for months. Can you imagine? Or, maybe not even until next year."

"We will wait," said Irina.

"But not here. It is the rain," Felix continued. "The rain. It reminds me of the day in London when I met with Widener. He always seems to win, that man."

"Mrs. Widener," Irina said. "She is a noble lady. A pity we cannot be friends."

"She must need friends. I think her husband has none," he said.

"He looked down his long nose at you, Felix," she said. "And, those fingernails now, did you notice? Like talons."

Felix turned from the window and for a moment held his eyes on his wife. "Yes," he said, "curved like a hawk. How can you trust a man with long fingernails? As usual, Irina, you have assured we live in comfort, as best we can manage in this place."

Irina had made sure their apartment was modern. Newly painted off-white, it had a new Frigidaire and a Westinghouse electric stove. They had not seen such conveniences in St. Petersburg because ice was plentiful, as were wood and coke for the stoves. Of course, their hands never touched anything of that sort back at home.

"I have made an appointment for us with Cartier tomorrow, Felix." Irina watched for his response. "They appear interested in what I have to show them."

"So we have come to that?" Felix said. "A Yusupov, and a Romanov, selling their jewels to survive, and having to live in this ignoble place! Fate!" He looked up and then down the street below. He sighed, running both hands through his thinning hair. "We will see what the American jewelers have to say."

"Dear Felix." She stood behind him putting her arms around his waist and her head on his shoulder. "We should be grateful we have something to sell, a way to survive. It will not be the end. There are many worse off than us—in Paris, in Russia, even in America."

"We have the other jewels hidden in Moscow," he said.

"Yes, and we are alive. We have each other, Felix." She hugged him tightly.

He turned and kissed her. "I am sorry. I have misbehaved, treating you badly at times."

"Yes, you have, Felix. But, what we do from now on is what counts. Past is past, forgiven, Felix dear."

"*Bon jour*, Prince and Princess Yusupov."

Irina and Felix felt comfortable being greeted in French. Cartier, the French jeweler, had been established in New York for fifteen years.

"My name is Dubois, Luc Dubois." He bowed and smiled, shaking hands with Felix. Taking Irina's in a courtly manner, he bowed once more. He was short, heavy, and peeked out at them through a disheveled mop of salt and pepper hair. He wore a white frock covering a black coat, and gray, striped, pants, and attached to the right lens of his thick, black-rimmed glasses was a small, pivoting magnifying glass. "You are known to us already, of course, in Paris and here," said the jeweler.

"Ah, yes," said Felix. "We are used to that now."

Standing next to Dubois was a lady in her fifties. She had squinting eyes, thick glasses, and was introduced only as Madame Clos. She carried a notebook in one hand and a fountain pen in the other. The jeweler held the chair for Madame Clos. They sat down across from the Russians at a walnut table covered with a white felt cloth.

"Such a pity to come to us to sell," Dubois said. "We would much rather you come to buy." When he smiled one gold tooth peeked out the right corner of his mouth. Madame Clos did not smile at all.

"We agree on that point, Monsieur Dubois," Irina said. She was wearing a green silk shift with bows at the hips. Her hair, circled with a band of gold and silver daisies, curled to her shoulders. She had brought a canvas shopping bag, and out of it she pulled a parcel wrapped in a common Turkish towel. She removed the towel and laid a red leather box on the table. On its top, embossed in gold, was the double-headed eagle of the Romanov monarchy.

Monsieur Dubois raised his eyebrows.

"A birthday gift from my uncle." Irina smiled. Madame Clos took notes.

Irina held her palm out to her husband. "May I have the key, Felix?" He took a small gold key from his jacket pocket. She joggled it into the lock, slowly opening the box. Monsieur Dubois leaned forward. His eyes widened. There in the red velvet compartments were jewels of the richest family in Russia. "These are only a few of them," she said. "The American customs officers still have a large part. This is what we have to show you today."

"May I?" Dubois asked, flipping down his magnifying glass.

"Please," said Irina. "That is why we are here."

Dubois opened a black piece of felt the size of a dinner napkin and spread it out on the white table covering. With the fingers of both hands he picked up a sapphire-and-gold necklace and shaped it into a circle on the felt, carefully positioning each jewel. He examined each of the three, two-carat, pendants in the center, and grunting a note of satisfaction, put them back into one of the red velvet compartments. He picked up a ring with twelve emeralds spaced evenly about a three-carat round diamond. It looked like a pocket watch and was almost as large. Subjecting it to his magnified eye, he turned the ring in his fingers and muttered, "Flawless," looking up to Irina and shaking his head in admiration.

Irina watched, silent, unexpressive.

She watched the jeweler looking at a ruby necklace and ear-ring set. Then he reached for a white silk draw-string bag of loose diamonds. He opened the little bag, shaking the diamonds out onto the black felt. With tweezers, the jeweler poked and turned some of them, then, mumbling approval, replaced them in the bag. Madame Clos took more notes.

Using both hands, Dubois lifted the top tray out of the leather box, setting it aside on the table. He hesitated, squinting his eyes and leaning forward. He moved up his magnifying glass and looked up for a moment at Irina. He lifted them out, his eyes caressing each dark gray sphere, one connected to the other. He draped the string over his left arm, one, two, three times, his fingers massaging them, feeling their warmth.

"Irina!" said Felix and he touched her hand. "You didn't tell..."

She put her finger to her lips.

He sighed and said no more.

"I have never seen anything like this," Dubois said. "Each is perfect. How long is it?"

"Twice around my neck to below my waist," she said.

"And how many pe...."

"I have no idea."

"Is this the famous strand that..."

"Yes, Marie Antoinette."

Madame Clos looked up.

They had been six months in America. Now, sailing again in First Class, they were ecstatic at returning to their home on rue Gutenberg. They had gained over three hundred thousand dollars from the sale of the jewels. Cartier had declined to purchase many of the items, saying they were overstocked with emeralds and rubies from Europe. Any diamonds under "VVS1 colorless" were not of interest. Irina's rare and famous black pearls alone brought $200,000.

Wrapped in their furs, standing on the windy Promenade deck, their hands on the railing, they watched the New York skyline vanish into the fog. With his hand on his heart, Felix confessed to his wife, "I feel a terrible responsibility for all of this. Having to sell your jewels just to keep us going. A Romanov! What an ignoble thing."

She was quiet for a moment, then put her hand on his. "Really, Felix, what are jewels anyway? They are cold, dead minerals from the earth carved and cut to impress the impressionable. But art, a painting comes from within, and when it comes from within Rembrandt, it is immortal. His portraits are alive. That is why we came to America, to take home the living, not the dead. Let's keep that hope."

CHAPTER TWENTY-SIX

THE TRIAL BEGINS

New York
April, 1925

T HE NEW YORK COURT HOUSE at 31 Chambers Street was a
Beaux Arts building of gray stone; seven stories high, eight
if the mansard roof was counted, with its ornate dormers and
statues of Peter Stuyvesant and De Witt Clinton. Its front windows
looked down with authority on City Hall Park, which was ablaze
with spring's floral reds, yellows, blues, and greens. Deep below
the park was the Chambers Street station, what the New Yorkers
called the most beautiful subway station in the world.

"I'm not happy at returning to this unfriendly city," said the
Princess Irina to her husband. "I hope this is over quickly so we
can return to our Parisian friends and home."

It was now a year later as they returned to the United States,
to New York—for *Yusupov vs. Widener*.

Princess Irina waited for the men to leave the elevator, then trailed
them out, inhaling the Aqua Velva after-shave of the lawyers

and, of course, of her husband, Felix. She noted the elevator door, polished walnut with a floral design in gilded iron.

Leading the pack into the fifth-floor hallway was attorney Clarence Shearn and his assistant, their arms filled with heavy books, a bulging brown briefcase, and pads of paper. Behind them were Prince Felix and Captain Maziroff. Irina followed.

The wall sign by the door to Department 17 read *Judge Davis*. Inside they found members of the press and others already there— for the trial deciding who would own the coveted Rembrandts.

"The room is quite small," said the prince, used to more glamorous chambers.

"As I explained," Attorney Shearn said, "there's no jury."

Princess Irina, for all her regal worldliness, was unfamiliar with the American legal process. Nevertheless, she felt confident in their legal representation. Clarence J. Shearn, she was informed, was a prominent New York trial lawyer with Root, Clark, Howland & Ballentine. She thought he looked intelligent, with an almost bald head and wire-rimmed glasses. His colleague, Leo Gottlieb, Harvard educated, was a partner in the firm. Both wore navy blue suits, white shirts, and red ties, as Irina noted did most of the men in the room. Felix was in a gray flannel suit, white shirt, and black-and-gray striped tie.

With a thump, attorney Gottlieb unloaded his case books, briefcase, blank paper and pens on the table, causing the water glasses to rattle.

Irina looked around at the bare, cream-colored walls. She closed her eyes for a second to inhale the clean scents of a passing early morning shower drifting in through the two half-opened windows.

Shearn directed the prince to sit beside him at the table. The princess, in a silver silk dress decorated with a double strand of white pearls reaching to her waist, was motioned to the bench reserved just behind them. Already seated there was their companion, Captain Maziroff, with his curled mustache.

Irina heard a man's voice: "Excuse me, Your Highness." A reporter, one of several in the back benches, stepped forward toward Prince Felix. With a pencil in his hand and another on his ear, he said, "I am from The *New York Times*, Your Highness," his pad at the ready. Other reporters crowded around. "Our readers are interested in the outcome of this fascinating trial, sir."

"They well should be," injected Princess Irina, "these are Rembrandt's finest portraits. They are from one of the most famous collections in Europe."

Felix turned away without a word.

"Do you expect to regain ownership, Your Highness?"

"Indeed we do," Irina answered. "The prince and I came to America for justice. That is all we ask."

"Your riches in Russia, will you retrieve them?"

"There is always hope," she said.

Felix grasped her arm, pulling her away to take their places in the Supreme Court of New York.

"It's all so uncertain, Felix," she said.

Since the Yusupovs' initial visit to New York two years earlier, the unsuccessful attempts by the prince's representatives to redeem the Rembrandts had been on the front pages of The *New York Times* and on the radio.

The American press was joined at this trial by journalists from London and Paris. They were in the back rows, all poised to record the process of American justice in this postrevolutionary Russian drama.

Against one open window sat attorney Nathan Miller, the Yusupovs' adversary, counsel for Joseph Widener. Miller acknowledged Shearn with a nod and a "Good morning, Counsel, lady and gentlemen." That was all.

"Governor," Shearn replied.

Irina knew that Nathan Lewis Miller, a partner in the respected firm of Miller & Otis, had been a judge of the New York Supreme Court, even elected for a short term as Governor of New York. She noticed his graying hair, parted down the middle, his mustache, his glasses pinched onto his nose.

Miller opened his coat, turned, and started drumming his pen on the table, waiting for the judge to enter. More reporters with notepads and pencils entered, filling the back benches.

From the end of the row of journalists quietly stepped a woman, dressed in black, with notepad in hand. She approached Irina from the left, sat on the edge of a seat behind the princess and said, in Russian, "Excuse me, Princess Irina, I am a journalist, too. But, really I am an artist, schooled in St. Petersburg."

Irina immediately turned to the woman, smiled, and answered in near perfect English, "That's nice to hear. What do you do in New York?"

"I write, mainly about art and artists. I am here for the *Art Journal*, a small, new magazine. I was in St. Petersburg in 1913. I remember you in the czar's box at the Mariinsky. It was *Swan Lake*. I was on the side balcony. I admired your beautiful, white dress and your black pearl necklace."

Irina turned her body to face the woman. "You have a great memory. What is your name?"

"Doris Anne Hill, and—"

The entry door snapped open. A man entered with a clap of authority.

"Hear ye, hear ye," called the gray-haired bailiff. He read from a paper on a clipboard, "The Supreme Court of New York is now in session in the case of Felix Yusupov, Plaintiff, versus Joseph E. Widener, Defendant; Judge Vernon M. Davis presiding. Everyone stand." In walked the judge. He routinely nodded his head toward the lawyers and took his seat.

Doris leaned to Princess Irina and said, "Judge Vernon Davis is highly respected. He has spent his whole life in the New York courts, first as a District Attorney, and then finally as a Supreme Court Judge."

"Does that mean we will win this contest?" said Irina. "I hope so."

"That all depends on the facts as presented," Doris replied. "I hope so, too."

With a rap of the gavel, Judge Davis opened the proceedings.

"I understand…," the judge looked out over his glasses from one lawyer to the other, "…this case concerns the rightful owner-ship of two Rembrandt portraits. Is that correct?"

The attorneys nodded. "Yes, Your Honor."

"Then, Mr. Shearn, you will please begin. The court will hear the background of this case and your opening statement for the plaintiff."

Doris Anne Hill settled into the empty chair to the left behind Princess Irina. "I have covered four court cases for the *Art Journal*," she whispered, "but none have been about such valuable art as the Rembrandts." Doris smiled at Irina, adding, "But, I know these two Rembrandts, Princess Irina. Our art class took a tour of the Moika Palace to see that wonderful collection. They were what everyone raved about."

"Really, Doris? How wonderful," Irina said, "Felix and I must have been in Europe on our honeymoon." She looked out the window for a moment. "If we only could return."

The judge leaned back and, running his hands through his white hair, looked about his courtroom—the lawyers, the desks of the clerk, the court recorder.

"Your Honor," Shearn stood and began, "in July 1921 the plaintiff, Prince Felix Yusupov, was the owner of two original oil paintings by Rembrandt, known respectively as *Portrait of a Lady with an Ostrich-Feather Fan* and *Portrait of a Gentleman with Tall Hat and Gloves*."

Doris Hill carefully recorded the proceedings on her notepad.

All were focused on attorney Shearn. They listened while, with measured words, he established the credentials of the Yusupov family, their large art collection, and their family's good stewardship possession of the Rembrandts for well over a hundred years. Mentioning the Yusupovs' reported former wealth in excess of five hundred million dollars, he stressed their reputation for benevolence, and their misfortune as a result of the Russian Revolution.

Irina leaned toward Felix, "That is no one's business. Not in this foreign country."

The prince sat with his clasped hands on the table, tilting his head to hear Shearn's remarks.

Doris Hill wrote faster as the attorney listed the credentials of the two Rembrandts, quoting The *London Times* in 1921 writing of 'the immortal, unchanging interest of these two superb portraits,' and of London's authoritative *Burlington Magazine* of 1911 that described them as 'among the greatest of all Rembrandt's creations.'

Irina turned to Doris and whispered, "Are you getting this?"

"Yes, Your Highness," said Doris, "what an intriguing story this is. Such depth."

Irina, holding her pearls, leaned forward in an attempt to better hear their attorney's presentation. Under her pretense of calm, she bristled at the uncertain prospects ahead and her inability to influence them.

Irina and Doris listened while Shearn, to establish the value of the paintings, cited offers including that of Sir Joseph Duveen in February, 1921, of 150,000 pounds sterling, which he estimated for the court was approximately $577,000.

The judge glanced toward the open window, distracted by the sound of honking horns and shouting on the street below.

Shearn, soberly posturing with his hands, related the prince's disguised escape from Russia with the paintings at great risk to his life. He told of the prince's intent never to sell the paintings, but to gain a temporary loan against them. Shearn turned, nodding in respect to the prince and to the princess, who, with a slight smile, nodded in return.

Doris wrote rapidly as Shearn detailed the London negotiations in the summer of 1921 when first Captain Maziroff and then Prince Felix met with Widener, asking a price of £200,000, but was offered only £100,000 in return.

Shearn covered the meeting of July 12, at which the prince again asked for £200,000 as a loan against the Rembrandts, with

Mr. Widener again offering only £100,000 and refusing a loan. He then described the final agreement which gave Mr. Widener one month to acquire the paintings for £100,000 with the option for Prince Yusupov to repurchase the paintings on or before January 1, 1924 for the same sum, plus 8 percent interest. Assistant Gottlieb handed the document of July 12 to the clerk who marked it for exhibit, then placed it in front of the judge.

Doris noted counselor Miller, leaning back with his folded arms, gazing blankly out the window, like he was disinterested in the plaintiff's claims.

"The next communication," Shearn continued, "received by the prince from Widener, was a cable on August 9, reading, 'Please communicate with my agent Sulley who has the money to take delivery.' My client, naturally understanding this to be the exercise of the option of July 12, that same day cabled his acknowledgement and agreement."

"Delivery of the paintings and receipt of money took place on August 12, completing the contract. We contend that the agreement dated July 12 is the contract in force, that it represents the intent of both parties at the time of signing. As such, it constitutes a chattel mortgage under the laws of the State of Pennsylvania, the two paintings being held as security there by Mr. Widener for the loan of £100,000."

Again, Doris took note of counselor Miller's apparent indifferent attitude, as he pushed his glasses up on his nose and began writing on a pad.

"However," Shearn continued, "On August 11, 1921, barely a day before the closing, the plaintiff received in the mail another document from the defendant under a cover letter dated July 25, 1921." Shearn shuffled some papers. "This new document," he said, "contained totally new language, a number of restrictive clauses that were not previously agreed upon, or even discussed, and which the prince would never have agreed to."

"With faith in the original contract of July 12, and on the advice of competent counsel," Shearn said, "the plaintiff having already made financial commitments, in full confidence signed the second document in order to collect the money promised by Widener. He wrote a letter to Mr. Widener explaining his trust in the original contract, but that letter went ignored, unanswered by Widener."

Doris and Irina glanced at each other, took a deep breath, and turned to hear more.

"Nevertheless," Shearn continued, "in the following months the plaintiff received funds from the sale of family jewels, and a personal loan. In November, 1923, the prince and the princess sailed to New York, and on December 13 of that year tendered to Mr. Widener the correct sum, in US currency, of $520,334 including interest, which in turn was refused outright by Mr. Widener."

Shearn took a sip of water. "He refused to surrender the paintings as agreed. We therefore contend that Mr. Widener is in breach of contract, and ask the court to find in favor of the plaintiff."

Finishing his notes, Judge Davis laid down his pen and asked, "Does that conclude your opening remarks, counsel?"

"It does, Your Honor." Shearn sat down.

A hopeful smile turned the corners of Felix's mouth.

Irina reached over, laying her hand on her husband's shoulder. "That is clear. Should be no problem, right?"

The judge called for a short recess while a clerk lowered the window half-way to cut the street noise, but still let in some fresh air.

Irina turned to Doris and said, "The issue is more than just the Rembrandts staying in the Yusupov family, important as that is. I have a personal commitment to a woman who is an actual descendent of the woman in the portrait. It is a commitment, since the revolution, to protect these paintings and ensure their proper security. I want to see them in a safe home—as they have always been in Russia until the recent upheaval."

"That is so noble, Princess Irina. They deserve to be admired by many, not just the Wideners."

The judge looked at attorney Miller. "The court will now hear the opening statement for the defense."

Attorney Miller cleared his throat, and spoke with the confident voice of a politician. "Your Honor," he said. "I represent Mr. Joseph Early Widener of Philadelphia, who, as everyone knows," the attorney looked about the room, "is a highly respected businessman and member of society. He is also a recognized connoisseur of art, with a notable collection of paintings, porcelain, sculpture, and other *objects d'art*." He raised his hand in emphasis.

"Indeed, Mr. Widener sought to acquire the Rembrandts in question. He already had twelve Rembrandts in his possession at that time."

Miller paused, turning to counsel Shearn, and nodded. "Counsel Shearn is, in general, correct, in his description of events leading up to the London meeting of July 12, 1921. However, Your Honor, some important details have been overlooked leading to the major point of law that applies in this case." Miller continued, looking aside as if it all was of little importance, "And, we know, of course, that the prince was desperate and was hocking his paintings all over Europe."

Irina frowned and glanced back at Felix. "How inconsiderate."

Miller reached back to his table, took a folder and removed a paper. "Indeed," Miller continued, "there is a legal contract in this case. But, it is not the contract described by Mr. Shearn for his client." Miller paced, as in thought. "Mr. Widener, returning to Philadelphia, raised the money to exercise his option, a challenging task in itself at that time."

Miller looked around as if addressing a full courtroom and jury, and caught the cold looks of Felix and Irina. "Mr. Widener's Philadelphia attorney prepared a proper Memorandum of Sale," he continued, "as any good businessman would, based on the general understandings in London."

Miller handed the clerk a copy of the Memorandum of Sale. "To meet the mail ship sailing July 26, one copy was mailed to Prince Yusupov and the other to Widener's London agent, Arthur Sulley, with a letter instructing Sulley that upon acceptance by the prince, he, Widener, would deposit the money, £100,000, into Sulley's account for payment to Yusupov."

"The cover letter to Yusupov," said Miller, "asked the prince to cable his agreement, if acceptable, which he did." Miller straightened his tie, stretching his neck like his collar was tight. "We contend that the prince, in fact, knew of the Memorandum of Sale. Mr. Widener, in receiving the prince's cabled acceptance of it, cabled Sulley advising the payment."

Miller paused, unbuttoned his jacket, and pushed up his glasses. "The sales agreement under letter of July 25," he said, "was duly signed by Prince Yusupov and witnessed on August 12. It is the terms and condition of that contract that governs the ownership of the Rembrandt portraits today." Miller paused, turning back to his table of documents.

"Is your opening argument finished, Mr. Miller?" asked the judge.

"Yes, Your Honor."

"Thank you, counsel," said Judge Davis. "Do you intend to enter a copy of plaintiff's acceptance cable of August 9?"

"Mr. Widener is expected in court tomorrow, Your Honor. He will bring the cable. I will enter it at that time."

Irina sighed. She leaned forward to Felix's ear, but he was listening to attorney Shearn. She turned to Doris Hill and whispered, "I don't understand. How can a simple agreement between two gentlemen be interpreted in two very different ways? Our paintings, and our honor, deserve better."

"It seems to me you have a strong argument," Doris said. She valued her new relationship with Princess Irina, but with Prince Felix, it was minimal. She laid aside her notepad and pencil. "That is why we have law," she said, "and courts to tell us what it all means. It is often confusing—we all know that. That is why it is so important to have agreements clearly understood and recorded to begin with."

Doris paused, knowing she was beginning to recall her conflicting observations in Russia. She felt uneasy voicing her arguable thoughts to this new and respected friend. She felt such love and admiration for so many friends and things Russian, and at the same time watched as their very civilization was washing away by their own fault. In the absence of common law, she learned that in Russia, a serious agreement, or contract as it is called, often seemed to be the beginning, not the end of negotiation. She decided to say no more.

Irina paused, looked deeply at Doris, sighed, then turned to Felix. When she saw that he was biting his fingernails, she reached up and tugged at his wrist. "Not here," she said.

"It's my turn next to be questioned," Prince Felix said.

CHAPTER TWENTY-SEVEN

THE YUSUPOV DEMAND

April, 1925
New York

THROUGH THE OPENED WINDOWS, the New York spring air was now still and warm. The judge asked attorney Shearn if he had any witnesses. Shearn said, "I do, Your Honor. I would like to call Prince Felix Yusupov of Russia."

Felix stood and straightened his jacket.

"God bless, dear Felix," whispered Irina as she squeezed his hand.

Doris smiled, writing rapidly in her notebook.

Felix approached the witness stand, sat down and was sworn in.

"Prince Yusupov," Shearn began, "these valuable Rembrandts were in your family how long?"

"It would be 137 years now."

The judge interrupted, "Could you, Your Highness, please speak a little louder?"

"Yes, Your Honor." He straightened, saying, "For 137 years the Rembrandts have been in my family." He spoke in near-perfect English with an accent polished at Oxford.

The prince retold of his escape, disguised as a common art student, to The Crimea with the Rembrandts, and the family's eventual rescue by a British warship.

"Did you bring anything else of value with you?"

Attorney Miller stood. "Objection, Your Honor. This information is irrelevant to the issue."

"Overruled, Mr. Miller, I would like to hear this."

Miller sat down, loosening his tie.

Judge Davis turned to the witness. "Please answer the question, Prince Yusupov."

"I brought many of the family jewels—wrapped around my body."

"Did you attempt to sell the jewels?" asked Shearn.

"We did. We have sold some. But, the market is not keen."

Irina, leaning forward to catch every word, smiled at her husband.

Doris whispered, "What a heroic story!"

"It's well known, Prince Yusupov, that you contributed much to help your fellow Russians exiled in Paris and London."

"Many were living like paupers," said the prince. "The money from the jewels was not enough. We were forced at last to borrow against the Rembrandts."

"Why did you agree to the Widener offer, Prince Yusupov?"

"Although the price was below their value, the agreement allowed me to buy them back as I intend to do," the prince said. "I was uncomfortable financially. I had to decide."

"Did Mr. Widener act on that option within thirty days?"

"As you described, he did that on August 9. We completed the sale, with stated reservations, on August 12."

"What happened next?"

Felix recounted his trip to America and Widener's rejection. Beads of perspiration formed on Felix's forehead, but he did not open his jacket.

"You did sign," Shearn said, "that second document received the previous August, did you not? And why?"

"I was compelled to do so at that point. But, I felt sure Mr. Widener was a gentleman and good to his word. My lawyers agreed that the first document was the only real agreement. When he later refused to honor it I was quite disappointed. I was personally hurt."

When time came for the cross-examination of Felix, attorney Miller placed his hand on the worn rail of the witness box. "Prince Yusupov," he said, "we are all familiar with the traumatic misfortune you and your family experienced. We do not want to add to your distress, but we are here to come to a rightful and fair decision about some very important property."

"Precisely, Mr. Miller," Felix said, "or I would not be here, so far from home."

"Yes." Miller hesitated. "We understand you were in substantial financial need in the summer of 1921."

"That is not news."

"Well then, Prince Yusupov, to start with, why did you not take the earlier offer of £150,000 from Sir Joseph Duveen?"

"It was an offer to buy. I did not intend to sell."

"You refer to the Russian refugees you were helping in London and Paris."

"Yes."

"You are to be commended for that, Prince Yusupov."

Irina smiled.

Doris whispered, "Such generosity. You are both to be honored."

"Will you tell me, sir," asked Miller, "how much you have spent on that charitable work?"

"I don't know," Felix answered, "I do not keep record of my charitable giving."

Miller removed his hand from the railing and continued, "In your June letter did you not offer your Rembrandts for sale?"

"No," said Felix. "I offered the paintings as collateral for a loan, with my option to repurchase at a future date. I invited Mr. Widener to see the paintings since he had not previously done so."

"And what did Mr. Widener answer?"

"He asked about price."

Miller produced a copy of that letter along with Widener's answer and handed them to the clerk.

"Now, Prince Yusupov," Miller replaced his hand on the railing. With narrowing eyes he leaned into Felix's face, "We know that Mr. Widener mailed you a formal contract under cover dated July 25. When did you receive that letter and contract sent by Mr. Widener?" He leaned even closer and before the prince could answer, raised his voice, repeating the question in measured words, "*When*, Prince Yusupov, did you receive that letter and contract? That is the contract you signed." He turned, and looked at Shearn.

Felix answered at once, "I believe it was August 11."

Miller straightened. "*Believe?* You *believe* it was August 11?"

"Yes, sir, I do."

"Tell me, Prince Yusupov, if Mr. Sulley received his copy of that contract before August 9, they both being mailed on the same day in America, why do you think it took until August 11, three more days, for your copy to reach you in the same city?"

"I have no idea, Mr. Miller. I can't answer for the British Post."

Miller turned to the judge and said, "Your Honor, we contend that the two letters, mailed in Philadelphia on July 25, went on the steamship America sailing from New York July 26, arriving in London 6:50 a.m. on August fourth." He continued with contingency scenarios of later mail ships, concluding that, "the contract mailed July 25th would have been delivered no later than Monday, August 8, in worst case before August 9."

Miller turned again to Felix, "We contend, Prince Felix, that you, in fact, received the contract you signed, on or before August 9, knowing full well of its contents before cabling your acceptance August 11, and signing that document on August 12." Miller handed the clerk a sheaf of official, published sailing schedules.

"While we agree, Prince, that you received the contract written July 25, we obviously disagree on when. But, you did sign that contract, did you not?"

Felix turned and looked at his attorney, Shearn.

At that moment, the fluttering of wings broke the suspense. A gray-striped bird with a red breast hit the framed glass of the open window nearest the judge's bench. It fell onto the sill, trembled in confusion, and tumbled to the floor. A clerk raced to grab the bird as it flapped across the floor, chased it, finally grabbed it, and threw it back out the window.

"Oh, what if its wing was hurt," questioned Doris who stood up to see the commotion. "It's a long way to the street."

The judge took a breath and looked about the room, "Can we have quiet, please?" He thanked the bird-catching clerk, then turned to attorney Miller and said, "Carry on, counselor."

Miller turned to Felix, "I repeat my question, Prince Yusupov. But, you did sign that contract, did you not?"

After a pause, Felix answered, "I had to."

"I understand. You said you were 'compelled to', is that right."

"Yes, I…"

"Who," Miller interrupted, "who compelled you? Who was with you when you signed the contract?"

"My business agent Captain Maziroff, and Mr. Rayner, my attorney."

"And," asked Miller, "did either of them force you to sign the contract of July 25?"

"Of course not." Felix looked at Shearn who was writing.

"Then how could you say you were 'compelled'?" Miller said.

"I was compelled by circumstances—my financial circumstances. I have explained that many times."

"I see. But, you did read and sign it?"

"Yes. Actually, I had my attorney read it and, yes, I signed it." Felix looked at the Judge.

"You signed it, but you did not agree to it, is that right?"

"Not all of it, no."

"Having put your signature to it, did you or did you not intend to honor that agreement?"

Shearn looked up from his notes, then dropped his head, rubbing his forehead with his fingers.

"My lawyer said parts of it were illegal," Felix said, "so I felt right in signing it, although I did not intend to honor the illegal conditions."

"May I have a 'yes' or 'no,' please, Prince Yusupov? Did you or did you not intend to honor the agreement you signed on August 12, 1921?"

"No. I intended to honor the contract of July 12—as I expected Mr. Widener to do."

Shearn cringed, giving a frustrated look toward Irina.

Miller turned to the judge, "I have no further questions for the plaintiff at this time, Your Honor."

Doris decided not to say a thing.

Irina leaned forward and whispered to her husband as he returned, "Not a word was mentioned about the despicable Rasputin affair. I am so glad for that."

CHAPTER TWENTY-EIGHT

THE WIDENER DEMAND

New York
April, 1925

PRINCESS IRINA, on this fourth day of the trial, in a fresh, white dress and her pearls, took her usual seat. She rubbed her hands in thought, looking about the room. She watched defense counsel Miller, sitting in the warm, spring sunlight slanting through the windows, remove his jacket. Next to Miller was the familiar face of Joseph Early Widener, in a pin-striped, three-piece-suit, leaning back, reading the *New York Times* through glasses resting on the end of his nose. They were all waiting for the judge to enter.

"That's he," Irina said to Doris, again behind her on the princess' left. "That is Mr. Widener, the man who wouldn't stand by the agreement and now has the Rembrandts."

Over the past three days several witnesses had been called by attorney Shearn, including Captain Maziroff who substantiated the testimony of Felix.

Irina leaned over to Doris, and said, "When will this ever end? We have heard the stories over and over. Either the judge believes Prince Felix, or he believes Mr. Widener. What a waste of time!"

"Yes," Doris replied, "There is an eventual truth. It is hard sometimes to see what that is. However, the longer it takes, the more money the lawyers make."

Judge Davis entered, his robe buttoned tight over his suit and tie. Everyone stood. He brought the room to order at ten o'clock sharp. Widener folded his newspaper and laid it aside.

"Will the council for the defense," the judge said, "continue with his calling of witnesses?"

"Your Honor," said Miller, "we are ready to continue. The defense calls Sir Joseph Duveen to the stand."

Duveen stood. He primed his mustache, straightened his jacket, and took the stand, where he testified that Widener was an honorable man and that he, Duveen, had sold over $350,000 worth of art to Widener, including Rembrandts, sometimes at no commission.

Shearn volunteered, "That seems to be the usual way with people who deal with Widener."

"Mr. Shearn," said the judge, "I warn you against such remarks."

To further establish market price, Miller then called his other art experts. There was Colin Agnew of Agnew's, Old Bond Street, London, the dealer Max Friedlander, and William Valentiner, director of the Detroit Institute of Arts, and published Rembrandt authority. The experts all agreed with Valentiner who testified that £100,000 was a fair market price for the paintings in July 1921.

Miller, wet circles spreading under each arm, pulled on his jacket. "I call Joseph Early Widener to the stand," he said.

Widener stood, straightened his tie, pushed up his glasses, and buttoned his double-breasted jacket. He took his place in the witness box and was sworn in.

After a repetition of all the unarguable facts, Miller asked the defendant, "Did you, sir, at any time say that you would consider loaning the prince money against the collateral of the Rembrandt paintings?"

"Absolutely not," said Widener. "He asked many times, but I made it clear that I bought for my collection. I am not a pawnbroker."

"Indeed," said Miller, "you have one of the largest collections in America, do you not?"

"The largest in America," Widener said. "The best, according to experts. It is the largest private collection of Rembrandts in the world."

"The price, Mr. Widener," his attorney said. "The prince obviously wanted to sell, at some price. Why were you so far apart?"

"That's simple," said Widener. "I told him no Rembrandts had sold for what he was asking. My offer was fair. He had inflated ideas, I'm afraid. I told him that." Widener looked at the judge and continued, "I sympathized with his situation. I knew how dear the Rembrandts were to him, but I could not take that into consideration." Widener glanced from his attorney to Shearn and the prince. "Every product has its price. They were hocked to a Jew pawnbroker, you know."

"But, you did sign an agreement with him on July 12?"

"Yes," said Widener, "it was a thirty-day option for £100,000 with an option to repurchase. He was quite confident of returning to his former way of life."

"Did you accept that option?"

"I did," said Widener. "After raising the money, I sent him a confirming Memorandum of Sale. He accepted it. I sent the money. He delivered the paintings in London to my agent. It was a clean sale. That's all there is to it."

"Thank you, Mr. Widener."

"And," volunteered Widener, "I will deliver his acceptance cable as soon as it is located."

"Thank you, Mr. Widener." Miller repeated as he swallowed that unsolicited admission of noncompliance from his client.

When it was attorney Shearn's turn to cross-examine the defendant, he began, "Now, Mr. Widener..."

Widener straightened himself in the witness box. "Yes?"

"Can you produce any other person who witnessed your conversations with Prince Yusupov on July 12?"

"No. Arthur Sully is not available." Widener tilted back his head, looking down his nose with half-closed eyes.

"I see, and..."

"Isn't my word enough, Mr. Shearn?"

Judge Davis interrupted. "Please just answer the question, Mr. Widener."

"Of course," Widener tilted back his head, pointing a long fingernail toward Felix's agent, "There was Maziroff, seated over there. But, he will give you the prince's story. That is how those people work."

"Your word, Mr. Widener, is taken as your testimony," said Shearn. "You claim the prince's cable of August 9 was an acceptance of your contract mailed July 25, yet my client says absolutely it was an acceptance of the option with its terms of July 12."

"I cannot help if the prince gets his facts and his dates confused, Mr. Shearn—or doesn't open his mail."

"You cannot, as you just confirmed," said Shearn, "produce a copy of the prince's August 9 cable, which you say accepted your contract mailed July 25?"

"That I *have* not does not mean I *will* not, Mr. Shearn. A search for it is underway. You have my testimony. I have twenty-five Pinkerton detectives searching Lynnewood Hall for it now."

Attorney Miller stiffened at the unsolicited information.

When asked why he rejected the full offer to repurchase the Rembrandts, Widener said, "The only contract at issue states that the prince must regain his former position in life. I have not heard of any return to the Romanov monarchy in Russia," Widener said. "Is the czar dead or not dead? There is chaos there. Anyone who can read knows that."

"But, Mr. Widener, you did give him the right to repurchase the paintings under certain conditions."

"Certain conditions? The return of his property by the Bolsheviks? Unlikely!"

From the row of press agents, murmurings turned heads, but Judge Davis was not distracted.

Felix sat expressionless. Irina, hearing those remarks, took a deep breath and hardened her look at Widener.

"You mean, sir," Shearn continued, "that you did not give value to the condition requiring the return to 'his former way of life' as you said."

"No, sir. The chance of that happening wasn't worth thirty cents. No, sir, not thirty cents."

Shearn turned aside and said, "Mr. Widener seems to be a sharp trader who has taken in a gentleman."

"Objection!" called Miller.

"I retract that, Your Honor," Shearn said, smiling. "Thank you, Mr. Widener."

Widener stood and exited the witness box, but hesitated. With a flushed face he said to Shearn, "The man is a buffoon, an assassin, a joke, a degenerate. Don't you know who you are dealing with, Mr. Shearn?"

"Mister Widener!" The judge's gavel came down hard. "You are out of order! Another comment like that and you will be held in contempt!"

Widener ignored the judge, but returned to his seat, muttering loudly under his breath, "It's this trial that's out of order. Any man who paints his face and darkens his eyes cannot be trusted. Did you know that, Miller?"

Felix looked at his shoes and Irina looked away.

Miller bent to Widener, raising his finger to his lips, "Please keep your voice down, sir. Davis can be tough."

"This pawnbroker thing," added Widener, "how demeaning!"

"And that Shearn. *Socialist!*"

CHAPTER TWENTY-NINE

THE SURPRISE

New York
April, 1925

"HOW MUCH LONGER IS THIS going to last, Mr. Shearn," Princess Irina asked their attorney. "It's been two weeks now and it's the same thing over and over. What difference to the decision do our personal finances have to do with it all?"

"It has to do with intent. The sides disagree," Shearn answered.

Felix asked, "And, what about the agreement cable Widener cannot produce?"

"As long as it is not produced, the court cannot know what it says."

Irina shook her head and sat down with Doris who said, "The reporters all believe it is almost over, but no one will guess what the judge thinks at this point."

Widener's attorney recalled Prince Felix to the stand, questioning him about his money. "You have stated that, indeed, you have approached a return to your former wealth, at least in the financial aggregate if not in your titled position." Miller looked about the room. "Is that right, Prince Yusupov?"

"That is right, sir."

"Can you describe some of this wealth, in addition, the money you offered Mr. Widener?"

"Objection, Your Honor," called Shearn, "that is privileged information."

"Overruled, Mr. Shearn," said Judge Davis. "Please answer, Prince Yusupov."

"I have a home in Paris and one in Switzerland."

"Can you tell us the approximate value of these properties, Prince Yusupov?"

"I can't tell you, I am not an estates appraiser." Perspiration began to line the prince's face. Felix continued, "I have substantial value in the family jewel collection."

"And, where is that located?"

"In vaults in Paris, and elsewhere. But, I cannot divulge that, sir."

"And, can you," Miller asked, "divulge the value of the jewels?"

The interrogation continued, listing the Polar Star diamond, the Morocco Steel diamond, the Marie Antoinette pendant, the diamond lavaliere, the case of snuff boxes and miniatures, and other items, all of which the prince estimated at over a million dollars. The prince allowed, however, that some has been sold and much of the rest pledged against loans.

"And, do you concede, Prince Yusupov, that there has been no change in the government in Soviet Russia that would allow you to return to your substantial assets there."

"This is true for the time being. However," Felix continued, "having the money to repurchase the portraits is tantamount to a return to my previous financial condition. But, that is not an issue here."

"Well, that may be," said Miller. "But, that is for this court to decide."

Irina pulled a linen handkerchief from her handbag and wiped her brow. She turned, saying something in private to Maziroff, and waving her hand in disgust.

"Prince Yusupov," Miller read from a paper, "we understand that on December 21, 1922, over a year from your deliverance of the paintings to Mr. Widener, you offered the same paintings to a Mr. Ruck for £140,000 although you did not own the paintings. Is that correct?"

Felix swallowed, hesitating. The judge bent over, watching for an answer.

"That was a misunderstanding," said Felix.

"Prince Yusupov," Miller stood back, hooking his thumbs in his suspenders, "I put forward, sir, that indeed there was, and is, a misunderstanding, and that not only do you not have any significant resources that would indicate a return to your former financial position under any stretch of the imagination," and he waved his hand, "but that you do not even own the money in the bank to pay Mr. Widener as you have proposed."

"Objection," Shearn jumped to his feet, "the counsel is testifying. Let him produce his evidence, if he has any, in acceptable form."

Felix was silent. He looked to Shearn, to the judge, his eyes open for instruction.

"Your honor," said Miller, "that the plaintiff received a loan was already established by his attorney. Exactly who loaned the money is material to this case."

"Objection overruled," the judge said, "the witness may answer the question."

"I have information here, sir..." Miller continued, waving a document in the air, "...that claims you have borrowed that very money from one Mr. Calouste Gulbenkian of Paris. Is that correct or not?"

Duveen, four rows back, looked about the room in an innocent pretense, dabbing his face with a cambric handkerchief.

"Correct," whispered Felix.

"The court understands," said the judge, "the witness answered 'Correct'."

"And furthermore," Miller continued, "that you have put up the Rembrandts as security for that loan, although you do not own them. Is that correct or not?"

"Objection, Your Honor," Shearn said.

"Overruled, the witness may answer."

"Correct," said Felix.

"I wonder," asked Miller, "what Your Highness is pretending to be, and if you understand what a contract is? We can only conclude, Prince Yusupov, that you consider a contract the *beginning* of negotiations, not the end of them. Is this the way you do business?"

"I am not pretending to be anything," Felix said, "just to be myself. In Russia we hold a man to his word, not a lawyer's paper."

Before the questioning could continue, the door at the rear of the courtroom burst open. The judge jerked his head toward the unscheduled event. A man hurried in, stumbling on a wrinkle in the carpet, and handed attorney Farr, Miller's associate, an envelope. Farr opened the envelope. Widener looked over their shoulders, then raised his eyebrows and smiled.

"Your Honor," called Miller, "May I call for a recess of ten minutes to consider the information just handed to me."

The judge agreed.

Shearn joined Felix, Irina, and Maziroff. They talked in low voices, wondering if the interruption was a dramatic ruse.

When the cross-examination continued, Miller first said to the court, "Isn't it interesting how truth surfaces at unexpected times." He turned to the prince. "The afternoon issue of The *New York Post* has an announcement that will not be gladly received, I have the duty of telling you."

Miller turned to the judge. "Shall I read the headline, Your Honor?"

The judge glanced at the paper, paused, then said, "Go ahead, counselor."

Miller opened the newspaper and read from the front page, *"Fortune in Yusupov Jewels found by Bolsheviks. Hidden in Moscow Estate."*

Felix's eyes widened. Irina gasped, holding her hands to her throat. Maziroff reached to steady her.

"Felix, our jewels!"

There was a buzzing in the courtroom. Everyone turned to observe the Yusupovs.

Finally, Judge Davis said, "Counselors, I had hoped to conclude the proceedings today, hearing the closing statements. But, with this new information, I will adjourn this trial today. The court will be ready to hear your closing statements tomorrow, same time." He looked at the two attorneys, asking, "Is that agreeable?"

"I will be ready to close tomorrow, Your Honor," said attorney Miller. "This charade has gone on long enough."

Shearn hesitated, then said, "Yes, Your Honor, I am ready to close."

Irina felt faint and reached for her seat. Doris took her arm and helped her to sit down.

Felix whispered to Maziroff, "I should have gone back for them—but, the ship was leaving."

"Felix," Captain Maziroff said, "You did your best. Look how much you did save, including the Rembrandts."

CHAPTER THIRTY

THE DECISION

New York
April, 1925

CLARENCE SHEARN, pacing back and forth, cupping his chin
in his hand, gave his closing statement. He addressed it
to the New York and European press as much as to the judge.
He positioned the trial as having an importance beyond the
personality of the plaintiff, or the value of the subject matter
of the litigation. "Such interest lies," he said, "in the fact that it
is going to be determined here whether the standards of business ethics of Mr. Widener are those supported by an American
Court of Equity.

"What a heartening message it will be." He looked to the
reporters in the back benches writing on their pads. "How high
Americans can hold their heads, when it is decided that in an
American court, a foreigner, one violently banished from his
homeland and stripped of his possessions, can prevail against
an American millionaire, and," he paused again with a glance
toward attorney Miller, "all the crafty tactics of cunning lawyers."

Attorney Shearn, recounting all the facts of the case, said, "It is clear that nothing else is of importance, not the tricky and dishonest contract supposedly mailed July 25, not the immaterial source of funds, which was freely admitted by the plaintiff at the start, and certainly not the unfortunate news in the *New York Post*." He paused again.

"The sale, Your Honor, without doubt is, and was intended to be, as signed on July 12 by both parties, a mortgage. The plaintiff is legally entitled under equity and the laws of the Commonwealth of Pennsylvania, and of England, to redeem his paintings. We hope the court agrees with this conclusive position, granting judgment in favor of the plaintiff."

Felix turned and looked at his wife, expressionless, unsure of the power of those gallant and to them, truthful words. She put her hand on his shoulder.

"Counsel for the defense? Your closing statement?" the judge asked.

"Your Honor," Attorney Miller paced before the Judge, "I will agree that the importance of this trial goes beyond the persons or the collateral of this issue, but to the clear and honest application of law." He went on to rehearse Widener's argument to buy, not lend against the paintings.

Miller, thumbs in his suspenders, looked at Shearn, stressing that Yusupov had received the contract, knew of its contents, and knew what he was signing days before signing it.

"And, further," said Miller, shaking his head in a show of disgust, "the prince has shown his disregard for either document, and common ethical practice, because he afterward offered the paintings for sale, first to Mr. Ruck, and then as collateral against a loan from Mr. Gulbenkian, in both cases," and, raising his hands in disbelief, "when he did not even have possession of, or title to the paintings."

Miller paced and looked at Felix, "This proves, Your Honor, the plaintiff's total disdain for the law…" he waved his arm in the air, "and that his real intent was to resell the paintings for a higher price if he got hold of them. We have proven that the prince has not returned to his former way of life as required in the agreement he signed, further disqualifying him from redemption of the art."

"Having exposed all the deception, and bad faith, on part of the plaintiff," he continued, "it is also clear that this trial may appear to be about the right of a well-meaning, but naïve, prince to retain his Rembrandts, but it is in fact about the right of Mr. Calouste Gulbenkian, one of the richest collectors in Europe, under subterfuge, to pry them away from Mr. Widener, their rightful owner."

Miller paused and looked to Duveen who glanced away, dabbing his face with his handkerchief. "The plaintiff, Your Honor, is merely a surrogate for Gulbenkian in this case. He has failed to prove his case in all points. We ask the court to dismiss the plaintiff's claim."

Judge Davis took a sip of water, leaned on his elbows, and looked at all the persons in the room, the attorneys, the prince and princess, Widener, the others. "The court," he said, "has heard all the testimony on both sides in this case, which was, in the court's opinion, professionally and convincingly put forth. The Court will examine all the evidence presented. Counsel will have their briefs to me by May 15. Judgment will be made before June 15." The gavel came down hard in the sweltering courtroom. Irina jumped in shock.

But, Shearn smiled. He encouraged his clients. "Don't expect the worst, Your Highnesses. We have a strong case and may well prevail."

Irina shook her head in disbelief.

Widener rose and in passing the prince and princess said, "I'm sorry."

Irina turned away.

Doris closed her notebook. She stood and faced Princess Irina. "Your Highness," she said, "Indeed, time may yet deliver the paintings back to the Yusupov family. I will certainly hope for that. You have certainly tried your best. You have shown strength under such challenging conditions."

Irina reached out and embraced the journalist. "You have been a solid supporter, dear Doris. This has been an ordeal for Prince Felix and me, so outside of our experience, and expectation. But, at least the art is safe for now. That is the most important thing. We will wait to learn of their next home."

"Felix," the princess turned toward her husband, forcing a smile, and took his arm, "the party this evening is at *L'Aigle Russe*, my favorite place. Everyone will be there. We must change. We are coming as Bohemians."

In early May, the prince and princess returned to France in a comfortable First Class cabin on the *Mauritania*, happy to see the tall buildings of disappointing New York slip below the horizon.

In July they received a cable from Root, Clark, Howland & Ballentine of New York, attorney Shearn's firm. Prince Felix insisted, "Irina, you read it." She haltingly read it for their unbelieving ears, placed in onto the piano top, and for days left it open there, untouched, as if it contained evil spirits.

"How did Widener do it?" Felix asked, "What wicked schemes did he invent?" Felix pushed at the cable with his finger. "How ironic. I thought I had won! I thought I would get justice in America."

His wife reminded him, "You tried, Felix. You said one should never admit defeat while there is a chance to fight. You fought hard."

Irina strolled over to the window, looking out onto the *Rue Gutenberg* from their second story. She thought about the Rembrandts. "They are not part of the Yusupov family anymore," she said, "but I can picture them on the Widener walls. I know they are safe, at least for now. I hope dear Anya will know that."

"But," Felix shook his hand in the air, "who knows what will happen next?"

Irina paused, looked out the window, and said, "God knows."

To put the remainder of their fortune to work, millionaire Baron de Zuylan, founder of Automobile Club of France, offered to help Felix to start a porcelain business. Irina modeled for their *Maison de Couture IRFE*, always with her pearls, but now not the black ones.

When the court decision from Judge Davis arrived by post, ten pages of fine type, it essentially agreed with the argument of Joseph Widener's attorneys. It concluded that the prince had acted with a disregard of his contractual obligations, and was not entitled to specific performance of the contract, and that the complaint be dismissed on the merits.

The prince appealed the case. When reviewed in 1927 by the New York Appellate Court, the trial verdict was upheld. This kept Mr. Gulbenkian at bay for two years until he had forgotten about the loss of over a half-million dollars since his walk in the park with Sir Joseph Duveen. He made up what he had lost many times over in his oil and other global endeavors.

In the meantime, Felix and Irina bought an estate on the island of Corsica, adding to their properties in France, and maintained a lifestyle which, while not as in St. Petersburg, was not one of social embarrassment amongst the residual royalty. Financially they were enhanced by a substantial libel judgment from Metro-Goldwyn-Mayer for a Hollywood film misrepresenting Irina's relationship with Rasputin.

They lived in Paris on the *Rue Gutenberg* for the rest of their lives.

CHAPTER THIRTY-ONE

THE GIFT

Philadelphia
November, 1927

E LLA PANCOAST WIDENER placed her gilded coffee cup on its
saucer. "You won the court appeal, Joseph. Congratulations."

"Let's take a walk, dear," he said.

She felt the warmth of his arm about her shoulders, and
remembered how often she had felt that comfort in the early
days of their marriage. They started toward the French doors
that led from the kitchen into the sunny garden where the flower
beds were empty, the bushes tented for winter. The aroma of
his favorite Sunday pecan coffeecake filled the air, but he had
eaten little of it.

Ella always knew that, when he said "Let's take a walk, dear,"
it was leading to one of those rare moments when he wanted her
opinion on something. She wondered if her husband was still
ruminating over 'that Russian prince affair' as he called it, that
bothersome struggle that had started at this same breakfast table
four years before.

"Now you can forget the whole thing, Joseph," she said, squeezing his arm. She always called him Joseph. Only his close men friends called him "Joe."

"No." He turned. "This way, Ella," he said, leading her through the galleries. She walked arm in arm with him, turning to watch his face as he lifted his tired eyes, glancing from wall to wall, the paintings stacked three and four high on the green, silk-covered walls in one room, silver in another. But, she thought, he was not looking so much at the art, but was assessing the collection like an inventory, as though he were a watchman on his rounds, checking if anything had disappeared in the night.

Ella had always known that, to Joseph Widener, Lynnewood Hall with its great art collection was hoped to be his ticket to acceptance and respectability amongst the affluent society. But, that hope had never been realized. It was as if he could never wash the butcher's blood off his family's hands. Even being married to her, a Pancoast, failed to achieve that goal. Instead, she was reduced, socially speaking, to his level.

When they entered the Rembrandt room, he stopped and dropped her arm. He turned in a complete circle, standing in a stoop with his arms by his sides, examining the fourteen Rembrandts on the deep-red velvet walls, saying nothing.

She waited.

He paused in front of *The Lady* and *The Gentleman*, his eyes inching over the brush strokes laid down by the Master two-hundred sixty-seven years before. She had never seen him so interested in these paintings for what they really were—representations of the human soul. The two Rembrandts were monarchs over the entire collection. She knew something had changed in her husband since the Yusupov affair. "They are safe here now, aren't they, Joseph?" she said, looking for a response.

"Ella, did you ever wonder who they were?" he asked. "This woman and this man? Sully didn't know. Something about a merchant—but weren't they all?"

"From her clothing," Ella pointed, "she was certainly a noble lady, a wealthy lady."

"She looks troubled, don't you think?" he asked.

"She is longing for something," Ella said, "something she does not yet have, maybe something she doesn't expect to receive." He has never shown much interest in the art itself before, she thought. In the collection as a whole, yes, but not in the individual art, the story in each painting. She watched his eyes, which were focused on those of the lady—and then whispered, "She is longing, as women do."

He glanced at his wife, but only for a second. "They are here," he said, "for what—six years now? Until the trial, I never got to know them."

"They were real people," she said, "with real lives."

"This place," he said, "is a museum." He pointed around the room. "We live in a museum, Ella."

"A special place," she said. "Our son and Gertrude were married in this room—right here, between The Lady and The Gentleman."

"The court says the Rembrandts belong here," said Widener, "not hidden away in Russia or Paris. But, Lynnewood Hall lacks permanence, respect, accessibility by the public."

"Where would you build a proper museum?" she said.

He turned and looked at her with a defiant squint in his eyes, "Not in the Commonwealth of Pennsylvania, I assure you. I won't give them a damn thing, those ungrateful bastards! After the way they have treated our family!" He coughed, took out his handkerchief and wiped his mouth.

"Your father," she said, "I know he always wanted the people to enjoy the art."

"Yes, but not here," he said. "Who comes to Philadelphia?"

"Exactly."

"These treasures," he added, "were shut up in a Russian palace for over a hundred years. They deserve better." Widener shook his head. "The prince..." he said.

"You called him some names, Joseph. Buffoon, I think."

"I called him a degenerate, a fool, too. He is a pathetic case. How can you feel sorry for a man who never counts his money?"

"I liked his wife, the princess."

He took a deep breath and winced a little from some deep down pain. "Mellon was talking to me, you know."

Of course, Ella knew Andrew Mellon. The Pittsburgh banker and industrialist was, in 1927, the US Secretary of the Treasury under President Calvin Coolidge. Mellon had told Widener of his plans to build a national museum in Washington for the nation's best art to be enjoyed free of charge.

"Will you join him?" Ella asked.

"This art," he said, "will last forever if it has a permanent home and care. Lynnewood Hall is not that."

Ella rested her hand on the top of a red velvet chair in that red velvet room, then sat down, pressing her fingers to her brow.

"Are you alright?" he asked. "Why don't you see the doctor as I said?"

Ella Widener was a willowy figure. The treatment recommended for her weakening condition was to 'take the waters' in the mineral spas of West Virginia, or at Saratoga when they attended the races.

"It is not just a museum, Joseph, it is our home. Is the art the only thing of value in your life?"

She had come to feel that she, his wife, was at best a second priority. He didn't even like her dog. Their son, Arrell, was a 'commoner' after driving a bloody ambulance with dying men down the rutted war-roads of France. Their daughter, Fifi, had married into society and left. If the art was gone, Ella knew that Lynnewood Hall could no longer have a purpose to Joseph. It, too, would be gone. The paintings would have a home if there was a museum, but she would not.

Widener looked up and down the corridors into the other gallery rooms. "I will miss these friends," he said. "You never know how much you value something until you are faced with living without it."

Ella saw his eyes moisten, which seldom happened. "They will find their home," she said, "they always have. You will make sure of that."

Ella retired to the music room where she spread her dress under her and sat at the piano, the polished, cherry piano that was a gift to old Peter A. B. Widener by William Steinway who was, in addition to his famed pianos, also in the trolley business on Long Island. She started to play Chopin, smiling, recalling Lord Byron's poem, "In solitude, where we are least alone."

Ella Widener continued to take her cures, but two years later, in 1929, Ella Pancoast Widener died.

Joseph Widener was at a loss. He resented the family's social mistreatment. He still mourned the loss of his brother and nephew on the Titanic in the icy Atlantic, and now he had to deal with the loss of his wife. He was alone. Unfulfilled by his wealth, the ailing

Joseph Widener decided to finally give the collection of art, all of it, to the new gallery being built with Andrew Mellon's money in the nation's capital, an act that required the intervention of President Roosevelt with Congress to pay the Pennsylvania estate tax. It was a condition for the gift as he refused to pay this to the state himself. That would, in a way, Widener thought, gain him a residence within credentialed society. But, that didn't happen.

Joseph Widener neglected Lynnewood Hall and let it fall into disrepair during the Great Depression, the gardens withering, the fountains dribbling to a halt. He just didn't care anymore. He lived there with his servants until 1942 when, with tears in his eyes, he watched his famous art collection, the Degas, the Corots, the Vermeers, and, of course, the Rembrandts, removed by sweating men in gray overalls who carted the art away to big, white trucks that hauled them down US Highway 1 to the new museum in Washington.

CHAPTER THIRTY-TWO

HOME

Sunday,
December 20, 1942
Washington, DC

F ROM THE BACK SEAT of the black Chrysler, she thrilled to see the steps and three-story, columned entrance to the new National Gallery of Art. On the front fender of the limousine, flapping in the winter breeze, was the red, white, and blue, horizontal-striped flag of The Kingdom of the Netherlands.

The driveway was blocked by a battleship of a black Rolls Royce with Union Jacks flying from the two front fenders. Two armed guards got out of the car and stood by the back doors. Then, out stepped the British Ambassador and his wife, he tall and stooped, she in a fox fur coat. The Rolls moved on, and the ambassador and his wife were escorted by their guards up the stairs to the main door.

In its turn, the Dutch car pulled up. Out of the front door of the Chrysler stepped the driver in a black suit and a brown leather cap. He walked around the rear of the car to the other side, and with a gloved hand opened the back door. The woman stepped out, followed by her escort; he in his late thirties, she younger, both in black coats down to their ankles. She pulled her fur stole tighter about her neck. With a finger she brushed aside a blond curl as her boots touched on the pavement stones. Under her arm was a weathered, leather valise closed with a brass clasp.

"It should be two hours, Schuyler," the man said to his driver.

"I'll watch for you, sir."

"Thank you, Schuyler," added the Dutch woman with a smile.

America was again at war, but for a welcome moment, there was an interlude in that preoccupation. Attending the event was the diplomatic elite, in their furs and felt hats, arriving in black limousines with their national flags. It was the opening of America's new National Gallery of Art, with a special reception honoring an important new collection of European art.

A man pushed snow from the granite steps with the deliberate speed of one paid by the hour. He stopped, turned, stood back, and watched the Dutch couple walk past into the marble building. Henryk glanced at the expressionless man leaning on his shovel, and tried not to notice his scarred face. "Poor man," he thought, and followed his wife into the fortress of a museum.

Following the British party, the Dutch diplomats passed through the high, mahogany doors under the three-story Ionic columns and portico. The guests were from the embassies representing the Allied powers. Denmark, like The Netherlands and France, was already occupied by the Nazis, London was in ruins from the Blitz, and The Soviet Union was under siege on three fronts.

The engraved invitation in the Dutch man's bare hand read,

Private Preview
for the
Washington Diplomatic Corps
The Widener Collection
Of European Art
The National Gallery of Art
Two o'clock, Sunday Afternoon,
December 20, 1942
R.S.V.P.

An attendant took their wraps on the first level, escorting the diplomats up the marble stairs to the Rotunda. Patterned after The Pantheon, this central structure was supported by twenty-four thirty-six-foot columns of *Vert Imperial* marble from Italy, the same source for the green marble columns gracing The Hermitage in St. Petersburg, now Leningrad. It was Christmastime and the center fountain, capped by the bronze Raghetti winged-victory figure of Mercury, was surrounded by arrangements of red and white poinsettias.

The Dutch couple paused along with others to comment on the peaceful beauty. "For a nation straining to fight a war on two fronts," said the Dutch woman, "this is a grand statement," She took a deep breath, absorbing the aroma of twenty ten-foot spruce trees standing against the encircling walls. "A lovely statement," she added.

Greeting the guests at the white marble entrance to the Garden Court were four men dressed in black ties and tails. One offered his hand, introducing himself as the Gallery Director, David Finley.

"Henryk van der Hoet, The Netherlands," said the Dutchman. "And, my wife, Anneke."

"Thank you so much for inviting us. It is an honor to be here," added Anneke.

In a wheelchair next to Mr. Finley sat a man, hunched over with bent head, looking at the guests through a set of eyebrows resembling untrimmed hedges. A thin ring of grey hair circled his balding head. Although his face was drawn and sallow, there was a sparkle of pride in the eyes of the man whose collection of art was being presented that day to the public.

"May I introduce you," Finley said to Henryk and Anneke, "to Mr. Joseph Widener of Philadelphia?" Finley's hand was on Widener's shoulder. The director bent close to the old man's ear. Widener offered a shaking hand with a firm grip, which the Dutch couple each held for a warm moment. Finley introduced them to representatives of the Mellon family.

Andrew Mellon had died five years prior, never seeing the completion of the nation's gallery, which he completely paid for—a building reported to be the largest marble structure built at that time.

Widener asked, his voice weak, "You are from The Netherlands?" A slight smile cracked the ends of his down-turned mouth. "You will find some of your countrymen here."

"We are honored," the diplomat said, "that you have included Dutch artists in this wonderful gift for all the world to enjoy."

"It's about time," said Widener. "They are all masterworks." Straining to straighten, he looked up to the visitors and said with pride, "It is the largest collection in America, you know."

The National Gallery of Art had opened the year before, but was yet unfinished. Widener's art joined that of The Mellon

Collection of 121 pieces, of which twenty-one were purchased from The Hermitage. Joseph Stalin had more need of money in his treasury than art in his national museum.

The Dutch couple joined a group of six others led by a docent, a young man with tousled hair and a ruddy complexion. The group included the British pair, a mustached man from Argentina, two smiling Canadians, and a thin, balding Russian with a sober face behind steel-rimmed glasses.

The docent, talking nonstop, led them though the room where the Bellinis, Titians, and other Italian art hung, then into the rooms with Gainsboroughs, Reynolds, Romneys, Turners, and the Sargent portrait of Peter A. B. Widener, the founder of the collection. Then they entered the rooms of Dutch paintings, van Ruisdael, Hobbema, Hals, de Hooch, and Vermeer. Falling behind the group, the Dutch couple discussed each one in a quiet and knowledgeable tone. They had never before seen these treasures by their country's artists.

Leading the group into the next room, the docent paused until all were together, and then with a wave of his hand announced, "Here we have the Rembrandts, the jewels of the Widener Collection."

Anneke placed her hand on her heart, smiling as if in a welcoming home. With her deep brown eyes, the woman looked at her husband, shaking her head in wonderment. Henryk leaned over, examining one painting, then another.

"Here is *The Mill*, a major Rembrandt," the docent said. It was in a large room with red velvet, padded benches for viewing. "Parliament tried to keep this painting in England, but could not match Mr. Widener's price." The British Ambassador's wife glanced at her husband as if he were to blame. He raised his eyebrows and shrugged innocence.

The docent pointed out other Rembrandts on the side walls of the room, *The Apostle Paul, St. Matthew,* and *The Man with a Tall Hat.* "And, here," said the docent, "is a portrait of Saskia, the artist's beloved wife, about the time of their wedding." The docent paused in front of Saskia's portrait, absorbing the gaze of the woman. "She supplied love and financial support to her husband for many years," he added. The docent hesitated, turned back for one more look, then moved on.

Anneke took a deep breath as the docent gestured with his hand, "And, here are the famous portraits called *Portrait of a Lady with an Ostrich-Feather Fan,* and its companion, *Portrait of a Gentleman with Tall Hat and Gloves.*" He paused while they all gathered. "These are the famous Yusupov Rembrandts," the docent explained, "smuggled out of Russia under the nose of the Bolsheviks by Prince Yusupov after he murdered Rasputin."

The English woman gasped.

"The Soviet government unsuccessfully demanded them back in 1925," the docent said with a smile. The Soviet diplomat remained expressionless. The docent added, "They are considered the finest of Rembrandt's portraitures."

"Who is the couple?" asked the Canadian lady. "Do you know?"

"No, that is a mystery," said the docent. "Speculations, yes. No, they remain totally unknown."

The British ambassador's wife stood back, saying, "They are somber, in control of their life, but not entirely happy. What is her secret?"

"An enigma, isn't she?" the British ambassador said.

"Both are," the ambassador's wife added. "Look at his eyes, so shaded. What were they thinking, those two?"

"The question is," the Argentine said, "what was Rembrandt thinking?"

Anneke, who was intrigued by the varied questions, spoke up, "We will never know." Her eyes focused on those of the lady in the portrait. "We only know what the artist represented—and that is for each of us to experience for ourselves." The docent nodded in agreement.

The Dutch couple settled on the bench before the portraits as the group moved on. Anneke held the leather valise in her lap. They heard the docent's receding voice introducing the El Grecos in the next room.

"The Lady and the Gentleman," said Henryk, "have found their home." Henryk van der Hoet was a typical Dutchman; tall, with a kindly face, and a large, a very Dutch nose. "Your mother," he added, "would be thrilled to know that, Anneke."

"She would be here, but for that German bomb on the hospital in London last year." Shortly the docent returned, and for a moment stood, watching the Dutch pair sitting, their eyes transfixed upon the Rembrandts. He moved behind the two, placing his hands on their shoulders and said, "Will our Dutch friends join us for the rest of the tour?"

Anneke turned to her husband, took his hand and nestled against him. "Another time," she said. "Thank you."

She laid the weathered valise on her lap, turned the worn brass latch, laid back the flap, and carefully pulled out the leather journal. She opened its fragile cover, and turned the yellowed pages as if they might break. They were filled with the faded script of different hands over the ages. Stopping at a sheet dated

December 12, 1660, with a quiet voice she read the ancient Dutch to her husband:

> "What is happiness I ask on this promising winter day? Surely to know that I am loved and protected and that come Saturday the door will be closed on the painful tricks of man and nature. We and our offspring will be forever safe under our roof and my secret will be forever silent. But, if destiny clouds the rays of hope and we leave this earth too soon, our souls will be captured on canvas by the Master's brush and if that is the closest we shall come to immortality, then it is still all worth it. After all, home, we know, is not a place; it is where we belong to each other."

They gathered their wraps and stepped through the mahogany doors into the fading evening light, their thoughts centuries away.

The End

ABOUT THE AUTHOR

FRED ANDRESEN has always taken the road "less traveled." Although he was born and raised in the West Texas desert near El Paso, he has extensively traveled, and has spent a great deal of his professional life working and living abroad. His time in the military and earlier business career took him broadly over Europe and Asia. The last nearly twenty years  were focused on business and culture in Russia, with six years in residence. Much time was spent with the art, literature, music, and drama, for which Russia is so well known. That experience has most inspired him today as a writer and as a world citizen.

His first book, a collection of autobiographical essays written during his residence in Moscow and St. Petersburg in the 1990s, *Walking on Ice: An American Businessman in Russia*, raised his profile as a writer and speaker versed in interpersonal relations abroad. For several years he wrote weekly columns for the prime Russian global web-news agency RIA Novosti, *(www.rian.ru)*. His writing was reviewed as "openly Chekhovian." His last book, *Dos Gringos*, is a work based on the true story of his Norwegian immigrant father's escapades during the Mexican Revolution. Andresen's literary focus is in the world of historical fiction.

See *www.fandresen.com*

The journey of the Yusupov Rembrandts—282 years.

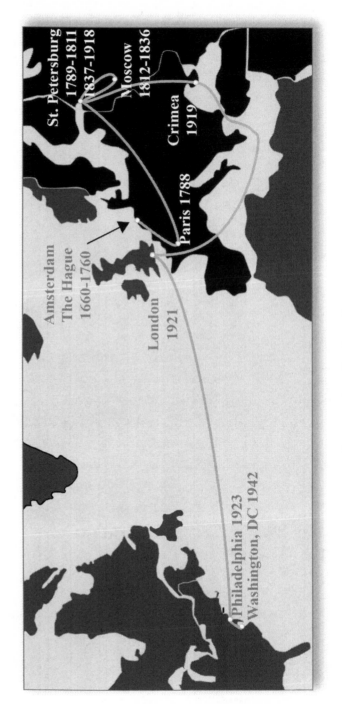

St. Petersburg
1789-1811
1837-1918

Moscow
1812-1836

Crimea
1919

Paris 1788

Amsterdam
The Hague
1660-1760

London
1921

Philadelphia 1923
Washington, DC 1942

The search for home.

Made in the USA
Charleston, SC
10 April 2016